Voyage To Secrets

Also by Greg Judge

Schea

Schea's Revenge

Voyage To Secrets

GREG JUDGE

Voyage To Secrets

Voyage To Secrets

Prologue

She saw the squall line off to the north, so she called to Peter, "Peter! We should head back in pretty soon."

"Okay mom. I'll make for the Buchard's." Peter was at the helm and turned slightly into the wind, while Olivia maneuvered the jib and mainsails of the small sloop. Once finished she moved the short distance to where Peter was standing. He was only 8 years old, but he was such a good seaman. It was in his blood. Well, truth be told, it was in the entire family's blood. She and her husband, Dan, had been sailing since they were young and the kids, Peter and Willa, had simply joined in as soon as they could crawl.

There were many boats out on the water today. Most of those she could see would probably return to their respective moorages. However, there were some larger, sturdier boats and yachts that could ride-out the squall. She and Peter definitely had to return. Their small sloop could not take the risk of whatever the squall line had to offer.

The two of them stood side-by-side watching the waters ahead of them. Occasionally, Olivia would turn to make a quick observation of the squall to make sure they were staying well ahead of it. She noticed it was getting a little closer, so she made sure that her life-preserver was secured tight and told Peter to check his too.

The skies grew darker by the minute, but she still felt they had plenty of time to make the Buchard's dock. She lost sight of all of the boats in the waters around them as they all scattered home, but one of the larger boats appeared to be on the same line to port as they were and was about a kilometer behind them.

Suddenly, Olivia's feet felt a large vibration somewhere on the sloop below the water-line. She also felt it begin to list to the port side. She bent down and leaned into the small space in the bow. That was when she saw the large tear in the port side of the hull. That was also when she was knocked unconscious.

The Coast Guard initiated a search, but found no sign of the small craft and no sign of debris in the water. They had to call off the search at around midnight and told Dan, Olivia's husband, they would start again the following morning.

Three days later someone called the local sheriff's office about finding a body washed up on the beach a few miles down the coast. It was eventually confirmed to be Olivia but, to this day, there has been no word as to what happened to Peter or the boat. The area where they were supposed to have sailed was searched extensively, but no evidence of the boat or Peter was found.

Willa and her dad stayed at their friends' house during all of the searches and investigations, but eventually returned to their home in Scarsdale, New York, two months after that nightmarish day.

XXXXX

It had taken Willa, Olivia's daughter, several years to shake off the sadness and pain of that day, but Dan had had a more difficult time and only recently began to come out of his melancholy. He had continued to be a caring dad, maybe even more so since the accident, but Willa would often see him sitting by a window staring out into whatever world he saw there.

Willa had started three or four years ago suggesting they make this trip, the trip her mom had wanted them to take years before, but Dan had kept saying, "Someday." Finally, six months ago, Willa put her fifteen year-old teenage foot down and said, "If you don't start making the arrangements, then I will."

1. On Our Way

The soft salt spray blew onto Willa's face and arms as the small craft cut through the light squall in the eastern Mediterranean Sea. As the craft came down into the swells, the spray flared up. Then, as the bow rose, a warm, sweet breeze wafted over her and dried her once damp skin. Her skin would be salty and sticky, but she didn't care. She loved the feeling. Willa was at the helm, which was all that mattered, while her dad was fixing some rigging that had come loose. Both were thrilled to finally be on their long-overdue family trip.

This was the trip the family had been waiting to make for over ten years. It was, had been, her mother's dream and she had wanted the four of them to make this around-the-world adventure. After all, they were a sailing family and all of them had been raised on or around the water. Willa and her brother, Peter, had been sailing since they were small and learned to pilot small craft when they were barely four years old.

Willa and her dad were now on the long dreamed of adventure. But, there were two very important people missing, Olivia and Peter. Willa's mom and brother had died in the boating accident ten years ago and it had been a long struggle for her and her dad to get to this point in their lives.

On that sunny, summer day ten years ago, the family had been visiting friends on Cape Cod. Olivia decided to take their twenty foot sail boat out with Peter. He was a handsome, bright boy who learned quickly and loved to show others what he could do.

Willa and her dad had already committed to going into town with the two daughters of their friends to see a movie. Well, truth be known, Dan volunteered to take the three girls to see the movie since Marilyn and Xavier Buchard needed some alone time. Willa, of course, had not known the couple was having some marriage issues. She just wanted some fun-time with Susie and Eden.

Everyone was upbeat about the day's activities and it was looking to be a very fun day. Willa might have wished to have been with her mom and brother, but she also enjoyed spending time with her dad, five year old Susie and six year old Eden. So, at ten am, Willa, her dad, Susie and Eden headed into town, while her mom and brother headed down to the dock to prepare the sailboat for a short trip out into the bay. Xavier and Marilyn prepared to stay at home to "talk".

Before the day was out, no one was thinking that this had been a fun day.

Willa's small group arrived at the theater, bought tickets, popcorn and drinks, then settled into their seats in theater number four to see the latest Disney movie. After the movie, Dan took the girls for ice cream at the nearby Cold Stone Creamery shop, where they lingered and giggled and talked about the movie for an hour or so. As it approached three in the afternoon, Dan began encouraging movement of the girls to the car and, after another half hour, he finally succeeded in getting them all to the car and buckled in.

When they arrived at the house, Xavier came out immediately. He smiled and told the girls to head inside because Marilyn had a surprise for them. The girls all scrambled off giggling with anticipation about what the surprise might be. Once the girls were beyond hearing range, Xavier pulled Dan aside and told him that Olivia had not yet returned and he was worried. A squall had been heading in the direction they had gone so they probably should have turned back hours ago. Dan nodded, but said not to worry. Olivia was one of the most accomplished sailors he knew and will likely be back soon. He was sure of it.

Two hours later, Dan was now worried and began pacing the dock while looking out into the waters off of the Cape. Willa was oblivious to all of this, as a five year old should be. There was no sense in getting her worried about her mom being in trouble when her mom would probably appear at any moment. However, even small children can be perceptive when circumstances do not seem to fit into their small, ordered world.

Near dinner time, Willa came to her father looking distraught. She asked him if mom was going to be late for dinner. She didn't want her to miss out on the clams, mussels and crabs they were planning to cook on the grill. Dan smiled, told her that her mom would be back any minute and suggested that she go and see what Susie and Eden were up to. Willa remembered walking off, but not running off. She somehow knew that something was wrong.

By nine pm, everyone was frantic with worry. Dan had called the Coast Guard office an hour before and asked them to initiate a search. He emphasized that although his wife was an excellent sailor, they had not taken any supplies, additional clothing or other gear with them. They had only planned to be out for about four or five hours at most, but it was now close to ten hours since they had left. He was also worried about the squall line which had gone through earlier. It hadn't seemed to be too severe, but he could not be sure of what they may have encountered out on the open water.

2. Reflections

Willa shook off the memory of that long ago time and focused instead on the squall line in the Eastern Med and her job at the helm.

XXXXX

In a small office in Moscow, a woman pounded her fist on her desk and yelled into her phone, "What do you mean you lost them? How could you lose them? It's a girl and a guy and they aren't trying to hide!"

"They just slipped away", said the man on the other end. "Don't worry, we will find them."

The woman disconnected without comment. The man didn't have a chance to tell her that the guy following them had gotten drunk and wandered off with some woman he met. The man would be dealt with later, but he now had to find the girl and her father before he, himself, was dealt with!

XXXXX

Dan finished with the rigging and headed back up to the helm. He stopped as he watched Willa expertly handle the boat in the choppy waters. He loved her so much, maybe even more so at that moment. She had been right to badger him into taking this trip. He had been in such a funk for the past ten years and knew it, but couldn't seem to pull himself out of it. And, of course, he was now feeling guilty about all of the years that Willa had had to put up with his moods.

She was perceptive, school smart and seemed to be street smart as well. Much of that, he was sure, came from her mother, since he was always the 'steady-Eddie' type in the family. Always calm, cool and collected.

Olivia had been crazy fun. She was always coming up with some new way to entertain the kids, from made-up games, to trips to weird parks, to family joke night, which was one of his favorites. The game required everyone to sit around the living room taking turns telling jokes, and the sillier, the better. Peter almost always provided the silliest jokes, while Dan provided the most un-laughable jokes. He missed those times.

At school, Willa was an accomplished runner and archer. Her cross-country team finished 2nd at the state championships last year and the school's archery team regularly won first honors.

She would say that she was not pretty but others would say she was. More importantly, everyone would say she was beautiful inside. She was of average height and weight for a fifteen year old girl – just shy of 5 feet 5 inches tall and about 110 lbs. and the running kept her figure quite lithe and graceful. She had natural dirty blond hair, but it had become very blond in the sun of the Mediterranean while her skin had become quite tan.

Dan smiled when he thought about Willa's given name – Wilhelmina. Her mother had thought of it. She had always admired two particular women with that name. One was Queen Wilhelmina of the Netherlands whose strength and fortitude during the two world wars in the early twentieth century helped her people and country survive. The other woman was Wilhelmina Vautrin. She was an American in China during the Japanese occupation in WWII, who had protected thousands of women from marauding Japanese soldiers. Willa had read a bit about both Wilhelmina's and learned how brave they were. She liked her name after that.

However, Willa quickly learned that her friends could never figure out how to pronounce it, let alone spell it. Dan and Olivia finally agreed to start using the name, Willa, on various official documents. But, they told Willa she would have to make the decision, when old enough, to change her name legally or not.

Willa sometimes used Will for her name when she was trying to fool boys, or girls, on social media. They thought they were dealing with a boy and it gave Willa a bit more insight into their real intent during their dialogues.

XXXXX

Within a month after the accident, Willa had closed herself off from the outside world. She managed to appear to be strong around her dad, possibly because she seemed to know he was a mess. At home, they settled into a sort of imaginary world of their own. They smiled at each other, laughed sometimes and chatted amiably about events of the day – Willa's school day, Dan's work, a new family in town, or something on the news.

But, outside of the house and away from her dad, Willa was a cold, shell of the once happy-go-lucky girl she had been and she pushed all of her friends away. Some of them made gallant efforts to help her, but she rejected their overtures.

Her grades suffered, not because she did not know or understand the material, but because she just didn't care to try. Her teachers made efforts to talk to her and called for conferences with her dad. During those sessions Willa would nod when they talked to her and say "Yes" when asked if she would try harder, but she never did. Dan would promise to talk to her at home and to help her, but he seemed to forget all of his promises once they were home, and Willa never reminded him.

Willa stopped participating in school activities, rarely went out of the house to play or to join in any of her usual weekend excursions. Her weight went up and her moods went down.

But, for some reason, four years after the accident, Willa started to come out of her fog. If asked, she might say it was a brief comment from a friend or a teacher. But the truth is, she had no idea. She just remembers waking up one morning to get ready for school, looking in the mirror and staring at who she had become. She remembers staring at herself for a long while and then seeing the tears beginning to cascade down her cheeks. She remembers feeling as though her heart had stopped beating and she had stopped breathing.

Possibly, if she had ever tried to explain this moment to someone, they might say that it was the spirit of her mom coming to help her, or maybe it was her brother, or maybe it was God trying to help her to come back to life. She had no idea. She just knows that she is thankful for whatever caused her to change.

She also remembers, while staring at her reflection, watching a small smile move across her face. At that point, she washed her face, brushed her teeth and headed to her room. She dressed, packed her school books and papers, ate breakfast, kissed her dad and walked out to the school bus. That day, at school, she began opening up to her friends, which surprised them at first, but then they simply started acting as though the last four years had not happened – the power of being young!

Willa is now an excellent student with exceptional analytical skills, which help her do well in the math and sciences. She is, however, brilliant with languages. Dan knows this is related to her mother's expertise in languages because Olivia had spoken five or six languages fluently. Willa has taken every language course offered at the school and Dan is lucky enough to be able to afford to send her to several local language academies. As a result, Willa now speaks Russian, Chinese, French and Spanish fluently. She is currently attempting to master Italian and German.

XXXXX

Dan's accomplishments are in the practical, business world. But, that is not where he had started. He had graduated from Harvard at the age of twenty-one with degrees in history and economics. On career day, midway through his senior year, he was approached by a man who asked him to have coffee with him at a nearby coffee shop. He did and was eventually hired by the CIA as a research analyst. He was told it would entail looking into various international organizations or countries for trends in their political, business and economic decisions.

He left the CIA at the age of thirty, not because he was unhappy, but because he just wanted a change. His experience there helped to get him a job at a large insurance company in San Francisco as a fraud investigator. It was there that he met Olivia.

He often needed to do research into changes in several California state regulations and used the local library to do so. The simple reasons were that they had an excellent legal documents section and it was very near to his office. He also liked getting away from his desk sometimes. On one occasion, he noticed a pretty assistant while he researched a case. He wanted to talk to her, but was too shy to approach her. He had never been very comfortable around girls in high school or college and, unfortunately, that had carried over into his adult life.

He needn't have worried. Olivia was not shy and, one day, as he bent over a large set of documents about some recent personal property insurance changes, she came over and asked if she could be of assistance. He looked up and saw the most beautiful face he had ever seen. She smiled and waited. He smiled and said nothing. Finally, she broke the stalemate.

And thank goodness she did. He had been stuck in some kind of space-time continuum and would have simply stared at her until the library closed. She asked again if he would like some help or would he like to go for coffee. Fortunately, he was smart enough to choose the coffee and, as they say, the rest is history. They were married a year later.

Peter, named after Olivia's grandfather, was born the following year and Willa was born three years after Peter. When Willa was two, Dan decided to go into business for himself and started a consulting firm that specialized in investigative research into insurance and business fraud. Olivia told him she had an inheritance they could use to set up the business.

He recognized that the market for his business was largest in New York City, so they left San Francisco and moved to Jersey City, New Jersey directly across the Hudson River from New York City. Two years later, when Willa was four, they moved to Scarsdale just north of New York City.

A year later the boating accident turned their neatly packaged world upside down.

XXXXX

Dan seemed to be fine for the first 6 months after the accident. He knew he had to help Willa get through this terrible loss, plus continue helping with his investigations. He also knew that he had to make sure friends and family were kept informed of any progress made in the efforts to find Peter.

What he didn't seem to know was that he was sinking into depression. He began taking on too much work but not doing it and he didn't notice that his colleagues secretly helped to keep the work moving forward. He didn't seem to realize he had secretly started to smoke and to have one or two drinks for lunch as well as after Willa went to bed, things he had never done before. He didn't notice his weight gain and his loss of breath climbing a short set of stairs. And, he didn't seem to notice that many of his former friends gradually stopped calling or asking him to do the things they had routinely done before.

Dan also didn't seem to notice when Willa began to come out of her depression. He was no longer asked to attend teacher conferences, except for the routine ones at the end of each marking period. He also didn't notice Willa having friends over and going to their houses for sleepovers.

If he was asked to explain how he had gotten turned around, he would say that it was Willa hounding him to take the long overdue sailing trip. He doesn't really remember all of the times he turned her down, but he does remember that day, several months ago, when she stood stock-still in front of him with hands on her hips and face set firm, telling him that they were going to go on the trip and that if he wouldn't help to get the planning started, then she would do it. She then turned, walked from the living room back to her bedroom and slammed the door.

He had been sitting in front of the TV not really watching some news program. As she left, he remembers sitting perfectly still for several minutes. Finally, he got up, went to her bedroom door and knocked. She told him to come in and, when he opened the door, he remembers that she looked at him with a smile and asked softly, "Ready to get started?"

He laughed and cried at the same time. "Okay, here's what we'll do. You plan our stops and routes. I'll search for a boat, check on moorage fees and research the various visa and legal requirements for entering the various ports-of-call. We'll plan to leave in early summer after school finishes but we'll need to check with the school since you'll be gone for about a year. I'll also discuss with my partners taking on my work while we are gone."

He noticed as he made this little speech that Willa continued to smile and nod at each statement. As he continued, he saw her rise from her bed, walk toward him and, before he knew it, she was hugging him. At that point, he stopped talking and hugged her back tightly. They finally pulled away from each other, both smiling.

After a several seconds, he said, "Okay", Willa said, "Good" and then he left her room feeling better than he had in years.

3. Getting Started

Dan bought their boat from a friend who had it moored in Piraeus, Greece, just south of Athens. It was an Alerion 41 and was the perfect boat for the two of them to take out on this around-the-world trip. It could handle the waters of the open ocean and be easily piloted by two people, especially two experienced sailors. They named it 'The Olivia'.

It had been well maintained by his friend who had added several additional features. One of which was a high-end navigation system for a boat this size. The other features had to do with upgrades to the interior compartments and storage areas.

Willa loved it as soon as she saw it. Dan thought she would love the beautiful paneling, roomy sleeping areas and spacious head with a good sized shower. Nope. What did Willa love most - the navigation and electronics systems, especially the upgrades to the navigation system.

Dan arranged with his friend to have the boat cleaned, stocked and inspected for their trip. He turned his business clients over to one of his partners, Greg, and told him he would be gone for about 1 year. He also gave Greg his and Willa's contact information.

Willa finished on a high note at school. Her year ended with her on the honor role, the state archery champion and her cross-country team finished second in the state. But, even with all of these accomplishments, her excitement was reserved only for their upcoming trip.

A few months ago, Willa and her dad had gone to the school counselor to discuss the impending trip. When they said she would be gone for all of the next school year, the counselor asked if she could still work on school assignments online. Willa said sure and agreed to work extra hard to make sure she kept up with her studies.

The counselor worked with the staff and Willa's likely teachers for the next year to make sure everyone was in agreement with the plan. Her English and History teachers were very excited and said they would create assignments which took advantage of her travel adventures and the places she visited. The science teacher said he would design assignments around the various animal and plant species she might encounter, as well as the local geography. The math teacher said that she would work closely with the science teacher to design Willa's math assignments in a way that would complement the data being collected for the science projects. If there were concepts she was covering in class which did not easily fit into the science assignment, then she would send a separate project for Willa to do in order to practice those particular concepts.

The school counselor reported all of this back to Dan and Willa a few weeks before their departure and both assured the counselor they would make sure to stay on track with all of the work sent to them. The counselor told Dan she would send regular reports to him about Willa's progress so he would know how she was doing and what the teachers were saying about her work.

Willa started packing the morning after her dad said okay to the trip. She knew space would be limited and that she had to be very careful about exactly what she brought along. Most of their route and destinations would have warm climates, so shorts, t-shirts, swimsuits and flip flops would be the dominant items.

However, on the open water, especially at night, it could get very chilly. Plus, they were planning on a stop in Cape Town during their spring season and then passing through the cold, treacherous waters around the Cape of Good Hope. For these reasons, she also packed raingear, long sleeve shirts, some warm fleece jackets, heavy socks and shoes. If needed, they could always pick up additional items along the way.

Over the next few months, she and her dad worked on the overall trip planning. They sat together and talked about the places they might want to see and the things they wanted to do while there. They reviewed what should be included in the ship's stores and created lists of food, gear and tools they might need. Willa remembered these days and evenings with heartfelt gladness. Her dad seemed so happy and excited during these sessions, which made her happy as well.

XXXXX

They arrived in Athens in the middle of June and made their way to Piraeus the following day. They contacted the agent for Dan's friend, since he was in London on business. The agent's name was Stavros and he had all of the necessary documentation for the boat. He reviewed the repairs, stocks and cleaning work done on the boat and spent a few days getting additional stocks of food and other last minute items. Stavros also spent time showing them the new nav and comm systems.

They had left one week after arriving in Greece and their first stop was in Istanbul, Turkey. They passed through the narrow strait that separates the continents of Europe and Asia and sailed into the Sea of Marmara. They sailed past the historic city of Gallipoli where a famous WWI battle had been fought, then headed straight into Istanbul, formerly Constantinople. They found a mooring, paid the fees, signed several documents and made their way into the city. Willa read about the city during the quiet days at sea and noticed there was so much to see here - the Golden Horn, the Bosphorus, the Blue Mosque, the Hagia Sofia, and so much more.

She and her dad decided to focus on the Blue Mosque, the Hagia Sofia and the huge central market. They spent their days exploring the city and their evenings sitting quietly on the boat watching sunsets, sunrises and the ship traffic in the area.

They departed Istanbul a few days ago and were currently heading for Malta. They were now located about fifty nautical miles north of the coast of the Greek island of Crete, once home to the ancient Minoan Civilization. They were now drifting silently since the brief squall had finally passed.

XXXXX

The English teacher's assignment for Willa was to document the trip using pictures and summaries of each stop's sights, people and sounds, while the History teacher assigned her the task of documenting the historical significance of each stop. The science and math teachers were sending her projects at each stop, but since their stops were flexible, Willa had to send the itinerary as they left one stop and headed for the next.

For Istanbul and the Sea of Marmara, the science teacher asked Willa to document with pictures and descriptions the important geography of the area, such as the confluence of the European and Asian Continents. The math teacher asked her to show all of the calculations for navigating to Istanbul and Malta, and to convert the distance to kilometers and the miles per hour to knots.

XXXXX

"How do you know?" asked the man in Moscow.

"We received a tip from an associate in Athens. She said they bought a boat and departed several days ago. She does not know their itinerary, but said she will have it soon."

The man thought for a moment, "Okay. Let me know what else you find out." He switched off the satellite phone, set it down slowly and leaned back in his chair. His mind was working hard on this development. *What are they doing? Is this simply a vacation or are they searching for something?* All he knew for sure was that he had to know the answers to those questions and soon. There was potential trouble for all involved depending on those answers.

He retrieved the satellite phone again and called a number. The call was picked up on the first ring, "Yes."

"We may have a problem."

4. Malta

Willa and her dad arrived in Malta on the 25th of June, a sunny Saturday afternoon. They secured a moorage in St Julian's Bay on the north side of Sliema and booked a room at the nearby Hilton Malta in St Julian's. It was on the bay and from their room's window they could actually see their boat moored a short distance away. They also had beautiful views out over the Mediterranean toward the island of Sicily.

Malta has a wonderfully warm climate year-round with a few cool spells in the winter months. It has lots of sun and fun in the summer and Willa was looking forward to some of that sun and fun at the beach. Dan was planning to go to a few boat shops to buy extra parts in case repairs were needed during the long stretch to Gibraltar and then on to Tenerife in the Canary Islands.

Malta became independent back in the 1960s after 150 years of British rule and had many other foreign occupiers for thousands of years before that. They are a fun loving, easy going people with freedom of religion, a stable government and a thriving tourist industry. Willa could not wait to get out and explore this pretty island nation.

After they settled into their room, Willa asked her dad if she could head out to do some exploring. He said sure since he'd be busy getting the spare parts but asked Willa to meet him for dinner at around seven pm.

Willa changed into shorts, a t-shirt and flip-flops then headed down to the lobby. She wandered over to the concierge and asked for a map of the area, including Valletta. He reached into his desk drawer and pulled out a map showing all of the major areas of the island. He took a few minutes to orient Willa and told her about some things she might consider doing in order to get oriented. One suggestion was to take the 'Hop On Hop Off' bus tour of the island. He told her there were three routes and gave her a brochure which showed the stops along each route.

He suggested she could get off at any stop in order to enjoy the area then go back to a designated 'On/Off' bus stop to catch the next bus and continue the tour. But, he advised her to stay on the bus for the entire one hour tour first since this would give her an excellent orientation to the whole island. She could then continue on the bus and get off at only those stops which sounded interesting to her. She thanked him and headed out to explore.

Willa strolled to the nearest 'On/Off' bus stop, marked on her map. It was on the Green Line and only a short walk from the front of the hotel. As she waited at the stop, she reviewed the brochure again and noticed the Green and Blue Line tours ended at around four pm while the Red Line ended at five pm.   It was now two pm, which would only allow her to take one tour and didn't leave much time to see anything along the route or to take any of the other tour routes.

She decided to take the Green Line to Valletta where all of the lines converged and stop by the company ticket office. She'd check on a ticket for the following day then spend the remainder of the afternoon and evening in Valletta. She would call her dad at around six pm to tell him to meet her there for dinner once she picked a place. She smiled and thought again about how great this trip was turning out to be for them.

The bus came about ten minutes after she got to the stop, so she hopped on, literally, paid for a ticket and found a seat on the top tier of the bus. It was a waste of money to buy the ticket since she was only using it for the short journey to Valletta but, hey, they were on a holiday. Why not splurge a little – right?

The next six stops took her through parts of St Julian and Sliema then to Valletta. She liked what she saw in Sliema, so she made a note to go back there. She arrived at the Valletta Castille or Castle and bought an all-day pass for the next day which included all three lines. She then headed into Valletta via Triq ir Repubblika, which was the main street into the town and eventually led to the waterfront.

She loved the look of Valletta. The architecture was cool, the old churches were fun to explore and she found the people she met really nice. She continued along the road until she came to a small plaza. She was getting a little thirsty for a good cup of coffee, so she looked around the plaza and saw a neat little place called the Café Cordina. The small plaque on the outside said it was over 100 years old. She decided it must be good to have been around that long and she entered.

The interior was amazing. As she entered, she saw a beautifully decorated spiral staircase leading up to another level. There were paintings along the walls that looked like they had been done by the great masters and there was even a chandelier hanging from the ceiling. *This is so cool*, she thought. She purchased a latte and took a seat in the back of the café. It gave her a great vantage point to watch the customers and to look more closely at the interior decor.

As she finished her latte and considered getting another one, a young man came over and asked if he could join her. His English was accented but she could not quite place its exact origin, *maybe France*, she thought. She looked up at him and figured he was a couple of years older than she, probably seventeen. He was cute, wore shorts, a t-shirt and boat shoes with no socks. Did she just think the word cute? She hoped he couldn't read her mind!

Willa smiled, "Sure. I was about to order another latte."

"Oh, please let me get it for you."

"Okay, thanks," and she gave him her preference. As he walked away, she watched him. He had an athletic build and moved with confidence. He was about four to five inches taller than she, with dark hair and quite tan. His eyes were brown and his teeth were white and straight. He obviously took care of himself. It was near five pm, so she had to call her dad fairly soon about their dinner plans but, unfortunately, she still hadn't identified a restaurant to recommend.

But now, she didn't really want to rush this experience, so she would see how things went before getting anxious. The young man was coming back so she smiled pleasantly as he approached and sat across from her.

"Here you go. I hope it is to your taste?"

Willa took a sip and smiled, "Perfect."

Smiling, he asked, "So, are you here on holiday?"

"Yes. I am here with my dad." *Oops, did she just say 'with her dad'.* Well, it was too late to take it back now. "We are on a sailing trip and plan to eventually work our way around the world."

He stared wide-eyed. "Wow, you're kidding! That has to be an amazing trip. Is it just the two of you the whole way?"

"Yup. It's just he and I all the way. We've been planning this for some time now." She decided to leave off any statement about her mom. Speaking of which, what was she going to say about her mom? What was she going to say about her age? Fifteen sounded so young. She had no real experience with dating and had only gone to a few school dances with guys, but that was it.

He had apparently been saying something because when she began focusing again, his mouth was moving. *Oops.*

She listened and heard, "… and my parents are as adventurous as your dad seems to be." He stared at her with raised eyebrows.

She realized he expected an answer. But to what, she had no idea. She took a stab at, "Yes, my family has always been into sailing and this trip has been waiting in the wings, so to speak, for many years." She hoped that would work.

Apparently it did because he said, "By the way, my name is Marcel."

"Hi Marcel, I am Willa. It's nice to meet you."

"And you too, Willa. I am from Corsica, which is an island off of the coast of France. My ancestors moved there from France about 200 years ago."

"I am from a small town named Scarsdale, which is located about an hour north of New York City."

They continued chatting this way for the next forty-five minutes. He told her he was attending the London School of Economics on an early admission, so he was smart. On her mom, she told him she died in a boating accident. On siblings, he said he has two younger sisters and she told him her brother died in the boating accident that took their mom. He said he was in Malta with friends from school on holiday. Age never came up.

She finally interrupted and told him she had to call her dad to tell him where they might go to have dinner.

"Oh, there are some really fantastic restaurants in Valletta. Where are you planning to go?"

"I don't really know yet. I haven't paid any attention to where we might go as I've wandered around this afternoon. Do you have any recommendations?"

"My friends and I have heard quite a few good things about Michael's restaurant. It is actually only a short walk from here. It is a little expensive, but it is said to be one of the finest restaurants in Europe. It is run by a father and son and they have served the likes of Madonna and Sir Roger Moore, of James Bond fame." He smiled. "I can take you there, if you like."

"That would be sweet." She didn't just say that, did she? Crap. She is such a goof. She got hold of herself and said, "Okay, let me call my dad and tell him to meet me there." She called, told him about the restaurant and he said he'd meet her there at around seven.

She put her phone in her purse slowly. She was frantically thinking, *now what? I don't want him to go, but he is here with his friends and maybe they are meeting up tonight. But, I also don't want to look desperate.*

She smiled and said, "My dad will meet me at Michael's around seven."

"Wonderful. That gives us another hour together. By the way, what are your plans for your visit to Malta?"

Did he just say they now have another hour? This can't get any better, but she hoped it would. "We leave in three days, so we don't have a lot of time to do much. I bought a ticket for the Hop On Hop Off Bus tomorrow and am planning to ride each line in order to get to see as much of Malta as possible." She hesitated then said softly, "Is that something of interest to you?"

"That sounds like a marvelous idea. I wanted to do that last week with my friends, but no one wanted to go, so I didn't do it. We have just been going to the beach in the day and to clubs at night. It's rather boring to me so I'd love to join you tomorrow."

Her mind was racing. *Okay, okay, it just got way better. Where am I? Here is this cute guy, from Corsica, here on Malta, and he is asking me if he could spend the entire day with me, riding a bus! And he said 'love to join you'!*

"That would be great. I'd love it." *Did I just say love? Oh brother!*

He smiled and said, "Great. I am looking forward to it."

They discussed where they would meet in the morning to get started on their day of bus riding and time flew by until he finally said he would walk her around to the restaurant. They left the Cordina, walked the short distance to the restaurant and stopped outside just as her dad walked up.

He stopped, gave Willa a brief hug and she nervously introduced Marcel. Marcel and her dad shook hands. Marcel said good evening then turned to Willa, "See you tomorrow" and wandered away. Willa stared after him for a few moments then looked back at her dad, who was smiling.

"What?" Willa inquired with a smile on her face. "We just met and he escorted me to the restaurant. That's all."

"Okay, okay. He seems like a nice young man. But, it seems that is not all there is to the story since you and he are seeing each other again tomorrow." He smiled and waited.

"We're just going to do the On/Off Tour. It's really no big deal."

"Sure. It's no big deal and it sounds like fun." He still had a grin on his face.

They finally went into the restaurant and were shown to the one empty table left. As they were seated, Dan ordered drinks, a local beer for him and water for Willa. They each ordered the Salmon starter, while Dan ordered the Rabbit main dish and Willa ordered the Smoked Sea Bass. Neither wanted dessert.

As they ate, Dan asked, "What else do you plan to do tomorrow?"

"As of now we only plan to do the On/Off Bus."

"Sounds like a great idea. Have fun. Please give me a call at about the same time tomorrow evening so we can have dinner again."

After a delicious dinner, they arrived back at the hotel at 10:30 and went to bed shortly after.

5. On/Off Across Malta

Willa and Marcel met at 10 am near the Valletta Castle stop where all three On/Off lines converge. She wore a sun dress with spaghetti straps, flip flops and her hair pulled back into a ponytail. She had taken almost an hour to decide what to wear. Her dad had looked on nonchalantly smiling while she asked, "How does this look?", then changed and asked the same thing over and over. The dress came to her knees and she didn't really know whether it was too much or too little or just right. Her dad only smiled, so she assumed it was just right.

Marcel wore flip flops as well, with a white t-shirt and dark blue cargo pants. *He looks so good*, Willa thought as she saw him walking toward her.

They exchanged pleasantries, chose to head out on the Blue line first and boarded the next one that came by. They knew it might be a stretch to be able to complete the circuits of all three lines and to get off at all of the places they found interesting, so they developed a plan of attack.

Each of them would take turns suggesting whether they should get off at a stop or not and there could be no argument by the other person about the decision. It sounded crazy at first but they soon found they had a lot of fun with it, but this changed when they moved onto the Green Line. They had tried to do the right thing on the other lines by getting off at historic places or at least, places where they could sightsee around the area. But, this went by the wayside once on the Green Line.

When it came to Willa's turn after a couple of stops on the Green Line, she chose the Santana Hotel. When they got off, Willa proceeded to give Marcel an outrageous description of the hotel, its amenities and the local neighborhood. She could see Marcel looking at her like she knew what she was talking about, but then his features started to change. His eyebrows came together, then one side would rise up, then he'd look away and finally he smiled at her. Willa looked at him questioningly. So, he put a serious expression back on his face as though this was the most interesting sight he had ever been to then they both started laughing.

On Marcel's turn he did the same thing at the Oawra Palace Hotel and Willa described the Hilton, where she and her dad were staying as a place for sports stars, movie stars, hicks, hookers and billionaires.

Marcel's next turn was at the Sliema Ferries. He was about to describe the ferry boats, when he saw Willa looking intensely at a leaflet pinned to a notice board at the ferry station. He stopped and came over to see what she was looking at so earnestly and saw that it was a notice for an archery tournament. It said all were welcome to compete in a tournament sponsored by the European Archery Federation. It was to be held on Manoel Island just out in the bay between Sliema and Valletta.

He asked, "Have you ever seen an archery tournament? Would you like to go to see it?"

Willa turned to him, smiled and said, "Actually, I want to compete!"

"You want to compete? Have you competed in archery tournaments before?"

"Well, yes, and I have done well. I love archery and this would be so cool."

Marcel grabbed her hand, "Let's go. We still have time to enter you into the competition and it's only right down the street from here." She started to resist then looked at his face. He was smiling ear to ear, so she shrugged and they took off.

They arrived at the small sports shop where a special room had been set aside for the EAF to sign up competitors. There wasn't much going on at the time and it appeared they were getting ready to shut down the signups. Marcel strode up to the table and said there was one more competitor.

The pretty lady looked up at him, smiled and said, "Okay. Please fill out this form."

Willa and Marcel moved to another table and Willa began filling out the form. Willa hesitated when she came to the entry for 'year of birth', but he didn't seem to notice that her entry clearly indicated she was only fifteen. Once she finished, they walked back to the lady and handed her the completed form. She glanced at it to make sure all was done properly but, when she noticed the name was Will Watson and the female box was the selected gender, she looked up at Marcel.

She smiled. "I think that you have selected the wrong gender. Please cross this one out and mark the male box."

Marcel smiled and pointed to Willa. "She is the competitor."

The lady looked at Willa and said, "Oh! Miss, you do know that this is an international competition and that many of the other competitors are quite good. Some are very well known."

Willa nodded and said, "I have competed in America and done well, so I hope to do well here also."

The woman shrugged, wished Willa good luck and filed the application with the others.

As they walked away, Marcel gave her an impulsive hug and said, "This is so cool. I can't wait to see you shoot."

Willa smiled warily then a look of shock crossed her face. "Oh my God, I don't have a bow!"

Marcel grabbed her hand again, "Then, we need to get you one. This store doesn't have any but I know where we can go." He continued to hold her hand as they walked through the streets of Sliema. He guided her along Testaferrata Street then stopped in front of a large sports store.

Willa stared at the storefront. "How do you know about this place?"

"I found it a few days ago with my friends. One of them wanted to get a new boogie-board so we came here. I am sure I saw that they sell archery bows. Maybe you can find one here that will suit you for the competition."

Willa gave his hand a squeeze and whispered, "Nice place! Okay. Let's go. I need to get a bow and try to get a feel for it before tomorrow."

They entered and, sure enough, there was a large stock of bows, quivers and arrows in the back right corner of the store. Willa began picking out bows, checking their weight, balancing them in her hand and trying to get a feel for it. She finally settled on one particular bow which was longer than she was used to, but its weight and balance were perfect.

At about the time she had settled on the bow, a store employee came over and asked if he could help. Willa turned and asked, "Is there a range where I can test the bow?"

"Sure." He guided them to a large, cavernous room below the store with an indoor range.

This is perfect, thought Willa. There was no one else there so she moved to an open shooting position. The clerk brought her a quiver full of range arrows. Willa nocked an arrow, took aim at a target twenty meters away and let loose. It struck the target, but it was well above the bulls-eye. She nocked another, adjusted her aim and tried again. This shot struck the red area just above the yellow bulls-eye. On the third shot and all shots thereafter, she struck the bulls-eye dead center.

After about fifteen shots, she turned to the clerk and said, "I'll take this one."

The clerk led them back to the register, rang up the bow, Willa paid and they exited the store.

As they reached the curb outside of the store, Marcel turned to her and said, "Wow, you are really good. I predict a first place finish for you tomorrow."

Willa smiled, "Well, that would be nice, but there are other competitors, you know. I have heard about some of them and they are really good. Also, I will be using a bow I am not used to!"

Marcel smiled, "Well, I know you will do great."

Willa suddenly remembered the time and saw it was already 6:30. "Crap, I was supposed to call my dad at 6:00." She pulled out her phone and called.

He answered on the first ring. "Hey Willa. I was wondering if you had forgotten about me."

"Sorry. We got hung up buying a bow." Before her dad could say anything, she said, "I'll tell you at dinner. Where do you want to eat?"

Her dad suggested the same place as last night and told her to ask Marcel if he'd like to join them.

After she put her phone away, Willa stood still for a second and stared at her hands. *What did he just say? Did her dad just tell her to bring a boy along to dinner with her?* Her world was spinning out of control, and she loved it.

Finally, Marcel asked, "Is everything okay."

"Sure." She still stood looking puzzled, but then smiled, looked at Marcel and asked, "Would you like to join my dad and me for dinner at Michael's?"

"Are you sure? I don't want to intrude."

"No worry. My dad asked me to ask you to come with us." Then she quickly added, "And I would love to have you join us."

Marcel smiled, "Well, with an invitation like that, how can I resist? I'd be happy to join you for dinner. From here, we'll be there at about 7:00." He grabbed her hand and they walked to Michael's.

Willa did not stop smiling the entire walk to the restaurant.

6. The Tournament

Her dad was waiting for them at Michael's. They all greeted one another and Willa explained the bow and the tournament with Marcel joining in, when prompted. Afterwards, her dad said he was delighted she would be able to compete and that he and Marcel would provide her with fan support and be her loudest cheerleaders. Willa rolled her eyes wondering if this could get any weirder.

Dinner went well and Willa's dad seemed to get along nicely with Marcel. They talked about boats and Marcel's studies at the London School of Economics. Willa almost fell asleep onto her plate when the school conversation continued through the main course. I mean, how much is there to say that's actually interesting about Purchasing Power, Exchange Rates and International Trade Sanctions. Fortunately, they moved on to other topics before she took the head plunge into her salmon.

At ten pm, her dad suggested they head back to the hotel. He paid the bill and refused any contribution from Marcel. They exited the restaurant and decided they would all meet at the tournament field near Fort Manoel at nine am. This would give Willa time to practice and for the guys to get good seats.

Once that was all agreed, Willa's dad did a little throat clearing and said, "I'll go and get a taxi to take us back to the hotel. The taxi queue is just over there." He smiled and walked away.

Marcel faced Willa, "Get a good night's sleep because I expect to be hugging an archery champion tomorrow after the tournament!"

Willa frowned and said, "Why hug them? Why not hug me?"

Marcel flushed and quickly added, "No, no! I meant you will be the champion and I will get to hug you!"

"Well, I don't know if I'll win, but even if I don't, you can still hug me." She quickly thought, *Oh my gosh. That sounded so lame.*

Marcel smiled. "I'd be happy to hug you anytime. How about now?"

"Sure." They hugged and as he pulled away from her, he smiled, "See you tomorrow!" As he walked away, Willa thought, *I think he might have wanted to kiss me. I wish he had or at least tried. I know I wanted to kiss him!*

Her dad walked up at about this time and saw her looking toward where Marcel had gone. He asked, "Ready?"

Willa smiled! "Yup. Let's go."

XXXXX

When Marcel got to his room, he immediately called the number he had been given a few days ago. When the person answered, Marcel said, "The girl and her dad are here but they will leave in two days for Tenerife. Should I follow?"

"No. We have someone else there already. Stay with them until they leave then return here."

The man hung up and Marcel slowly set his phone down and sighed. This type of mission made him almost hate his job. He was glad this would only be for another day.

XXXXX

Willa was still smiling when she woke the next morning. She bounded out of bed and got ready to go. They left in a taxi for the tournament field at 8:30. They were dropped off near the fort and they walked to the sign-in desk. She gave the young man her name and he gave Willa an identity bracelet and a slip to use to check out as many arrows as she needed for her practice session.

He added, "This event is not a sanctioned event by the International Governing Body, so not all standard tournament rules will be followed. Competition arrows will be distributed as each level of advancement is reached. Ten arrows will be given to each competitor for each session and each arrow will contribute ten points to the competitors score. The scores for each session will determine if a competitor advances to the next level and the scores are not accumulated over all sessions." Willa nodded in understanding and exited the area.

Willa passed through to the tournament field, while her dad went to the viewing area to find Marcel. She glanced over at them when she reached the practice field and saw her dad and Marcel up in the stands waving at her. She was still having trouble adjusting to the fact that her dad was sitting with a guy that she had only known for a little over two days, and who had almost kissed his fifteen year old daughter the night before.

She went to the stock of arrows and showed the lady her permission slip. The lady gave her a bag of twenty arrows and told her to come back if she needed more. "But," the lady said, "Practice ends sharply at 9:45 and the first level of competition begins promptly at ten."

Willa walked to an open practice position at the range and began shooting. It took about five arrows to get used to the weight, length and feel of her new bow again, but she eventually started hitting the bulls-eye on each shot.

The tournament began promptly, as the lady said, at ten with Willa competing in the individual women's group. Willa easily qualified for the next level, which began at one pm. She walked over to the stands to find her dad and Marcel. They both said good shooting as they moved to the concession area for a light lunch. At 12:30, Willa went back to the tournament grounds.

Willa passed into the final round which began at three pm. She didn't go to the viewing stands this time. Instead, she went to the practice range to make any final adjustments she thought necessary. As she shot her final practice arrows, she wondered how she would do in the finals. The other finalists were all top shooters from around the world with impressive international experience. Willa had never competed internationally or against such a top notch field.

The finals began promptly at 3:00. The women were up first and each competitor was given their arrows. Their total score after shooting their arrows would determine the overall winner. It was getting quite warm now and several of the finalists seemed to be having trouble with the heat. Willa had seen them shoot better in the earlier rounds.

They were finally down to two arrows and Willa had a score of 78 out of 100, which put her in second place. She figured she needed to hit the bulls-eye with each of her remaining two arrows in order to have a chance at winning. She concentrated on each shot and two bulls-eyes gave her a total score of 98. Willa saw that the one remaining competitor had one arrow left and needed a bulls-eye to take the title. Willa watched as she pulled back, aimed and let her last arrow fly to the target.

Bulls-eye! Willa had taken second place. She couldn't help smiling as she turned to look at the viewing stands where she saw Marcel and her dad wildly cheering and waving their arms. There were actually many people cheering for her. Maybe all of this cheering was because she was an unknown and so much younger than the other competitors. Or, it actually didn't have anything to do with her and they were mimicking the cheering of the two guys who were acting like crazy men. She didn't care. She was only thinking about how cool it will be to show her second place medal to the team when she got back to school.

As Willa was gathering her things and getting her medal before making her way over to the viewing stands, Dan turned to Marcel and asked, "Would you like to come back to the hotel with us for a celebratory drink at the hotel bar and dinner at the restaurant? We must be on our way tomorrow, so you can take the opportunity to say goodbye to Willa. I know she would like that."

"I'd love to join you for a drink, but I must decline dinner since I am meeting my friends for dinner later. I have been putting them off for the last couple of days." He smiled and so did Dan, both knowing why he had been putting his friends off. They turned as Willa came up to them.

Dan gave her a hug and told her how proud he was of her. Marcel also gave her his promised champion's hug. As they made their way out, Willa gave her bow to a young girl who had congratulated Willa on her shooting. The girl seemed excited and started showing it to her friends.

They took a taxi to the hotel and went directly into the lounge area. Dan had a beer, while Willa and Marcel had orange juice. They had one more drink before her dad said, "I am going up to the room to change for dinner. It was nice meeting you, Marcel, and I wish you the best in your studies." Dan smiled and headed to the elevators.

"I'll be up in a minute, dad." Willa called after him.

After her dad left, Willa walked Marcel out to the front of the hotel so that he could take a taxi back to his friends. As they stood, seemingly wondering how to say goodbye, Willa turned to Marcel and gave him a hug. She pulled back smiling. "Thanks for sharing these past days with me. I had a really great time." She paused then added, "I hope my dad wasn't too boring."

Marcel quickly said, "No, no. I am the one who should be grateful. I mean it isn't often I get to spend two days with such a pretty girl and then get to tell my friends I dated a European Archery Champion!"

"Actually, I had a second place finish and it wasn't a sanctioned event!" Then she stopped speaking. *Wait, did he say she was pretty and they had dated? As in, she was pretty and they had been on a date?* This story will be even better than the archery story when she tells all her friends at school.

Willa then did something else new for her. She got up on her toes, leaned in, put her arms around his neck and kissed Marcel right on the lips. They held the kiss for a few seconds then pulled away from each other.

He broke the silence and said, "I need to get going. Maybe we could keep in touch?"

"Absolutely, I'd love to." Willa gave him her email address. He smiled then headed to a waiting taxi.

Willa waved as the taxi drove off, stood for a bit then headed up to the room. The good thing was that her dad didn't say anything, other than, "He seems nice."

She responded with, "Yeah, he was very nice."

They decided to have dinner on the balcony of their room and talk about the trip.

Tomorrow they would be off to Gibraltar, but tonight, Willa was looking forward to her dreams. And, maybe an email!

7. Gibraltar and Tenerife

By nine am, she and her dad were at the boat packing everything away and getting ready to set off on their next leg. The plan was to head to Gibraltar where they would restock for the next leg to Tenerife in the Canary Islands. It was a shorter leg than the leg to Gibraltar, but it would be out in the rougher waters of the eastern Atlantic Ocean. Storms and a busy set of sea lanes would be their main concerns.

Willa estimated that it would probably take them about a week to reach Gibraltar, a tiny speck of rock connected to southern Spain by a narrow stretch of land. This tiny speck is part of Great Britain and was ceded in perpetuity to Great Britain in 1713 by the Treaty of Utrecht, but Spain would now like it back. However, all referendums by the citizens for choosing Spain versus Britain have overwhelmingly been in favor of continued British rule.

They planned to spend a couple of days on Gibraltar then head to Tenerife to spend at least a week refitting and restocking the boat for the very long journey to Cape Town, South Africa. And, at least in Willa's mind, she was definitely going to enjoy the sunny weather and white sand beaches in Tenerife.

On the second day out of Malta, Willa was relaxing on the top deck while her dad was at the helm. She had been enjoying the sun in her bathing suit for the past couple of hours but finally got up, put on a t-shirt and flip flops then walked over to her dad.

"So, dad, are you enjoying the trip so far?"

He smiled. "Of course I am! What father wouldn't enjoy being out on the open sea, sailing under blue skies and spending some very lovely time with his delightful daughter?"

"Oh dad, stop trying to be such a softy. I know you are a tough old brute," smiling sweetly at him.

"Yeah, that's me.

Willa was quiet for a minute or so then asked, "Dad, sometimes I don't feel focused on my future. I mean, I know I am good at school and really good with languages. I also know that I am very good analytically and have that eidetic memory thing working for me. But, what does all that mean? How does that help me to map some kind of plan for my future?"

Dan hadn't expected a question like that, but he was getting used to his teenage daughter coming up with challenging questions for him. He looked out ahead of them then asked, "Willa, when you look ahead, out over the water here, what do you see exactly? I mean, what do you see that is a sure thing for the next leg of our journey to Gibraltar?"

Willa looked where her dad was looking. After a moment, she said, "Well, at least for the near distance, I see calm waters and 'smooth sailing' for us. But, as we know, much can change out here on the open water when so many elements are yet unknown. Weather, the shipping lanes and our boat may present us challenges, but we can never be sure. However, I know we will do great."

"Life is like that. We can look at what we know and what our experiences tell us, but we just don't know what life will present us. We simply need to be prepared to take action when it throws us 'a curve' we don't expect." He turned to her at this point. "Willa, you are well prepared to handle what life throws at you. Don't worry. You have years before you have to decide on some type of life's work and, when the decision presents itself, you will make the right choice." He smiled. "If things change then you will adjust and make it work for you."

Willa became quiet and continued looked over the bow at the water. As Dan watched her he noticed a small smile. He finally interrupted her thoughts and asked, "Anyway, do you have any thoughts on what we should do or see in Gibraltar?"

"Well, we could hike up the Rock of Gibraltar then take the Cable Car back down. That is supposed to be pretty cool. I also wouldn't mind wandering some of the streets and checking out the architecture. We could also check out St Michael's Cave, but I'm not interested in the Gibraltar monkeys, unless you are?"

Dan smiled. "Nah, monkeys aren't my thing either, but I definitely like the idea of the hike and the Cable Car ride."

"The truth is, but I am really more excited about Tenerife and ..."

"The beaches?" Dan interjected.

"Now how did you guess that?" She said with a big smile.

Gibraltar proved to be a fun short stay. After finding and paying for moorage, they headed into town to search for someplace to eat. After eating, they walked the streets for a while. But after a couple of hours, both of them started to feel a little drowsy, so they decided to head back to the boat for the night.

The next day, they were up and about with lots of energy for the first of only two full days in town. They headed to the 'Rock' to hike up and then to take the cable car back down.

The hike up the mountain wasn't difficult and they had plenty of time to stop to take in the views of the city, the blue waters of the Mediterranean, Spain in the near distance and the coast of Africa in the far distance. They snapped pictures of the views, took some selfies, asked folks to take pictures of the both of them and, all-in-all, it was a fun hike.

Before heading down, they walked the short distance to St Michael's cave. It was a pretty site. The stalactites and stalagmites were amazing and many of them were greenish in color. They also thought the chapel deep inside the cave was fantastic. There, they both took a few moments to sit and offer prayers for Olivia and Peter.

The Cable Car ride down was cool and they eventually found a small pub down near the water. They each ordered a Shepherd's pie then wandered the town. The next day, Dan busied himself with preparations for the next leg of the trip, while Willa wandered the town, checking out the shops and architecture.

XXXXX

"They are headed to Tenerife and then to Cape Town." The caller said.

"Is this reliable?"

"Yes. Our friend has been very helpful and I'll pass on your heartfelt gratitude!"

"Whatever." He clicked off and then got back on the satellite phone. He entered the number and it was answered on the second ring."

"What?"

"They are heading to Tenerife then to Cape Town. Do you have help in Tenerife and Cape Town already?"

"Yes. Do we know what they are up to yet?"

"Not really. Having a fun trip is all we can figure out at this point, but it could be a ruse for something else. Their communications are routine and her uploads have been scanned by our best code breakers but they can't find anything out of the ordinary in them. We'll keep watching."

XXXXX

The Tenerife leg wasn't as long as the one to Gibraltar, but it was mostly on the open Atlantic Ocean and they had to be ever watchful for ship traffic and storms off the coast of Africa. After all, most of the hurricanes that strike the Caribbean islands and east coast of the United States are spawned in these waters and it was hurricane season now.

Luckily, they didn't encounter any trouble and made it to Tenerife in a little over a week. Tenerife is one of a number of islands that make up The Canary Islands, which is administered by Spain. The islands, Tenerife in particular, are a very popular holiday destination for European travelers and most of the island's residents speak fluent English for that very reason. However, Willa was anxious to try her Spanish during their stay.

They planned to be in Tenerife for at least a week since the next leg was extremely long and could be very dangerous for a number of reasons. The weather and large ship traffic were just two of those dangers. And, they would be passing along the coastline of Africa that contained numerous 'political trouble spots'. These were mostly governments, or factions within those countries, who were very unhappy with their own circumstances and were out to make changes and trouble in the area.

There were a few safe harbors along the way if they needed one, but they would likely be on their own until they reached Cape Town.

But, right now, they were in Tenerife and Willa planned to make the most of the sunny weather and the beautiful, warm, sandy beaches.

Willa and her dad secured the boat, paid the moorage fee and headed into town. They chose the Hotel Silken Atlantida in Santa Cruz. It was about 800 meters from where the boat was moored along Avenue Tres de Mayo. It was a very nice hotel with free WiFi and breakfast.

They also decided to rent a car. The island was not large but, with a car, you could get almost anywhere within an hour. That was all great, but Willa only cared about finding beaches!

After dinner in the hotel restaurant, they headed back up to the room. There was a mini-frig stocked with various drinks and snacks. Dan grabbed a beer and a soda and headed over to Willa, who was sitting outside on the small balcony. They were on the sixth floor, so they had a very nice view out over the water and the waterfront.

He handed the soda to Willa, sat, popped his beer and took a sip. "So," he started, "how is the trip going so far for you? By the way, did you hear from Marcel? He seemed like a nice guy. I liked him and I really enjoyed talking with him at dinner and at the tournament."

"No. Not yet anyway." She smiled and continued, "And yes, the trip is going great. I mean, I met a cute guy my dad actually likes!" and they both smiled. "And, I won a trophy at an International Archery Tournament. But, most importantly, I am definitely getting one of the nicest tans I have ever had. What could be better?" Willa smiled and glanced at her dad. He was sort of smiling, but he also seemed to be staring at some small point off in the distance.

Willa looked away and ventured, "Thinking of mom and Peter?"

Dan turned to her smiling sadly, "Yes. I can't but think they would have been so happy to be here with us."

"Are you regretting our decision to come on the trip without them?"

Dan immediately turned to Willa and said, "Absolutely not! This is the best thing we could have done to honor their memories. It was silly of me to have put it off for so long and I am glad you kept insisting we do it. You were right and I was wrong to have delayed."

Willa set her drink down and came over to her dad. She climbed up onto his lap like she used to do, not that long ago. She put her arms around his neck and hugged him tightly. He did the same to her and she whispered, "I love you, dad."

After a bit, she smiled at him and went back over to her chair. Dan was quiet for a moment then said, "Well, I am happy too, but maybe you should start running again. You seem to be putting on weight. My legs fell asleep while you were sitting on them."

Willa blinked, looked at him and saw a big smile. She laughed and said she was actually thinking the same thing. "I think I'll start running first thing in the morning! After all, I should also make sure I keep in shape so that I look nice. I want to be fit and trim to go along with this new tan. Then, when we get home next year, I can adjust my outfits to make sure people can see how good I look. Maybe I'll add some new slimmer and shorter skirts. Oh, and yes, I need to get some of those little bikinis so many girls are wearing now at the beach. Maybe, I should also consider getting more tight little spaghetti-strap t-shirts and tank tops. Of course, that will mean getting some new bras and panties that don't really show through these new tight clothes."

She was looking out over the city as she said that, but as she finished, she surreptitiously glanced over at her dad. His look was priceless. You would have thought she was asking him what he thought of her taking a job in a Girlie Club serving drinks to men with more than drinks on their minds. She looked at him innocently and said, "What? What's wrong dad?"

When his look didn't change, she laughed and told him, "I'm just kidding. Don't worry. I'm not going to do all of that. Well, except for the teeny, tiny bikinis."

Dan harrumphed and said, "I'm getting another beer." He turned away from the balcony and walked into the room with a smile on his face. Then, the smile faded and thought. *She was kidding. I am sure of it.* But, he wasn't so sure. Boy, raising a daughter was harder than he had expected.

8. The Beach

Willa was up and out of the room by seven am the following morning. She dressed in shorts, a t-shirt and running shoes then headed downstairs to the concierge desk. In Spanish, she asked the gentleman if he could recommend some safe areas to go running.

He pondered the question a moment then responded in Spanish, "I am not aware of a specific running route, but there are wide walkways and several small parks along the waterfront that might be suitable. While you are gone, I will check with some of my colleagues about running routes and will have some ideas ready for you when you return."

She thanked him and headed out. She ran toward the water along the avenue then turned south. He had been right. The walkways were quite wide and she had no problem navigating her way around people and crossing streets. There was a small park about a mile along the route so she turned into it. There were a few short trails that at least gave her something different to look at other than cars and tourists. After about thirty minutes, she turned and headed back to the hotel.

As she entered the hotel lobby, the concierge hurried over and handed her a towel and a glass of cold water. She was a little surprised at this service gesture, but smiled and thanked him.

"I have checked online and with several of the staff about running routes but they are not aware of specific running trails. However, there are numerous wilderness and hiking trails outside of the city and those could certainly be excellent trails to run on."

"Great, and thanks for checking."

Dan was up and eating breakfast when she entered the room. He told her she could call room service now and her breakfast would be ready for her after her shower. She called then headed to her room.

After her shower and breakfast, she asked, "So, what is on our agenda for today?" She had a big smile on her face, expecting to hear about a beach trip.

"Well, I figured we could get our car and drive along the northern part of the island to look for a nice spot to have lunch. Then, we could pick up some travel brochures to see what fun activities there might be around the area. I hear there is a theme park down south that might be fun. Also, they are supposed to have a very interesting zoo with many indigenous island species." He stopped and continued to look out over the water knowing full well what Willa was doing.

Willa was staring at him like he had just told her to get a job babysitting in order to help pay for the trip. She could not believe he was suggesting a theme park and a zoo! Did he think she was ten years old, again?

She was about to say something, when he looked at her with a big smile, raised his eyebrows and said, "Gotcha!"

"You, you, you ...", she couldn't think of anything clever to say, so she finally laughed too.

"Come on. Let's go find a nice beach to explore for interesting rocks and shells."

"Sure, great idea."

The hotel had a car rental agency they regularly used, so they called and rented a car based on what Dan had specified. The hotel also got him a twenty percent discount on the rate and the agency delivered the vehicle to the front entrance. While Dan was taking care of this, Willa went over to the concierge desk and asked for a map of the island. The concierge gave her several that highlighted roads, parks, beaches and trails.

When the car arrived, they loaded up their stuff and drove off. Willa would be the navigator, just as she was on the boat. She directed her dad along the TF-5 Hwy that ran west, then south along the coast. She had found a black sand beach there called Playa Jardin when she was researching beaches the night before. It was about fifty kilometers from Santa Cruz.

They arrived a little after eleven am, parked and decided to grab a quick lunch before making the short walk to the beach. They also weren't sure if there were changing rooms at the beach, so they used the restaurant's restrooms to change into their swim suits. They bought water then headed to the beach.

They walked around the corner of a sand dune and looked on in wonder at the black sand beach. It was stunning and the sand was so dark. Many of the black sand beaches around the world, like the ones on Maui and Santorini, are grayish due to the mixing of lighter sand with the volcanic sand. But, this one was almost pure black.

Willa had read that the beach was man-made back in the early 1990s. An investor thought it would be a great tourist attraction and serve the surrounding hotels, restaurants and shops very well. And it had! The black, volcanic sand was literally hauled up from the sea floor nearby then dumped in an area of beach which had been stripped back to make room for it. The beach was divided into three sections separated by large stone walls. This was done to prevent excessive erosion of the black sand.

Willa didn't care how it was made or why. She just wanted to get on it, go for a swim then lie in the sun on the warm, black sand! Dan smiled when he glanced at Willa's face. She was so happy, which made him happy that he could afford to do this for her. It had been too long since they had spent time together just having fun.

They wandered to the section furthest to the left and picked a spot for the blanket they had bought the day before. They dropped their borrowed hotel towels and backpacks on it, took their shorts and t-shirts off, lathered on sunscreen lotion then headed to the water. The sand was warm and soft on their feet and the water was the perfect temperature.

After about twenty minutes, they wandered back to the blanket and lay down. Dan put his t-shirt back on since he was not much of a 'sun worshipper'. Willa was and, since she was wearing a cute two piece bikini, lathered herself with more sunscreen lotion before lying on the blanket.

Dan could see that she was not going anywhere anytime soon, so he nudged her and said, "I'm going to do some exploring."

She kept her eyes shut and said, "Sure, see you later." Dan wandered off.

Willa rolled onto her back after twenty or thirty minutes, added more sunscreen then closed her eyes. She was totally into black sand beaches. She and her dad had taken a few pictures earlier and she planned to send them to her friends as soon as she got back to the hotel. She could send them now, but she didn't want to spend time doing something that took her mind off of the beach and the sunshine. She could also use the history and uniqueness of the beach in one of her school projects.

She wasn't sure how much longer she dozed, but she opened her eyes when she felt a shadow move over her. At first, she thought her dad had come back, so she smiled and said, "Hey, dad. How was your walk?"

When he didn't respond, she opened her eyes and began to focus. It wasn't her dad. It was a stranger. She quickly sat up and grabbed her t-shirt. She stood and stared at the man walking away from her. He looked like a beach bum.

She scanned the beach for anyone else and finally noticed several people gathered down on the far right section of the beach. They weren't paying any attention to what was happening at her end and she didn't see her dad anywhere.

The man wandered away into the dunes and grasses which ran back away from the beach area. Before he was out-of-sight, Willa grabbed her smartphone, snapped off a couple of pictures and watched him go until he was out of sight. He had been about her dad's age, probably in his mid-fifties, dark hair down to his shoulders, dark skin, ragged clothes and sneakers. He was around six feet tall and maybe one hundred and forty pounds.

People told her in the past that she'd make a great witness in a police investigation. She seemed to be able to remember almost everything about a person even if she only saw them briefly. She had learned later that she had an eidetic memory. She was somewhat flattered by that, but secretly hoped she'd never have to put the skill to actual use.

She decided to move closer to the people to the right. She would have to watch for her dad so he didn't freak out when he returned and didn't find her where he had left her. She put on her shorts and sandals, packed up their stuff and wandered in the direction of the group at the far end. She stopped a few meters away, laid everything out again, then sat on her blanket.

She glanced toward the group and noticed they were a group of six teenagers near her age. There were four boys and two girls, and they were speaking English. Some of it was British and some of it was English accented with French. It seemed that the boys were the Brits and the girls were the French. She also noticed that a couple of the guys kept glancing over at her. One of them nudged the girl to his right, said something to her, she nodded then started walking over to Willa.

The four boys were all cute, about the same height, around five and a half feet tall, trim and fit with light tans. They each wore shorts and t-shirts of various colors.

The girl approaching Willa was about Willa's size and had long, dark brown hair tied back in a blue ribbon. She had shorts that showed off her tan, shapely legs and her t-shirt was worn loose. She had a nice smile with a couple of slightly crooked front teeth. Her eyes were brown and her nose was pert and a little turned up at the tip.

The girl standing back with the boys looked about the same height, but she was blonde and, some people would say, voluptuous. Her shorts were tight and barely covered her butt. She wore a tube top that Willa supposed was struggling to do its job successfully.

Willa looked away and waited. The girl finally reached her blanket and spoke to her in halting Spanish. She asked Willa, "Are you here alone?"

Willa responded in perfect French, "I speak French and I am here on vacation with my father."

The girl squealed and started yelling to the other girl in French to come over to her. The other girl ran over and the first girl told her she had found another French girl.

Willa smiled, stood and in French said, "I am actually American, but have learned to speak French and a few other languages. My name is Willa."

The first girl said, "My name is Bernadette and this is my friend Santine."

Bernadette continued, "Those boys are from England and we are all here to run a local charity race. It is just a ten kilometer race, but it raises money for an orphanage here in Tenerife. We are on a French girls' team."

"I think that is so wonderful that you are doing this. Your parents must be very proud of you."

Both girls giggled then admitted, "Well, they are, but we may have also wanted to do the race in order to come here for a short holiday."

Willa laughed, "Well, no sense in coming all the way here and not enjoying the beautiful beaches and sunny weather."

Santine grabbed Willa's hand and dragged her to where the boys were. "This is our new friend, Willa. She is French, but she also speaks American English very well." She glanced at Willa and winked. Willa decided to go along with the charade.

The boys smiled and introduced themselves as Brian, Thomas, Jeremy and William. Willa smiled at each and nodded.

The girls helped Willa bring her stuff over to their little camp then they all sat. Willa asked, "Tell me about the race."

Brian took charge. "The race was organized about ten years ago to benefit an orphanage here in Santa Cruz. The organizers were part of a British tour group here on vacation. They had seen how much the kids needed the orphanage and decided that a charity race might be a good way to attract money and donations for it."

"They started out using their own tour group the following year and raced just two teams. At first no one really competed. They just ran for fun and wore funny costumes. On the third trip here, one of the people in the tour group happened to be a marketing representative for a large sports drink company in Britain. He saw the advantage to his company and to the orphanage to grow the race and to make it more competitive. He also felt that it should have teams representing all of Europe."

Santine cut in, "When he got back to London, he pitched the idea to his company. He suggested that they should sponsor the race, put up some prize money for the winning teams and to give a donation to the orphanage. The company loved the idea and he spent the next year organizing and promoting the race around Europe. The race grew like crazy and now there are teams from all over Europe and even North Africa. There are a total of forty-five teams this year with each team made up of five runners. The event holds five separate ten kilometer races and each team puts a member of their team in each race. The combined lowest total time for a team wins the prize money and the trophy."

"There are twenty-five boy teams and twenty girl teams. These boys" and she pointed at the boys with them, "are four members of the British boys' team."

"Cool. When is the race?" asked Willa.

"It is three days from now on Saturday. You should come and watch. The Parque Maritimo is the race's staging area. It is a large park between the bay and Constitution Avenue and they close off a section of the avenue. The runners for each ten kilometer race start in the area in front of the Parque Maritimo, run five kilometers, turn and run back to the finish. The times are recorded and once all five races have been completed, the times for each runner are added and a team total is determined. There is a boys' team winner and a girls' team winner. There are also awards given to the top three individual boys and girls based on their time in the 10k leg that they ran. The whole event lasts from seven am to around four or five pm. Afterwards, everyone heads out to party! Woo hoo!"

"It sounds like so much fun. I'll definitely try to come and watch."

The teens hung out and swam and chatted at the beach. Several times the girls would change to speaking French just to annoy the boys, but it was always in good fun and no one took offense. The boys finally retaliated by starting to speak with Cockney and Geordie accents.

After three or four hours, her dad finally wandered back down to the beach. At first he panicked when he didn't see Willa at their chosen spot, but then he heard the kids all laughing and figured she had joined the group so he walked toward them. She saw him coming and trotted over to meet him.

When she got to him, she hugged him and whispered, "The boys think that I am French."

He looked at her, smiled and nodded.

"This is my dad, Dan." Willa proceeded to introduce each of the others by name and they all said hi. Santine noticed his American accent and smiled.

He saw her smile and said, "Yes, I am American and Willa's mother was French. She passed away years ago, but Willa kept up her French even while we lived in America. She is a French citizen as well as an American citizen."

Willa smiled, but her mind was racing. First, because it had been a little over a week since she had had to tell someone that her mom was dead and the finality of the statement still hurt a little. Second, because her dad said she was a French citizen and seemed serious about it. This was the first she had heard it and she'd have to ask him about it as soon as possible.

It was getting close to five pm when Dan quietly suggested to Willa that they head back to the hotel. She nodded and said bye to everyone. Bernadette asked, "So, where are you staying?"

"We are at the Silken on Tres de Mayo," said Willa.

"Oh, okay. That's not too far from where most of the teams are staying. Maybe we'll see you again before the race."

"I'd like that", said Willa and gave Bernadette her phone number.

They all waved as Willa and her dad headed to the car. When they had everything stowed and were seated, Willa turned to her dad and asked, "Am I really a French citizen?"

"Actually, you are. Your mother had French citizenship because of her dad. So, citizenship can be passed to the child of a citizen. We filed for it right after you were born, as we had done for Peter. However, we never arranged to get you a passport because, well, you didn't need one and we didn't really have any plans to go to France for any length of time. However, you could get one now if you wanted to apply once we get home. By the way, you also have Russian citizenship. Your grandmother was a Russian citizen, as was your mom and as are you. You could get passports for both countries, if you like."

Willa could only say, "Way cool!"

9. The Event

As things turned out, Willa was now on the French girls' team. During her run on Thursday morning she met up with Santine and Bernadette, as well as two other girls on the team, Andrea and Chantal. They all started running together and Willa asked in French, "Where's the fifth girl on your team?"

Bernadette grumbled, "Francine, Andrea and Chantal went off shopping yesterday instead of coming with Santine and me to the beach. As they walked along one of the avenues, they were talking and laughing. Suddenly Francine screeched and told the others to look over to the other side of the avenue at some boys that were checking them out. But, as they continued walking, they did not pay attention and Francine stepped off the curb, twisted her ankle and fell to her knees."

Willa asked, "Is she okay!"

"No. Her ankle is swollen and her right knee sustained a severe bruise. She will not be able to run on Saturday."

"I'm so sorry."

As they ran along, they chatted about the trip, boys and beaches.

They ran for another thirty minutes then made their way back to the girls' hotel. Once there, they stopped, went into the lobby then made their way to sit by the pool.

They picked up bottles of water from the huge cooler nearby, wandered to the pool, took their running shoes and socks off then sat on the edge of the pool dangling their feet in the water.

Santine looked back toward the lounge chairs and saw Francine on one of them reading. She shouted over to her, "Hey, Francine, how's the ankle?"

"Still swollen", as she said this, she slowly rose, grabbed a crutch and hobbled over to the pool. She eased herself down and sat with the others dangling her feet in the water.

"Francine, this is Willa."

Willa and Francine smiled and said hey.

Suddenly, Santine smiled, looked at Willa, then at Bernadette and said, "I know who we can get to take Francine's place on the team!"

"Who?" Bernadette said excitedly.

Santine let her eyes drift over to Willa and smiled. Bernadette followed Santine's eyes and then her face lit up. "Yes, that's a great idea!"

Willa looked back at them with a half-smile on her face because they seemed so happy, although, she wasn't sure why they were. Then it hit her. She was their choice to take Francine's place on the team. "No. I can't do that. I'm not a team member and didn't come with you and haven't trained like you guys." Her mind whirled trying to come up with more reasons why she couldn't do it.

Bernadette was now smiling at her even more broadly. "You are the perfect replacement for Francine. We know you and we have run with you so we know you are good. Plus, you are a French citizen!"

"But, I do not have a passport!"

"That's no big deal. The consulate here can check online for your citizenship. They don't need a French passport so you can show them your American passport, which they can use to get your personal information correct. Our coach will be thrilled. She was thinking we'd either have to forfeit our entry or run it with only four runners. Willa, please, you are the perfect choice and we would not have to forfeit."

Willa thought for a minute then looked between Santine and the other girls. She could see their excitement. She gradually started to smile and finally said, "Sure, why not."

Everyone immediately stood and discussed what they had to do next. As they did that, they started moving toward the hotel lobby. Once there, Bernadette reached for one of the hotel phones to call Coach Sabin.

When the coach answered, Bernadette quickly explained their solution to her. She mumbled "um and we and Willa" a few times then hung up. She turned to everyone and yelled, "We are a team!"

They all shrieked and laughed and hugged, even Willa. Then, she remembered her father. Oops, she needed to make a call. She explained this to Bernadette and went off to the side to make the call.

When Dan answered, she explained what was going on and, just like Bernadette's call to Ms. Sabin, there were "ums, yeses, okays and sure" on her end of the conversation. She hung up and went back to the girls. Bernadette had told everyone what Willa had to do so they were all watching her with expectant looks as she walked over to them.

As she walked over, she smiled and exclaimed, "I'm in!" More shrieks and hugs were exchanged.

XXXXX

So, on this bright Saturday morning Willa, her team and all the other teams gathered in the Parque Maritimo. The consulate had checked Willa's personal information on Thursday afternoon, confirmed her citizenship and gave her an official form to indicate her French citizenship. Ms. Sabin had taken that to the race officials and explained what had happened to the other girl and why Willa was their substitute. Thank goodness for the French and Spanish laissez faire attitude because the officials stamped the changes that permitted her entry into the race without any questions.

Willa had gone for another run with the girls on Friday and afterwards the girls gathered at poolside to discuss their race strategy. Francine sat nearby with a pained look on her face.

Francine had originally been assigned the last leg, but now they were discussing different strategies. Maybe Willa should go last or first or third, but then others would have to switch around their legs. Finally, Santine interrupted the conversations and said, "Look. It is the day before the race. We should just let Willa run the last leg so the rest of us can keep the legs we have been training for."

Everyone had been quiet for a moment then they all smiled and said "Good idea". So, the racing order would be Bernadette first then Andrea, Chantel, Santine and finally Willa.

XXXXX

Dan was on the opposite side of the start line and waved as the girls lined up for the officials to mark their race bibs. Once this was done, no other team members were allowed into the start area and no runner could leave the area, except for health, injury or emergency reasons.

They were now ready to start the first leg of the race, so the first group of runners shuffled up to the start line. The boys would be started first then the girls about ten minutes later. Once all in the first group of runners finished, they would do the same with the second group and so on until all of the runners on each team had finished.

The race was using chip timers. This was older technology, but the race officials had decided not to add any new expenses to their costs. Each runner had been issued a chip to tie onto their running shoe and the chip would record the time the runner crossed the five kilometer point before turning back to the finish line. Once the runner crossed the finish line, their chip would be taken off and collected. The times were automatically recorded for each runner and the results would be known instantly at the end of the race. Team and individual honors would be awarded within an hour of the completion of the race by all teams and runners.

Group one runners were now lined up at the start line. The starter raised his air-horn, held it for a second then squeezed the trigger. The blast was met by cheers, screams and stomping feet as the boys took off. Immediately, the girls in the first group started to line up at the start line. Willa and her team members gave Bernadette high-fives and words of encouragement as she headed to the line. Ten minutes after the boys started, the horn went off again and the girls took off.

Depending on the ability of the runner, a ten kilometer race takes anywhere from a fast thirty minutes to an slow and easy sixty minutes, or even longer. About thirty-five minutes after the boys started, the first boy came across the finish line. Within a few minutes, more boys came across. The first girl crossed the finish line about thirty-eight minutes after she had started. Bernadette finished in an excellent time of forty-three minutes.

Once the officials knew the course was clear, they started the second group of boys then the second group of girls. The same process unfolded for this group and the next and the next. They finally got to the fifth, and last, group at almost two in the afternoon.

Willa's team was doing well. Andrea's time was forty-four minutes, Chantal's time was a quick forty minutes and Santine's time was forty-two minutes. Willa had been resting, drinking water with some energy drink added and had eaten an energy bar about two hours before. She was nervous, but felt ready. Dan yelled encouragement as she moved over to the start line and she smiled back. Then, she got serious.

With about a minute to go before the start, Willa did some jogging in place, shoulder stretches and arm waving to get loosened up. As she worked her neck back and forth, her head suddenly came to a complete stop as though frozen in time. She was looking directly at the beach bum and he was looking at her. He then quickly turned and walked away.

The horn sounded but Willa stood there staring at the crowd. Suddenly the noise and the runners bumping into her forced her back to the present moment and she started to run. She didn't lose any time because the chip time would not start until she crossed the start line.

It took her about a mile to get her head back into the race and when she did, the adrenalin rush of seeing the bum kicked in. It was like she was trying to get back to the finish line as soon as she could in order to confront him about who he was and what he was doing following her.

She made the five kilometer turn in twenty minutes. She knew that the fastest race times for most runners came when they ran a negative split, a slower first half and a faster second half. She bore down on the course and put everything she had into the next five kilometers. She was exhilarated. She was passing runners, both boys and girls, every few feet and crossed the finish line with a time of thirty-eight minutes.

Willa immediately started searching the crowd. Anyone watching her might think she was searching the crowd for friends and family, but that could not be further from the truth. The bum was not a friend and certainly not family. She smiled as her teammates came over to her and began high-fiving each other. If they wondered why she wasn't as excited as they were, they didn't ask.

Willa didn't see the bum, so she finally began to celebrate with the rest of the girls. She also made her way over to her dad who hugged her and said, "Great run! The return 5k had to be sub-twenty minutes!"

"Yeah, it was. My watch showed around thirty-eight something. I guess I was just excited to get the race over!" She smiled but was thinking she was not going to tell her dad about the bum. At least not yet!

The boys' competition was much tougher, so the Brit boys finished in sixth place. However, the French girls finished in second place and won a trophy while Willa's time earned her a third place medal.

Once things settled down, Willa's dad congratulated the team on their finish. As they stood slightly apart from the other girls, he congratulated her again then said, "By the way, I have some last minute work to do on the boat but I'll meet you in the room at around nine this evening." He smiled and whispered, "Have fun celebrating, but not too much." He chucked her shoulder, said great job to the girls again and walked away toward the marina.

Willa had brought a change of clothes with her, so she went to the girls' hotel room. They all showered and changed then hung out chatting about the race, how each girl did, the boys and finally, what would they do to celebrate. They finally agreed to go and find the Brit boys to see what they were going to do. Francine sat sullen while they all left.

XXXXX

Once the girls were gone, Francine walked easily to her room and pulled out her phone. She keyed in a number and it was answered on the third tone.

"Yes?"

"I am in with the girls' team but faked an injury to get the girl to be a member of the team. This gave me a better chance to keep an eye on her. What do you want me to do next?"

"Make sure that their next stop is Cape Town and call if it isn't. When the girl and her dad leave then make some excuses and come back here."

Francine shut her phone down and smiled. She was glad that she was leaving these silly, brainless girls.

XXXXX

They caught up with the boys as they gathered in the hotel's lobby. Willa stood to the side with the other girls as Bernadette, Santine and William did the negotiating.

While she was standing there, Brian came to her side and said, "Wow, you really ran a great race."

Willa smiled, "I guess I just wanted to get the race over as quickly as possible. How did you do?"

"I ran just over forty-two minutes."

"That's a great time. So, what's next for you guys?"

"Well, we're here for another couple of days then we head back home. School, you know."

Willa smiled and said, "Yeah, I know. I'm behind on my assignments and need to catch up during the next leg of our trip."

"I think it's fantastic that you and your dad are doing this together. My dad works so hard he never has much time to spend with me and my brother."

"I guess I'm just lucky."

Just then, the three organizers gathered everyone together and said they were all going to a club a few blocks away from the hotel. Bernadette added, "For those of us who are underage, the drinking laws here are pretty lax, but they also serve many non-alcoholic drinks so don't be stupid. Anyway, tonight they are having a local band playing in celebration of the race and a percentage of the money that the club takes in will go to the orphanage."

Willa wasn't all that keen on going to a bar with people she hardly knew, but she would simply keep her wits about her and leave if she grew worried.

Willa needn't have worried. A couple of the boys drank beer and Chantal drank what looked to be champagne, but the rest of them drank juice or soda. No one seemed to be drinking too much and everyone enjoyed the band and the dancing. Willa danced with each boy at least once.

When it approached nine, she excused herself and went outside to call her dad. When he picked up, she said, "Hey dad." After he said hi, she continued, "I'm out with the team and we are at a bar called "Clam Bake" which is not too far from our hotel. Would it be okay if I stayed another hour? And, don't worry, I am only drinking orange juice and I am keeping my glass with me at all times. A couple of the boys have had a few beers, but no one is getting crazy." Willa waited for her dad to respond.

Finally Dan said, "Okay, but I will meet you outside of the bar at ten sharp."

"No problem dad and thanks." She clicked off and went back in. She was actually glad that her dad was going to wait for her. Not because of any of the boys, but because she was still a little worried about the Beach Bum.

Willa danced a few more times and chatted with the girls while Brian sidled up to her a few times to talk and dance with her. He was nice and she enjoyed hanging with him, but she was leaving in a day or two and didn't really feel 'the vibes' to exchange contact information.

She left at ten after making plans with the girls to head to the beach the next day. Her dad was waiting as she came out of the front door and she immediately went to him and gave him a hug. She pulled back and told him, "You are the best dad ever."

"Yeah, I know." Dan was smiling from ear to ear as they headed back to the hotel.

XXXXX

Willa met the girls outside of their hotel the following day at noon. No teenage girl in her right mind would attempt to have an early day when they have no school and they are on a beautiful island with lots of beaches. In Willa's case, she had actually gotten up at 7 am and gone for an easy run.

The girls walked to a nearby beach and spent the afternoon talking about the race, the club, and boys. It seemed that each of the girls had met someone they had liked. When it came to Willa to disclose her true heart's feelings, she smiled and said, "Well, Brian was nice, but I leave tomorrow and will be gone for another seven or eight months, so it doesn't make sense to make a connection now."

The girls mumbled things like, "Sure.", "Makes sense.", and "That's smart." But, they quickly moved on to other more important topics.

They swam, sunned and ate some packed lunches the hotel kitchen had put together for them. They wandered back to the hotel at six that evening and Willa said bye to each girl then walked the short distance back to her hotel. She did not see the 'beach bum' all day.

10. Cape Town

Willa met her dad at the hotel bar when she got back to the hotel and he smiled when she came over to his table. He had a beer and ordered an orange juice for Willa when the waiter came by.

"How was the beach", he asked.

"Fantastic! We really didn't do much except swim, sun and talk for six hours." She smiled knowing that guys could never understand how girls could just sit around and talk for such a long time.

"Well, I am glad you had fun and it was really neat that you met those girls at the beach a few days ago. It turned out to make the last few days of our visit here quite exciting."

"Yeah, I know. The race was a lot of fun."

They were quiet for a few moments then Dan broke the silence, "Okay, tomorrow we begin our long journey to Cape Town. Oh, and by the way, while we are in Cape Town, you will turn sixteen, unless of course, we are delayed in our voyage. Any thoughts on what you'd like to do to celebrate it? I mean, it is the 'Sweet Sixteen Birthday'!" He smiled at her.

Willa rolled her eyes. "Right. Number sweet sixteen. Hmm, what's the typical thing that is supposed to happen on that birthday? Oh right, the girl gets her first kiss!" She smiled and looked at her dad like, come on, really?

He looked at his beer, "Well, okay, maybe it won't be your first kiss and I would certainly understand if you didn't follow that tradition." He glanced at her and she looked impassively back at him.

He finally said, "Fine. Anyway, let's head out to the boat at around seven in the morning after breakfast. That means we will need to be up shortly after five so we can pack up and get to the boat."

"No problem. Sounds good to me."

XXXXX

They moved smoothly out of the harbor shortly after seven and headed for the open sea. While Dan managed the helm, Willa checked the navigation system and plotted their course. Their plan was to head south by southwest until the twenty-second parallel, then turn due south to the equator. This should get them past any of the trouble spots that might be active along that part of the African coast.

Once they crossed the equator, they would turn east to the Greenwich Meridian then head south by southeast toward Cape Town. This would probably be their second longest leg of the entire trip. The longest would be crossing the Pacific Ocean, but they hadn't quite decided where that would occur.

When she finished plotting the course, Willa came up to the helm and stood next to Dan. "I have plotted our course and calculated the duration of this part of our trip. It looks like we have about 15,000 kilometers or around 8000 miles to cover. Based on our slightly jig-jag course, it looks like we will be in Cape Town, depending on the weather and other unknowns, in three to four weeks."

"Sounds good, but regardless, I trust your work. We should have enough supplies to last until we get there. We are stuffed to the 'gills', as they say, which will slow us for the first third of our trip but, once we start whittling down our weight, we should make up all of the time lost, and maybe then some."

Willa went back into the cabin to enter the course details. She also decided she would start researching Cape Town for stuff they might do while there. Her dad said they might be there five to seven days depending on supplies needed, any repairs that were necessary and what they planned to see and do. They would need lots of food and supplies, because the next leg was likely to be to Singapore and it was about as long as this one.

But, unfortunately, first things first and schoolwork was calling to her loudly. She had lots of homework to catch up on and was already late on her math and science assignments. She thought she might butter up those two teachers by adding all of the research and navigation calculations she had just done for the trip to Cape Town. They'd like that!

It was smooth sailing for the first week and they had been lucky because they had a steady wind, not a strong one, but a steady one. They were now heading into the equatorial waters, which usually experienced a serious lack of air movement. If they were lucky, they'd have a steady wind for the next four to six days and would be beyond the The Doldrums.

Willa spent most of the time working on her school assignments. She had finally finished her assignment for the Tenerife stop, which included the nav calculations. And she had been correct because the math and science teachers loved the work. The math teacher loved it because she used a lot of algebra and geometry. The science teacher loved it because Willa had to incorporate estimated winds, currents and tides in all of her work. They returned the 'favor' by giving her the assignments for Cape Town and the Cape of Good Hope. Ugh!

Her dad had been great the whole time. He hadn't asked her to take on any extra work because he knew she had lots of school work to do. But she was finished now and wanted to pitch in more so she put her laptop aside and went up top to hang out with her dad.

"Hey," she said as she came up beside him.

"Hey," he replied. He looked over at her and asked if she was done with her school assignments.

"Yup, but now I have my assignments for Cape Town and the Cape of Good Hope."

"Well, you have time to think about them." He paused then said, "I am a little worried about the leg from the Atlantic waters to the Indian waters because the seas there can be horribly rough. Many larger and sturdier boats have been lost over the years and I am just hoping we can make our passage when it is somewhat mild."

"Don't worry dad, we'll do fine. I know you will get us through."

"Ah, the confidence of youth," and smiled at her.

Willa was quiet for a time then, "Mom and Peter would have loved this stretch as well as the next one, for that matter. They really enjoyed just being out on the water. I think if they could have lived out on the open sea, they would have. Just sitting on the boat and feeling the up and down movements of the swells and the rolling waves would have been heaven to them."

"Oh, I definitely agree. Your mom would always beg me to stay out 'just a little more' when I would suggest we head back."

Willa leaned over the port side and stared at the waters as they passed by. She finally asked, "Did mom ever talk much about her parents and siblings. I mean, I know that her mom was Tatiana Tissot, that her dad was Antoine Tissot, that her dad had a sister, Ludmilya, that her mom had two sisters, Celine and Anna, but I don't know anything else. They were gone when I was old enough to ask. Do you know anymore?"

"Well, I don't know much more. Tatiana had passed when I met your mom and she said her dad had gone into seclusion after Tatiana died. Your mom said they were so much in love he was literally heart broken. Eventually, she lost track of him. She did say that her mom was a translator for one of the large French industrial companies, but I don't remember which one and that her dad was a language teacher at the local high school in the town where they lived. Apparently, the sisters of both families didn't approve of the marriage for some reason and never kept in touch."

"Wow! I now have even more questions than I had before."

"I know. I'm sorry that I didn't probe more back when, well, I could have." Dan grew silent.

Willa came over to him and hugged him from behind. "Sorry dad. I'll stop bringing this up."

"No, I'm sorry. Don't worry. You keep asking me stuff and bugging me about information. After all" and he looked around at the boat and the waters, "that is why we are out here. You rightly bugged me to do this until I did and I couldn't be happier. You always make me happy."

XXXXX

They were now about a week away from Cape Town and Willa had spent the last few days researching the area for things to do. When she did her research into towns, cities and areas they were going to visit along the voyage, she also checked any local tour agencies just to see what they recommended to visitors. She did not hire one to actually plan their stay, but merely 'stole' their ideas about what they thought was best to see. However, she did find a tour operator in Cape Town that she just couldn't resist contacting and, maybe, use their services.

The tour company is called 'Spirit of the Cape' and the guide whom she thought would be great for them was named Daleen Smit. She found an email address, sent an email and briefly described who they were, what they were doing and how long they might be in Cape Town.

Today, Willa received an email response from Daleen. It was four pages of tours, sights and other things to do. Daleen knew they wouldn't have time for all of it, but she wanted to give them a full plate of things to choose from. She also told Willa she had a dear friend who was a member of the Royal Cape Yacht Club and he would be happy to arrange moorage for them if they would like. And, she found a neat looking hotel near the center of town she thought would suit their needs.

Willa passed all of this to her dad that evening as they ate dinner. "Yes, definitely tell Daleen we would love to get moorage at the Club and ask her if they can be flexible on our arrival and departure dates. The hotel sounds fine to me and I suggest you pick the things you'd like to do while there. I may or may not be available to go on certain days if there are repairs or other things I need to do to make us ready for the next leg of the trip."

That evening, Willa sent an email to Daleen explaining their request. Daleen wrote back the next day and told Willa there were several spots available at the Yacht Club, so it shouldn't be a problem fitting them in. She also said she would love to meet with them when they arrive and help them to get settled. She included her mobile number so Willa could give her a call when it would be most convenient to do so. Willa was actually looking forward to meeting Daleen. She sounded really nice and someone who would be fun to hang out with. Well, that is, if Daleen didn't mind hanging out with a teenage girl.

Willa estimated they would arrive on 1 September, near noon. She emailed Daleen to tell her this and said she would call as soon as they were approaching the harbor. She also emailed the hotel and made a reservation for their arrival for six nights. They were now set for their stop in Cape Town.

Willa was at the helm as they approached Cape Town. Cape Town is located on the extreme southwest coast of South Africa and is only a short distance from the southern-most point of the continent of Africa. The two primary languages spoken there are English and Afrikaans with Xhosa, the language of many of the black population, appearing more and more. It is a relatively small city when compared to Johannesburg, Pretoria and Durban, but the residents are fiercely proud of their city and will go out of their way to make you see the 'light'!

The skies were clear and blue as they approached the city and the harbor. She could see Table Mountain easily in the distance just behind the city. She had read that the mountain was over 600 million years old, which made it older than the Himalayas and the Rockies. As the name implies, the top of the mountain is as flat as a table top. The other thing Willa marveled at was the scene in the harbor itself. It was beautiful. There were colorful buildings, various boats of all sizes, and warehouses, which were now shops and restaurants. It was one of the most beautiful harbors she had seen.

Willa called Daleen while Dan took over the helm. Daleen answered on the first ring and told Willa that she and her friend, Norman, were waiting at their moorage. Daleen handed the phone to Norman and Willa handed her phone to Dan. Norman guided Dan to the moorage space and helped to secure their boat.

Once all was tied down and secured, Dan and Willa stepped down onto the dock and met Daleen and Norman. Daleen was a beautiful blonde and stood a few inches taller than Willa. She wore a white blouse and pastel green slacks. Norman was a handsome man with short hair and very tan arms and legs. He wore white shorts, a pullover blue shirt and boat shoes. Daleen spoke first and Willa heard the pretty accented English that most Americans loved when they met someone from Cape Town.

"Welcome to Cape Town. I am Daleen and this is Norman."

"Hi. I am Willa and this is my dad, Dan."

They all shook hands and Norman asked if they'd like to relax a bit in the club before heading to their hotel. They nodded and Norman led them into the club.

As they headed to the entrance, Willa walked next to Daleen, while Dan walked with Norman. "The harbor is so beautiful. I was at the helm as we came in and was just stunned by the view of Table Mountain in the background and the pretty harbor all around me."

Daleen smiled, "Many people feel the same way. We, who live here, feel the same way too, by the way."

They entered the club and went into the bar area. Norman motioned for a waiter and they each gave him their drink orders. Once the waiter moved off to fill their orders, Daleen turned to Willa and Dan and asked, "So how has your trip been going so far? From what Willa has told me in her emails, it sounds like a marvelous adventure for the two of you."

11. Sightseeing

As they were leaving the Yacht Club, Daleen and Willa headed for the restroom. As soon as the girls were out of sight, Dan turned to Norman and said, "Willa will be having her sixteenth birthday in five days and I'd like to have a surprise party for her. Do you know of a nice pub or restaurant that we could use where a small party could be held? I'd also like to have a cake made somewhere."

Norman thought a moment, "I think that Paddy Malone's might be a good spot. Underage people are allowed in bars here, so that will not be a problem. They have an area upstairs that might do just the trick for what you want and they have an excellent menu. Even if they do not do cakes, I am sure they'd be able to find a bakery that could fit the bill for you. It is located in a really nice area down by the Victoria and Albert Waterfront."

Dan saw the girls returning so he thanked Norman and said he'd check it out.

As they walked over to the men, Daleen asked, "Where are you staying?"

"I went with your suggestion and booked The Grand Daddy Hotel."

"That will be an experience."

Willa wasn't sure how to interpret this comment, after all, it is just a hotel and had chosen it because she liked its location at the center of town. It also had a cool name.

They all headed for the hotel after grabbing their bags from the boat. They walked along the harbor and Norman pointed out several yachts. He also talked to Dan about moorage and various sailing rules for the harbor.

While the men seemed to be engrossed in sailing talk, Willa slowed so that Daleen would slow with her. When she felt they were out of hearing, she turned to Daleen and quietly said, "It is my sixteenth birthday on the sixth and I think my dad will try to plan a surprise party. I do not want to ruin his surprise, but I'd also like to surprise him since he has been so wonderful on this trip. If you could find out where he is planning to have the party, then I could plan something for him as well. Would you mind letting me know if you hear anything?"

"Sure. After all, we girls must stick together."

After a short walk they turned and headed up toward the center of town along Long Street. The view in front was of Table Mountain and the view behind them was of the harbor. Willa still couldn't believe how beautiful the city and the surrounding area were.

Willa recognized the hotel from the picture she had seen on its website. It was four stories high and had a greenish, 'antique' looking exterior. They walked through the entrance and up to the reception desk on the left. They were pleasantly greeted by a pretty young woman who took their name, keyed some data on her computer then looked up, smiled and said, "You have two accommodations and here are your keys. Take the elevator up to the third floor, exit and turn right. Proceed up the stairs and exit onto the roof. Please enjoy your stay and do not hesitate to let us know if there is anything we can do for you."

"Did she say roof?" Willa asked Daleen as they grabbed their bags and headed to the elevator.

"Yes, she did."

Willa thought, *what are we doing, camping out on the roof? I hope it doesn't rain.*

They stepped through the door onto the roof and looked around. To the right, they saw an old Airstream Trailer. To the left, they saw a bar with stand-up tables and stools. At this point, they looked down at the tag attached to the key they had been given and noticed for the first time they did not have a room number. The tag had a name on it and Willa saw that hers said 'Gold Rush'.

As they continued to the left, they saw the rest of the roof. It looked like a typical trailer park in the states, albeit a small one. Dan remarked, "I guess we look for one with the same name as is on the key tag."

Dan's was called 'Wagon Train' and he found it located along the back of the roof while Willa's 'room' was located just to the left of his. They entered Dan's first and, as Willa scanned the interior, she thought, *this is so cute.* It was certainly small, but the bed was a queen size and the living area in front of the bed had a small fridge, sink, flat screen TV, coffee table and sofa.

To the right was the bathroom, which was really, really small. But, it had everything in it that one might need. She noticed that the shower was actually the entire bathroom. That is, there was no separate enclosure for the shower. The water would simply go all over whatever was in the bathroom.

While the others were looking around Dan's accommodations, Willa backed out, went over to hers, entered and smiled. It was similarly apportioned and very cute. The colors were gold, whereas Dan's were a light brown. This was just too cool for words. She would have to take pictures and send them to her friends.

She tossed her bags on the bed and the bags landed, she heard a knock on the door. She opened it to see Dan, Daleen and Norman. She motioned them in. "Isn't this cool?" They all smiled.

After a minute of looking around, Daleen announced, "Well, it looks like you guys are getting settled in very nicely." She looked at Willa, "Maybe you could look over the tour ideas I sent to you and give me a call tomorrow morning as to what you'd like to do during your short stay."

"Will do," said Willa.

Daleen and Norman left, while Dan and Willa got settled into their 'rooms'! Once she finished, Willa wandered over to Dan's trailer, knocked and went in. When she entered, Dan turned to her with a big smile on his face. "I have not seen one of these things since I was a kid. These used to be a big deal in the states for people to travel around the country during summer vacations."

"Yeah, it's pretty cool to be using them as accommodations at a hotel. I wonder why they chose to do this and how the heck they got them all the way up onto the roof."

"I'm about ready, so let's go explore the area and find someplace to eat. The hotel has a restaurant so we could just plan to eat here."

Willa said, "Sure. Let me change and I'll meet you at the bar before we head down."

While Willa went in to her 'room', Dan changed his shirt. He came out shortly after, walked over to the bar and found a few people already there with Willa one of them. She was sitting at the bar chatting with the bartender. He was a young man with close cropped hair. He smiled as Dan approached and asked if he could get him something. Dan smiled and said, "Thanks, but I am just stopping by to get my daughter". He glanced at Willa and she smiled then said bye to the bartender.

Willa and Dan walked the stairs all the way to the ground floor and Willa went to the front desk to ask for a map of the area. They walked out to the curb and turned right since they had already been down to the left when they approached the hotel's location.

As they walked along the street, they saw a surf shop, more restaurants, souvenir shops and mini-stores. Dan commented that they should check out the surf shop to find out about renting scuba gear. They were both certified divers, so maybe they might want to do that one day. Willa had also seen an On/Off bus stop and suggested that might be an idea for something to do.

As they walked through the area, they marveled at the mix of old-world charm and modern conveniences. Many of the building facades were multi-colored and seemed to reflect the multi-cultural makeup of the population. After about an hour, they decided to head back to the hotel to eat. They entered the restaurant and sat at a table along the windows that faced Castle Street. They ordered the daily special, which was roast, while Dan ordered a glass of white wine and Willa had water.

Near the end of their meal, Willa sat chewing on her roast beef special while staring out the window at the people wandering Castle Street she suddenly stiffened and almost jumped out of her chair.

Dan saw her reaction and quickly asked, "What's wrong?"

Willa didn't say anything but kept staring out at the street.

Dan turned to look too, but only saw people wandering left and right. He asked her again, "Willa, what is wrong?"

"Nothing. I mean, I thought I saw someone, but, I don't know. He looked like…"

"What are you talking about? Who looked like who? Come on Willa, what did you see?" He asked more forcefully.

Willa was quiet then sighed and told her dad, "There was a man who just walked by that I am sure I saw in Tenerife. But, I may be wrong."

Dan knew about Willa's ability to remember details, so she was not wrong. He now was worried because, even if she wouldn't admit it, there was someone following them, or worse, her.

Dan got up, went to the side door of the restaurant and out onto Castle Street. He looked both ways along the road and, of course, had no idea who to look for, but it made him feel better to at least check out the street. He went back in and sat across from Willa again. He leaned toward her, "Willa, tell me when and where you have seen him before."

She frowned and told her dad about the two incidents in Tenerife. She added that she was sure he was here now, but she had no idea why he was following them. He had not threatened her in the previous incidents and he didn't threaten her a few minutes ago. He didn't even look in the window.

"I'm sorry dad. I should have told you before. But, they were so quick and harmless and I didn't think anything of it."

Dan reached over and put his hand on hers. "It's okay. I understand why you did what you did. But, I think we need to figure this out and try to determine what that man is doing following us around"

"I agree and I promise that I will tell you if I ever see him again." She gave her dad a detailed description of the man in case he sees him.

They finished eating, paid and went up to their 'rooms'. Dan insisted that he come into hers just to make sure there was no one around. He also made Willa promise to lock her door and to move the coffee table in front of it. She said she would.

XXXXX

The following day at breakfast, they talked about what they might like to do, but neither of them mentioned the subject of the man. They decided to go to the surf shop to check out dive equipment rentals and potential dive sites. After that, they would do the On/Off bus tour. Willa also showed Dan the tours Daleen had put together and they discussed which of them they might like to do. Willa said she would email Daleen their choices and they agreed to meet at the rooftop bar at eleven am before heading out for the day.

Willa emailed Daleen as soon as she got to her room. She told her what they had planned for today and that they would like to tour with Daleen tomorrow to the Hout and Camps Bays as well as the coast road. She also suggested that the seal colony tour would be interesting. She told Daleen that the day after, she and her dad were going to go diving for the day then on Friday, the fifth, they would like to continue touring with Daleen to the Cape Point Nature reserve, Cape of Good Hope and the Penguins colony. On the sixth, they would wander the city a little and make sure they had everything ready for their departure on the seventh.

She added, "Have you found out what my dad is planning, yet?"

She actually received a reply before she started out the door to meet her dad. Daleen's email said she would be happy to put together tours for both days and would send her the itinerary later. She also added, "He's planning a party at Paddy Malone's in the Victoria and Albert Waterfront. There will be music, food and a cake and start at around 6 pm. Good luck with your surprise!"

XXXXX

Willa and her dad exited the Grand Daddy, turned right and walked the 100 meters to the surf shop. They walked in and were met by a pleasant young woman in shorts and a tank top. She was dark and could have been very tan or light skinned African.

She asked, "Can I help you?"

"Yes, we are interested in renting scuba gear. Can you help us with that?"

"Absolutely. Please follow me." She led them to a small area along the side of the large shop that had a desk, books, pictures and diving gear. Willa followed her dad and waited while he discussed equipment types, areas to dive, what they might see and how they would travel. Willa finally wandered away. Her dad knew her abilities, preferences and equipment needs, so she didn't need to be there with him.

Willa wandered around a little picking up items, examining them then moving on to another display. As she was looking at some running shoes, a cute guy walked up and asked if she needed help. She glanced at him, smiled and said, "Well, I am looking for a new pair of running shoes and I am not sure about the sizes here when compared with the sizes in America." She actually was, but she really wanted to chat with the cute guy. *Wow*, she thought, *I am really getting bold*.

"No problem. We have a chart you can use to make the comparisons. What size do you wear in America?"

"I wear a women's size seven."

He smiled, moved to her side and held the chart in front of the two of them. His arm was gently touching her arm as he moved it to show her the size comparisons. It caused little electric sparks to tingle her skin since he had a t-shirt on and she wore a sleeveless shirt. She wasn't really paying any attention to his explanation of the chart.

He finished and asked, "So, does that help?"

She spluttered, "Oh yes. That was great. I really feel better about my choice now."

They were smiling at each other when he finally said, "Umm, would you like to look at some shoes in your size now?"

"Absolutely. Can I see that one and those two?" She pointed at the shoes.

He left and she sat on a small stool. She had shorts and flip flops, so she kicked off the flip flops.

He came back with several boxes and began taking out shoes, undoing or loosening the laces and talking about the qualities of each shoe as he helped her try them on. But, before he put the shoes on, he also helped her put little socks on. There was lots of touching by him of her feet and ankles. After each shoe was on, she would walk a short distance away acting like she was seriously looking at the design and getting a feel for the shoe's comfort and fit.

She finally said she would take the last pair. He said great, removed the shoe from her foot placed it in the box, removed the little sock from her foot and set that aside. He left the other boxes, picked up the box with the shoes she had chosen and walked over to the register with her.

As they walked, Willa asked, "So, do you go to school here?" This was another first for her. She had never initiated conversations like this with guys. This trip was truly a learning experience for her.

"Yes. I will attend the American International School as a senior this fall then plan to attend the University of Cape Town next September. I am planning to become a lawyer and work for the United Nations Human Rights Commission."

"That sounds wonderful. It seems you are pretty sure about what your future will entail. I wish I was so sure. But, I still have two years of high school ahead of me, so I guess I have time to work all of that out."

As she was taking her receipt and the shoes, Dan came over, smiled and told her, "We will pick up our diving equipment the day after tomorrow and Miss Varty has arranged for a driver to take us to the boat that will take us to the diving areas."

"Sounds great, I can't wait." She glanced quickly at her dad and, was about to say bye to …, wait, *I don't know his name*. She turned to the cute guy and said, "Well, maybe we'll see you around. By the way, my name is Willa." She put out her hand. *Please say your name, please, please, please say your name.*

"It was nice talking with you Willa. My name is Darius."

"Great. Thanks. See you later, Darius."

Once on the street, Willa's dad turned back toward the hotel. She had already turned right toward the On/Off stop. When she saw that he wasn't next to her, she turned and saw him walking away from her. She caught up to him and asked, "Where are you going? The stop is that way!"

He smiled at her. "Are you planning on carrying your new shoes all over Cape Town today?"

"Oh, okay, right, I'll leave them at the front desk."

"Good idea."

It only took a couple of minutes to get to the hotel, leave the shoes with the front desk and get back to Dan, who was waiting just outside the door. As she walked up to him, he commented, "Well Darius must be a great salesman."

"What do you mean?"

"Because your current shoes were bought just before we left on this trip and they seem to look fine to me, but he must have convinced you that you needed new shoes. Otherwise, you would not have wasted his time trying all of those shoes on and then buying shoes you really don't need."

"Well, um, my old shoes were, well, a little tight, so I thought why not get a new pair while we were in a shop that sells running shoes."

"Uh huh, right. Makes sense to me." He was smiling as they walked to the On/Off stop.

They spent most of the day on the tour getting off at stops that seemed interesting. Stops like Table Mountain, the castle, the Slave Museum and the waterfront area where they both surreptitiously took a look at Paddy Malone's as they walked around the area.

They ate at the hotel restaurant again and headed up their rooms. Willa went to her room and worked on her school assignments. Dan sat outside in the lounge area reading before heading to bed.

XXXXX

They left with Daleen early the following morning. The tour was fantastic. Daleen explained everything they were doing and provided a running commentary on the history and significance of each stop. They had lunch in a little beachfront restaurant and returned to the hotel at eight in the evening. They grabbed a sandwich from the restaurant and ate it up at the roof bar. They chatted about the day while Dan had a beer and Willa an orange juice. Willa finally went to her room while Dan stayed to finish his beer.

After Willa left, Dan noticed a lady at the bar sitting alone. She had been there the night before when he and Willa had briefly stopped by. Maybe she was staying at the hotel too. He turned back to his book.

He glanced over at her a little later and she suddenly turned toward him. He quickly looked away. Apparently, the woman she decided to take the 'bull by the horns'.

She walked over to where Dan was sitting and, as she approached, he thought. *What do I do now? I was shy when I met Olivia and haven't changed. I don't have a clue.* But, the woman was suddenly at the table and smiling, so he had to do something. He smiled.

"Hi. I'm Amy." She offered her hand.

Dan took it and said, "I'm Dan. Please join me." He thought, *that sounded pretty good.*

Amy sat. "Are you here with your daughter? I think I saw you with her yesterday, as well as tonight."

"Yes. Willa and I are sailing around the world. It's been great fun and a wonderful experience for us."

"Wow, it sounds amazing and what a great thing to be doing with your daughter. I am divorced and never had children, which might have been one of the causes of our break-up. Anyway, I decided to take a vacation here since it's a place I have always wanted to see."

She told him about her work – she was a successful realtor and owned her own company. He told her about his work, the loss of his wife and son and Willa's influence on him. Amy admired his relationship with Willa.

He bought her a drink and had another beer. Finally, he suggested that he needed to get some sleep since they were scuba diving the next day. As he got up, he said, "Maybe I'll see you around." She nodded and waved as he left.

XXXXX

Willa and Dan left the next morning for the surf shop as soon as it opened at 9:00 am. They said good morning to Darius and Ms. Varty and their driver arrived about ten minutes after they had. The equipment was loaded into the van along with Dan and Willa's bags containing their diving suits, change of clothes and other personal items.

Dan and Ms. Varty had searched several websites, maps and brochures at the shop the other day to decide where they should go. They had decided to head first to the Atlantic side to dive at Coral gardens then head to the Indian side to dive at two spots, Quarry then Spaniard and Gibraltar. They opted to have an experienced diver with them at each site in case they needed help or got lost.

At the end of the long day and because the dives had been exhausting, on the drive back to the surf shop, they both fell asleep. The corals at the first site were amazing and the other two sites were equally beautiful but much more exhausting since they needed to swim fifty meters deep and more than a hundred meters along escarpments and ridges.

Willa didn't wake up to go in to see Darius when they reached the shop. It was just as well, since only Miss Varty was in the store. Dan finally woke her once all the equipment was transferred to the store and the driver needed to get going. Dan carried their bags as they trudged back to the hotel. He helped her into her Airstream, locked her door and suspected she was asleep before the door closed. He decided to have a beer at the bar.

Amy came through the door to the roof about fifteen minutes after he sat down. She waved, ordered a white wine and walked to his table. "Mind if I sit?"

"I'd be upset if you didn't!" He smiled at her, stood and pulled her seat out. There was a lounge type area in the center of the roof with sofas, comfy chairs and tables and Dan suggested they move there where it would be more comfortable.

"Great idea." Amy got up and began walking to the area with Dan. They sat next to each other on one of the sofas. She was a little shorter than he was and appeared to be in her forties. She had on a beige pullover shirt with collar and several buttons down the front. The top few were open, stopping just above where it would be too much. Her slacks were black and her shoes were beige flats. She was trim and looked to be one of those who spent time in the gym.

"How was the scuba diving?" Amy asked after they settled into the sofa.

"It was fantastic! Do you dive?"

"No. I never seemed to have the time or the right people around me to learn. Besides, I grew up in Oklahoma and there aren't many places to dive there. Maybe someday I'll take the time to give it a try."

"You would enjoy it, I think." He got quiet and stared down at his beer. Finally he looked at her and asked, "What do you have planned for tomorrow?"

"Not much. I am impressed with the tour guide you guys are using, so maybe I'll contact her about doing a tour with her. I leave for London on the 9th of September, so I still have time to sign-up for some tours." She stopped and waited. She knew what he was about to ask, so she wanted to give him time to collect his thoughts.

Sure enough, after a minute of looking at his beer, looking at the sky, looking at the Airstreams, Dan turned to her, "Would you like to spend some time with me tomorrow?"

"Sure. But, I thought you and Willa would be spending the day together."

"She is doing another tour with Daleen, but I plan to bow out since I haven't done any work on getting the boat ready for our departure in a few days. It shouldn't take all day, so I thought maybe we could meet for lunch then spend the afternoon together. Willa and I are planning to have a nice dinner tomorrow evening, but I am not sure where yet. Maybe you could help me with that?"

"I'd love to. I'll meet you at the hotel restaurant at noon then we can decide where to go."

"Great, I'll see you then." They both stood, stared a little at each other, smiled and then Amy moved in and hugged Dan. As she pulled way, she kissed him lightly on the cheek.

XXXXX

The following morning Willa and Dan were up and in the restaurant having breakfast when Daleen came in. "How did the diving go?"

They both said things like, wonderful, amazing, great, and spectacular. Daleen smiled because she knew they would love it. Cape Town had some really great dive areas within easy reach.

Daleen sat and ordered coffee then asked, "Are you guys ready to go?"

"Absolutely", said Willa.

"I am afraid I will need to bow out for today. I haven't done any preparations for our departure in two days. There are some repairs to do on the boat and supplies to replenish. I hope you don't mind, Willa."

"No dad, I am okay, but I wish you'd let me stay and help. I can help with whatever you are going to be doing you know."

"I do know and I appreciate your offer. But, I want you to enjoy the time you have here in Cape Town. Besides, you need to make sure you have enough information to complete your school assignments. Anyway, you and Daleen can spend some 'girl' time together."

"Okay. But, we are going for a nice dinner tonight when we get back, just you and me, right?"

"Sure, sounds great. I'll make a reservation later today or I'll ask the front desk to do it for us. What time would work?" He looked at Daleen.

"We should be back between six and seven, so I suppose eight would give Willa time to freshen up and change. What do you think, Willa?"

"Sounds great. I am not high maintenance so it certainly won't take me any longer than thirty minutes to get ready."

They were about finished, so Dan rose, paid the bill, told them to have a great time and headed up to his room to get ready to go to the harbor.

Daleen turned to Willa and asked, "Ready?"

"Yup!"

Daleen had planned each of their days to be personal guided tours, so it was just she and Willa. They walked around the corner to a parking lot and got into Daleen's car. As they drove away, Daleen smiled and said, "Your dad is actually going to spend a couple hours tomorrow with Norman arranging your party at Paddy's."

"Do you think we can take a couple of hours at the end of today for me to plan my surprise for him? Also, do you know of a really good artist? I know it is short notice, but I'd like to present my dad with a painting of our boat with us on it. I have a picture of the boat that I took while we were moored in the harbor in Istanbul. I'd like the artist to use that as the basis of the painting and then add us onto the boat using a picture of the two of us in Malta."

"Absolutely. I have a wonderful artist in mind for you. In fact, let's stop at his studio before we get started. This will give him extra time to work on it and you can answer any questions he might have when we get back this afternoon."

Willa was so happy Daleen knew an artist and was being so flexible after only knowing her for a few days that she hugged her, saying "Thank you so much. You've been so sweet to me this whole trip."

Daleen was so surprised at this sudden show of affection, but she hugged her too.

They stopped at Daleen's friend's place and Willa explained what she wanted him to do. She gave him the photos and he looked at them while she talked about her idea. She said she would like to pick the picture up on the afternoon of the 6th. He didn't say anything during all of this until finally, "Okay. Stop by later today and I will show you what I have."

XXXXX

The tour involved lots of driving because they were heading to areas far outside of Cape Town. The Seal Colony, Nature Reserve and penguins were a good distance away.

They were all wonderful visits but Willa enjoyed the penguins most. She would have liked to have spent more time there, but Daleen reminded her they needed to get going if she was going to have time to prepare her surprise and then get ready for dinner.

They stopped by the artist's studio once they were back in town. The artist was in the back but came out when he heard the tinkle of the little bell above the door. He smiled when he saw them and went into the back room again. He came back carrying a canvas painting mounted on a stretcher frame. It looked to be about twelve by sixteen inches. He walked over to a table and set the painting on it so Willa could see it.

Willa couldn't take her eyes off of what she saw. It was beautiful. He had painted the boat exactly as it looked, but with the sails slightly waving in a soft breeze. Willa was next to her dad pointing at something out in front of them while looking up at him. The painting showed her in profile with her dad at the helm looking at her and smiling. The background showed blue skies and ocean spray over blue-green seas. In the far background there was a land mass that could have been Malta or the Golden Horn.

She kept staring at it. She couldn't look away. It was perfect. Tears began welling up in her eyes. She finally mumbled, "This is so beautiful. It's perfect." She looked at the artist then Daleen who smiled back at her.

Willa turned to the artist and said, "Thank you so much!"

He smiled. "You are welcome, but I am not done. I still have some touch up work to do on the lines, the background and the ocean. But, do not worry. It will be ready for you to pick up tomorrow afternoon."

Daleen decided to call Norman after they left the studio in order to update him on what time she would be home. But, it was really to find out what he and Dan were doing.

"Hey, Norman. I should be home in a couple of hours." She smiled at Willa. "Okay, I'll see you at six at the club. Right, see ya."

"Okay, they are somewhere down by the waterfront. So, if we stay in the city center than we shouldn't cross paths with them."

"Actually, you can drop me at the hotel now if you like. It would give me time to shower and get ready for my dad."

Daleen nodded and dropped Willa at the hotel, got out with her and walked over to Willa. "It has been such a pleasure to have met you and to have helped you to enjoy your short stay here in the Cape. I hope you have a wonderful birthday and I am glad the painting turned out so well. Spenser is an amazing artist so I knew he would do a great job."

Willa smiled and came into her for a hug. She wondered how she had become such a hugger. Maybe it was because she was having so much fun thanks to all of the wonderful people she was meeting on the trip. She didn't care what the reason was. She just planned to continue to enjoy it.

"I want to thank you too, Daleen. I couldn't have asked for a better friend and companion during my stay."

12. Surprise!

Dan figured to spend the morning at the boat. Norman came by a little before noon to see if Dan needed anything. "Not yet, all is going well but would you mind telling Daleen this afternoon, if she calls, that you and I are busy?"

"Sure. What have you got anyway, a hot date?" Norman chuckled, but Dan suddenly looked like he had just gotten caught in the girl's locker room in high school. Norman stared, smiled then said, "You do have a date! That's brilliant. You are 'the man'!"

"I don't know about that but, I met this gal at the hotel bar and, well, we have enjoyed spending some time together."

"Hey man, no need to justify it to me. I am happy for you. It seems like it's been too long for you, so I say go for it. If you are worried about Willa, I think you are way off. She will not only understand, she'll be happy for you. In case you didn't know it, she's a smart kid!"

"I know, I know. Thanks. By the way, I am not sure if you and Daleen have the time tomorrow, but I know Willa and I would love to have you come to her birthday party."

"I'm open, but I'll need to check with Daleen. If we can, we will definitely be there. And," he winked as he said, "have fun this afternoon."

Dan watched him leave, smiled and thought. *He is right. This is good for me, and Willa will understand.*

XXXXX

Dan met Amy at the hotel restaurant shortly after noon. She was sitting in one of the booths sipping a cup of tea, so he went over and sat across from her. "Hey!"

"How are the preparations going for the trip?"

"Great. I finished all of the repairs that needed to be done and had a little time left to inventory the supplies. We need to restock all of our foodstuff and water, but I think we are pretty good on spare parts and other miscellaneous items. I can check those again tomorrow as I restock to see if there is anything else we absolutely need."

Amy nodded as he told her this. When he finished, she smiled and he asked, "What?"

"I was just thinking how nice it was for you to let Willa go off on her tour when she probably would have been a big help to you."

"She deserves this time to enjoy the trip. We've been to some amazing places and met some wonderful people." He smiled at Amy and she smiled back. "She has met some pretty neat young people on the trip, including a really nice young man in Malta. I also suspect that she might meet up with Darius, who works at the surf shop down the street."

"Have you been fine with all of that?"

"Definitely. Willa is a great kid. She is smart and really good at sizing up people. I trust her completely and she has never, ever disappointed me." He looked away.

Amy reached over and touched his arm. "You are a lucky man and she is a lucky girl."

"Yeah, I am." After a pause, "she actually competed in an archery competition on Malta against some of the world's best and came in second. Then, she competed in a relay race on Tenerife and her team came in second, while she took an individual third place award. These are all things she will treasure all of her life."

"Wow, she is amazing alright. I hope to get a chance to meet her before you guys leave."

Dan smiled, but his mind was racing. "Well, we are planning to have a nice dinner tonight as I told you. Would you like to join us?" He thought, *Please say yes.*

"But, didn't she say it was to be just the two of you?"

"I know, but I think that she would love meeting you. She is great around adults, unlike many teens her age. She and our tour guide, Daleen, act like they are sisters."

Amy smiled and said, "Okay. I'd love to join you and Willa."

"Good," was all that Dan could say, but inside he was scared, excited, worried, and confused. But, mostly excited!

They left the hotel and headed down to the waterfront. As they walked, he told Amy that he still had some planning to do for Willa's party tomorrow. He also told her that Norman was covering for him this afternoon and Amy smiled at all of this conspiracy stuff. Inside, she figured that Willa probably already knew what was going on. She also suspected that Daleen and Norman have been part of the whole charade as well. The only one who thought it was all still secret was probably Dan. It was all so cute and she smiled at Dan as he explained the 'secret plans' involved.

When he finished, he told her they needed to go to Paddy's now to reserve the room, place the food order and find out about a cake. He asked for her help picking out something nice as a present for Willa and he'd also like her opinion on where they might eat dinner tonight.

Paddy's visit went smoothly. The room was available and, since the party was going to be buffet style, all they needed to do was pick the items to include in the buffet and give them an estimate of the number of people. Finally, the manager told him they would take care of the cake because they had recently hired a pastry chef who would be happy to use his skills for the first time cake order.

They next went to the Duncan Dock and checked out the restaurants. They didn't find anything there that struck them as the right place for this evening, so they headed back to the Victoria and Albert Waterfront, where there were many restaurants to choose from.

They finally settled on the Nabu. It was a beautiful place and very upscale. It was probably a little over the top, but Dan was now going to be accompanied by two pretty ladies and he wanted this to be an evening everyone would remember. He made the reservation for 8 pm.

It was already 5 pm, so they headed back to the hotel. Amy was in one of the normal rooms and invited Dan in to check it out. As they entered, he looked around admiring the furnishings and décor, which were all styled as nineteenth century vintage. She had a queen bed, small work area with a desk and chair, a coffee table and a large HDTV. The bathroom was three times the size of the Airstream's.

"Nice room!" Dan said. It was close to 6 pm so he suggested, "Willa should be back in about an hour. How about if we meet in the roof bar at 6:30 and I'll bring Willa to introduce you guys? We can head to the restaurant at 7:15?"

"Sounds great." They walked to the door and, as she opened it, Dan turned back to Amy, leaned forward and kissed her lips softly. She responded and pulled him a little closer. Once he pulled away, they smiled at each other and Dan went out. *That felt wonderful*, and he continued up to the roof.

Dan saw that Willa's light was on, so he figured she must have just gotten back. She'd probably be another hour, so he would have time to go to her Airstream to tell her about Amy before they left.

About five minutes later, Willa emerged wearing a light green skirt and a pretty, yellow cashmere top. She wore one inch black pumps and walked over to the bar, said "Hi" to the bartender and he poured an orange juice for her.

A few minutes later, Amy came up the stairs and turned into the bar. She saw Willa, hesitated a second about continuing then thought, *Why not*. Amy walked over to the bar, ordered a glass of white wine and sat next to Willa. Willa wasn't sure how to take this since there were plenty of seats open around the bar. After Amy got settled onto the stool, she turned to Willa and said, "Hi, Willa. I am Amy. I met your dad the other day and think he is a wonderful man. He has told me much about you and I am happy to finally meet you."

Willa was a little taken aback at first when Amy started to talk to her but, when she heard that Amy had met her dad and they had apparently been hanging out together, she relaxed. By the time Amy finished, Willa was secretly happy. Her dad had finally met someone and they appeared to be getting along nicely.

Willa smiled and said, "Nice to meet you Amy. I am glad that my dad has gotten to know someone his age on this trip." She smiled, as did Amy. "He has been hanging out with teens during the whole trip and I'm afraid he is starting to act like one and is becoming very annoying to me and my friends. Hopefully, you can take him off my hands for a little bit."

Amy chuckled. "Yeah, adults who don't act their age can be so annoying. I tried online dating a few years ago and became totally frustrated with the process. Guys would post pictures of themselves when they were at least ten years younger. If I agreed to meet them, some would show up dressed like we were going to a college dance. If it hadn't been so funny, I think I would have been scared."

Willa laughed and they continued to chat. Just then, Dan emerged from his trailer and, without looking, walked over to Willa's trailer to make sure she was still there. He didn't see the light on and turned around in a panic. He looked over at the bar and saw Amy and Willa sitting at the bar talking and laughing. *Oh no. What should he do now?* He finally realized there was nothing he could do and just headed over to the ladies.

Amy saw him coming first. During a pause, she quietly said, "He's coming."

Willa knew what she meant so she didn't turn around.

When he got close and before he could say anything, Amy got off of her seat, moved to Dan and kissed him right on the lips. He was stunned and stood there like a telephone pole. Amy pulled away and without pausing said, "I want to introduce you to a friend of mine. I just met her and she is wonderful. We've been having so much fun talking about her trip and her friends and all kinds of things." She didn't give him time to say anything as she emphasized this last part.

Willa quickly turned and said, "Hi dad. I just met Amy. She is really cool. Did you know that she is staying here too? It's such a small world. From here, she is going to London. Do you think we could go to London sometime?"

At his point, both girls stopped and simply looked at Dan. His look was priceless. He looked like he would rather crawl into a hole than stand there. His eyes went from Willa to Amy then back. Both girls simply kept staring at him, waiting.

Finally, Willa went to Dan, gave him a hug, smiled and said, "Gotcha!"

Once Dan had recovered, they left the hotel and took a taxi to the restaurant. The dinner went really well and everyone got along. They told stories, laughed, listened attentively when talking about some of their life loses and left with Dan holding Amy's hand.

13. A Busy Birthday

They had agreed after returning to the hotel to meet for breakfast the following morning. Willa left Amy and Dan sitting at the rooftop bar and went to her Airstream. She spent the next couple of hours catching up on her English assignment by summarized the sights, sounds, and culture that she had seen in Cape Town over the last few days.

She also sent an email to her friends and told them about Darius, as she had done with Marcel.

She finally got ready for bed and crawled under the comforter. As she lay there, she smiled as she thought of her dad and Amy at the bar. She really hoped they had made a connection, even a small one. He looked so happy at dinner and Willa could see his eyes light up every time Amy looked at him and said something, even if it was just "Please pass the salt."

XXXXX

Amy was in the restaurant already as Willa and Dan walked in for breakfast. They all sat in the booth with Willa sitting opposite Amy and her dad. The waiter brought them some coffee and took their orders. They discussed the day's plans while they waited for their breakfast to arrive.

Willa started. "I think I am going to check with Darius to see if he has some time today to hang out. Maybe he can show me around the local neighborhoods."

Amy figured Willa was leaving it open for her dad to tell her about his birthday surprise, but he kept up the charade and said, "That sounds great. Amy offered to help me finish getting supplies for the boat today, so we'll be busy with that." He smiled at Amy and she smiled back.

The breakfasts arrived and they started buttering toast, cutting sausages, using condiments and eating. As they finished, Dan asked for the check and turned to Willa. "Amy and I are thinking of heading to dinner this evening around 7 pm at Paddy's Pub. Why don't you and Darius join us?"

"I'll have to ask Darius. He might have something else in mind, so I don't know. But, of course, I'll be there."

Willa went up to her Airstream while Amy and Dan had another cup of coffee. Amy asked him, "Aren't you afraid they might decide to go somewhere else this evening and your surprise will be ruined?"

He smiled, "Nah. Darius and I had a conversation yesterday. He knows the plan."

Amy thought, *Maybe he is not as clueless as I thought.*

XXXXX

Amy and Dan left the restaurant and headed to the marina. Dan wanted to show Amy the boat then start getting the last minute supplies they would need. He also wanted to leave enough time for Amy to help him find something nice for Willa's birthday present.

In the meantime, Willa responded to a few emails, including one from Marcel that she thought was a little strange. It was the first time he had written and all it said was 'watch your back'. She supposed it could mean the usual 'hey, be careful, but have fun' or something like that. But, it was still strange that his only email should say just those three words.

She changed into a pair of dark blue shorts and a white t-shirt she had bought in Malta. The back was plain but the front had the words 'Malta' written in two inch block letters with a caricature of the sun below it. She slipped on a pair of tennis shoes and headed out.

She had emailed Darius yesterday morning to ask if he would be around today and he had said that he had the day off so he'd meet her at the surf shop at ten am.

As she walked into the shop, she saw Darius inside talking to Ms. Varty. She headed to the two of them and said, "Hey." Darius came over and hugged her. She approached Ms. Varty and noted that her name tag said her name was Amita. "The recommendations you gave us for our diving adventure were fabulous. Thanks so much."

"Oh, it was my pleasure. I am happy you had fun. Anyway, I know you and Darius have plans for today, so I'll leave you to them." She walked over to a customer who had been examining some surfing outfits.

Darius asked, "So, where to?"

"I was hoping you would know. Maybe we could explore some neighborhoods this morning then have some lunch."

"Sure, I know just the areas to explore. Let's go." As they headed out the door, he turned to her and said, "You look great, by the way."

"Thanks. You look pretty good yourself." He was wearing green shorts that fell just below his knees, a light brown polo shirt and sandals. He was nicely tanned while his hair was blonde and stuck up here and there, but not in a goofy looking way.

They headed up Long Street and he explained that this was generally where the party people hung out in the evenings, which she had figured because she heard the 'fun' happening from the hotel's roof top bar each evening. They then headed to the left and walked through a park called Company's Garden in front of the Planetarium. He apparently knew a good bit of biology because he was able to tell her the names of most of the trees and plants there.

Their next stop was the Green Market Square. As they headed there, they passed St George's Cathedral and Darius told Willa that was the cathedral where Bishop Desmond Tutu preached. They arrived at the market then noticed that it was getting close to 1 pm so Darius asked Willa if she was ready for some lunch.

"I thought you'd never ask".

"Right. Follow me."

Willa came up next to him and grabbed his hand. "I guess if you hold my hand, then you won't lose me along the way." He smiled and clutched her hand a little tighter. He led her to the Rose Corner Café. It was located in the historic Islamic area of town with lots of brightly painted houses. They each ordered a spicy curry dish.

They left about an hour later and, as they turned right to head to the District Six part of town, Willa suddenly pulled to a stop and stared across the street. She and Darius were holding hands so he had to stop too.

He looked at her, then where she was looking, then back at her. "What's wrong?"

Willa hesitated then said, "There's a man who seems to be following me around. He was just there on that corner but then headed away along the street."

"Has he ever done anything to you?"

"No, but he was also in Tenerife and near my hotel the other day."

"Come on." And he led her quickly in the direction where the man had gone.

She had to rush to catch up to him. "Hey, we don't need to do this. He hasn't done anything to me or even threatened me."

"Yeah, not yet, but you can't take any chances with these guys."

He continued to rush in the direction where Willa had pointed, so she simply ran along with him. "Tell me when you see him again."

As they crossed Long Street, Willa suddenly pulled up and pointed to the left, "There".

Darius looked and saw the back of a rather tall man with short, brown hair wearing an old brown jacket.

They rushed after him. The man turned, saw them and headed toward Company's Garden on Green Street. Darius turned on Pepper Street and yelled at Willa, "Continue following him, but do not approach him. I'm going to cut him off."

Willa continued rushing along Green Street but could barely see the man a block ahead amongst the people out on the sunny day. Suddenly she saw Darius rush at the man from the left and knock him against a truck parked on the street.

People around them started scrambling to get out of the way of the two crazy men. Darius went into the man and caught him with a punch to the stomach. Willa was now about ten meters away and saw the man swing at Darius and hit him on the side of his head. Darius went down but managed to grab the man's leg causing him to stumble to the ground. By now, they could hear sirens off in the distance.

Darius hung on, probably hoping the police would arrive soon and help him, but the man was strong and nowhere near ready to call it quits. He kicked Darius with his free foot and Darius let go. The man quickly scrambled to his feet and rushed off across the park.

Willa was now at Darius's side. "Are you okay?"

He sat up on the sidewalk, groaned and said, "Yeah, I'm okay. I'll just have a headache for a few days."

"I'm so sorry. We shouldn't have chased him. As I said, he hasn't done anything to me."

Darius looked at her, "Yet. Men like that cannot be trusted to just look. Eventually, they will act. My cousin thought that some guy was harmless until he raped her. I was not going to let that happen again. If he was harmless, then he could have simply explained himself to the police and promised to stay away, but he ran."

The police arrived and one of them came over to Darius and Willa while the other officer went over to several bystanders.

Darius told the police officer what had happened and what they suspected. Willa also told him about seeing the same man twice in Tenerife and at the hotel. The officer took notes and asked a few more questions.

The other officer finally came over and the two officers conferred for a few minutes pointing, checking their notes and looking at Willa. They finally came back to Willa and Darius.

"Well, it appears that you, young man, were the aggressor here. But, given that this man has been following the young lady around the world, maybe there was reason to attempt a confrontation. However, that was not the way to do it. You should have contacted the authorities and let us handle it. With Willa's description, we would probably have found him in a reasonable amount of time and, until then, she and her dad could have taken precautions."

"We are letting you go with a warning and a recommendation. First, do not attempt something like this again. Second, miss, you need to inform your father about this incident and make sure you let authorities know if you see him again before any action is taken. Do you both understand these conditions?"

They both said they did and thanked the officers for their help and understanding. The officers wished them well and made sure Willa knew they were serious about telling her dad what had happened. She promised she would.

The crowd dispersed since there was no more excitement or bodies or fighting or even blood. Boring!

Willa and Darius started walking to the waterfront since it was now almost 5 pm and Willa had to pick up her dad's painting. She invited Darius to come along and stay for her party. "Absolutely, it sounds like fun. Well, not as much fun as chasing bad guys, getting punched, kicked and chastised by the police, but still fun."

"So, now you know what it is like to hang out with me!" She smiled.

XXXXX

They reached the artist's studio at 5:30. He was working on another painting but, when he saw her, he immediately went into the back room and came out with her painting. She looked at it and got tears again. The boat with she and her dad seemed to emerge from the canvas the longer she looked.

He wrapped it for her in some nice colorful paper and pastel tape. She guessed that his expertise was art and not wrapping packages. She didn't care about the wrapping. It could have been wrapped in pages from a newspaper and she wouldn't have cared. She paid for it and they left the studio.

Outside, she held her painting gently against her chest. Darius asked, "It was beautiful. Is it a painting of your boat?"

"Yes. It also includes my dad and me on the deck. Spenser did such an amazing job and I know my dad will love it. By the way, I need to call my dad about dinner."

"I thought you said party?"

Willa smiled. "Well, things are not always what they seem. It's my sixteenth birthday today and my dad has been planning this party since we arrived. He is out with his friend Amy and they have invited us to have dinner with them at Paddy Malone's, so that is where the party will be."

Darius dutifully nodded and smiled but, of course, he already knew all of this. It had been his job to keep Willa away from the area around Paddy's until at least 6:30 pm.

Willa called her dad, listened for a bit, said "sure" a couple of times then put her phone away. She smiled at Darius and said, "We have half an hour to kill. Any ideas?"

"Well, it's a pretty good walk from here, so let's just head there now. Besides, we can take this time to talk about stuff beyond diving, Cape Town history and bad guys."

And, they did. She talked about the trip, school and briefly mentioned the death of her mom and brother. He talked about his family – mother, father, two sisters – all living just north of Cape Town on a small farm. He said that he was a pretty good rugby player and an excellent shot with several different rifles. "You had to be a good shot when living on a farm and trying to protect crops and animals from predators on four legs or sometimes two."

They arrived at the bar and stood outside for a minute. They decided that Darius would carry the painting so she could go in with her arms and hands empty. She took a breath, looked at Darius, who smiled, and then entered.

Her dad met her just inside the front door. He shook Darius' hand and hugged Willa. He told her they had a table upstairs and led them up. As they reached the top of the stairs, Willa heard, "Surprise!" then the song "Happy Birthday to You". She acted suitably surprised and, frankly, she was kind of surprised that he had gone this far with her birthday party.

She brought her hands to her mouth then hugged her dad tightly. She whispered in his ear that she loved him and this was her best birthday ever. He just kept hugging her.

When they pulled apart she saw there were more people than she had thought. Of course, there was Darius and Amy, but there was also Daleen, Norman and even Amita. Amita had also brought a friend with her. As she scanned the rest of the room, she saw that there was a small buffet set up and the table was decorated with pretty plates, cups, napkins, and other birthday paraphernalia. There were even balloons floating above them with one tied to each chair.

She moved through the room thanking everyone for coming. She hugged Daleen, Amy and Amita, who introduced her friend Zamir. Finally, her dad lightly tapped his knife against his glass and everyone moved over to the table. The table was a large round table with eight place settings. Dan and Amy sat with Willa next to her dad and Darius next to her. Amita sat next to Darius with Zamir on her left. Finally, Norman sat next to Zamir and Daleen sat between Norman and Amy.

Dan picked up his water glass and proposed a toast. "I would like to welcome all of you to Willa's sixteenth birthday party. This is a small group, but an important group for us here in beautiful Cape Town. We leave tomorrow for our next destination but I hope we can keep in touch with those of you who wish it." Willa noticed that his eyes glanced ever so slightly toward Amy.

"This party is not just for Willa's birthday. I also wanted to share with you this wonderful, lovely, caring young lady. She is the love of my life and a diamond in my eyes. When my wife and son passed away years ago, the one person who got me through those terrible times was Willa. She was only five, but she seemed to know what to do even though she was dealing with a lot as well. She also knew when the time was right to get me out of my funk. So, a few years ago she started bugging me about this trip, a trip that we had planned years ago with her mother and brother.

"Somehow, Willa knew it was time to do it, but I did not and I resisted. Fortunately, she was patient and kept at me. Now we are here and I couldn't be happier. Please, if you have not had a chance to meet her or talk with her, do so tonight. You will not regret it." He paused, raised his glass at Willa and said, "I love you!" Tears fell down his cheeks.

Willa was also tearing up. She raised her glass to him, took a sip, set it down and grabbed her dad.

Finally, they all sat and people started talking and laughing. Dan stood after a minute and told everyone to help themselves to the food. He mentioned that drinks could also be ordered from the downstairs bar, if they liked.

There was lots of shuffling of chairs and clinks of dishes and spoons. After people filled their plates they wandered back to their seats. Norman went downstairs and brought up a couple of beers for himself and Dan and a bottle of wine for Amy and Daleen to share.

As they were about to finish, Dan clinked his glass again and everyone got quiet. He moved off to the side, brought a nicely wrapped package back to the table and handed it to Willa. He said, "Happy Birthday!"

Willa thanked him, gave him a hug and opened the package. Once opened she saw a pretty sun dress, lifted it out and commented on how beautiful it was. Then she pulled out another one and then another one. After the last one, she pulled out three cute bathing suits.

Her dad smiled. "I was thinking of getting you a more formal dress, but Amy suggested there would probably not be many opportunities to wear it and suggested some nice sun dresses and bathing suits might be more useful."

Willa hugged her dad then moved around her dad to Amy. She hugged her and said, "Great idea. Thanks." Amy smiled and nodded.

Willa walked to the front of the room and looked back at Darius. He pointed to a spot near the right of the door where he had stashed the painting.

She moved there, found the wrapped painting and brought it to her dad. "I know it's my birthday, but it is also sort of a special day for both of us. This trip has been such a blessing to us and" She paused, "our friendship. Yes, you are my dad and always will be. But, you are also my best friend. Thank you." And she handed him the package.

He stared at her and a tear or two started falling again from his eyes. *Man*, he thought, *I am such a cry baby*. He carefully opened the package and stopped when he saw the painting. He had to sit down. He stared at it for what seemed like forever. He slowly looked at her and told her, "I love it. I absolutely love it. This is amazing. Oh my gosh, I love this."

He held it up and invited everyone to take a look at it. People started to get up and look at it as well as the dresses she had gotten. They all commented on how lovely the dresses were and how cool the painting was. No one else brought presents. Dan had emphasized the need to not do that since they were very limited on space and they all abided by his wishes. But, some did give her cards and some had money in them.

Willa thanked everyone for their gifts and for being part of this special event.

She wandered over to Daleen and told her, "Thank you so much for recommending Spenser. The painting is amazing and my dad loves it."

Daleen smiled. "I'm just happy that it all worked out so well."

After another hour, people started to move off. Amita and Zamir left and wished Willa and Dan a safe trip. Daleen and Norman left shortly after and also wished them a safe trip. Willa hugged both of them and thanked them for being so wonderful to them during their stay.

Finally, Dan suggested they get a taxi back to the hotel. He asked Darius, "Do you need us to drop you off somewhere?"

"No, that won't be necessary. I have an apartment not far from the surf shop, so I can walk there from your hotel."

When they got to the hotel, they all went up to the rooftop bar. Dan got a beer and Amy a glass of wine. Willa and Darius had orange juice. They all sat in the lounge area in the middle of the Airstream Trailer Park. They sat, talked and reminisced. After an hour, Darius excused himself and said he had to get going since he had to work early the next day. Dan and Amy said their goodbyes and Willa walked him down to the front of the hotel.

As they stood outside, Darius said, "You know you need to tell your dad what happened today with the strange man."

"I know, I know. I'll tell him tomorrow as we leave the harbor. I don't want him delaying our trip and trying to find the guy. He's probably gone anyway."

"Okay, but you need to tell him. Promise me that you will."

"I had to promise the police that I would and now you! Wow, I am really in the 'hot seat'."

She smiled and leaned in to him for a kiss. He obliged. As they pulled back, Willa said, "Well, I finally got my sweet sixteen kiss! I thought I'd have to ask the front desk clerk to give it to me."

Darius laughed and said, "How about two?"

Willa smiled. "Now that will make up for me having to wait." He kissed her again.

They separated and Darius asked if he could contact her sometime. She smiled and gave him her email address.

He kissed her on the cheek before walking off. She watched him for a little bit then headed back up to the roof.

When she got upstairs, she went over to Amy and her dad and said she was pretty tired so she was going to head to bed.

Amy and her dad rose. She hugged her dad and started to say bye to Amy, but Amy stopped her and said she was going to go with them to the marina to see them off, so they could say goodbye tomorrow.

Willa smiled and noticed the smile on her dad's face. She nodded and went to her Airstream.

Dan and Amy sat back down.

XXXXX

The following morning, they were up at six am. They checked out and Amy accompanied them to the marina. Taxi dropped them off and they got their bags then tossed them onto the boat.

Willa said bye to Amy and gave her a hug. Willa told her, "I hope you and dad will be able to keep in touch."

Amy said, "Me too." and winked.

Willa got onto the boat and began to stow their bags and other items.

Dan and Amy stood a little apart then hugged. They pulled back then kissed deeply and long. Finally, they pulled back, smiled, said bye and that they would keep in touch.

Dan boarded and waved to Amy. Then, he started helping Willa prepare the boat for departure. As they began pulling out, they both waved to Amy who stayed to watch them leave.

As they grew smaller against the blue sky, Amy turned and made her way back to the hotel.

XXXXX

As they were moving out of the harbor area, Willa came and stood next to her dad who was at the helm. She put her hand on his back and gave it a little rub. He glanced at her and smiled.

Once they cleared the harbor and began moving out toward the open ocean, Willa told her dad what had happened with the man, Darius and the police.

She feared he was about to lose it, but he finally said, "Okay, I guess I understand why you didn't say anything yesterday but, next time, you need to tell me right away. This is getting serious and, frankly, scary. I can't, and won't, let anything happen to you. Do you understand?"

She hugged him from the side and said, "I do, I really do. I promise I will tell you as soon as possible if I see him again."

They sailed for an hour or so then Willa took the helm and Dan checked that the supplies were stored and secured tightly. He knew that the passage from the Atlantic Ocean to the Indian Ocean could be treacherous, so they needed to be well prepared.

As he moved from one cabinet to another, his phone buzzed. He looked but didn't recognize the number, then saw that it was a text message. He opened it and read, 'Imp truth. Ans phone call'.

He read it again then shook his head. He had no idea what it meant, who it was from or what he was supposed to do. He tried calling the number, but was told the number was unknown. He shrugged and said to himself, "Whatever."

14. The Man

"Where are they now?"

"They spent about a week in Cape Town touring and restocking their boat and left yesterday. By the way, a guy that Willa was with a few days ago got into a fight with our guy on the street. Our guy ran off and Willa and her friend were left to deal with the local police."

The caller was talking to Homer Simpson, who was head of the Counter Espionage Group. And, yes, he hated the jokes made about having that name. "Where are they headed?"

"We don't know yet, but we will soon. We are getting copies of their port filings as soon as we can make contact with our connections in the places where they stop. Frankly, it's hard to keep up with them."

"Whatever. Do we know yet if this is just a trip or are they on some kind of mission? I don't like this at all. They have been quiet for 10 years and suddenly they take off to sail around the world? There must be more going on than we know. I want you to personally handle finding out what they are doing. I want updates each week, or more frequently as information becomes available. Understand?"

"Yes sir. I'll update you as we get more info."

15. Another Man

"Have you found them?"

"Yes. They have just left Cape Town, but we do not know where they are heading next."

"When will you know?" asked Dimitri Visiliev. Dimitri was the head of Russia's new Espionage Recruitment division. He and many of his group were former KGB employees.

Heinrich replied, "We will know soon. Our man will find out within the next day or two and I'll personally pass it on to you."

"You know how important this is. If they are doing what we think they might be doing, then we could have an incident on our hands."

"Don't worry, be assured that we will handle this."

16. The Storm

Dan piloted the boat out into the open waters of the Atlantic Ocean just northwest of the Cape of Good Hope. They would hug the coast all the way around the Cape in order to minimize the danger of any severe weather and currents.

Meanwhile, Willa was plotting their trip to Singapore and, rather than head far into the open seas for too long, they decided to island hop to Singapore. The plan was to make stops at Mauritius, Diego Garcia and Sri Lanka before heading into Singapore. Each of those legs would only be a week or so long and, hopefully, the weather would hold for them.

"Okay, dad. I have plotted our route and I think we'll make Singapore in four to six weeks, depending on the weather and any repairs required along the way. Our stops look good. Mauritius and Colombo are friendly ports and will have good moorage and supplies available. You said you would take care of Diego Garcia."

"Yes. I will handle getting us into Diego. It is a US Naval Base and doesn't really cater to tourists, but I will call a friend at the CIA when we depart Mauritius. We should be fine. We don't plan to stay long and we'll stay in unrestricted areas on the base as their guests." He smiled.

Willa knew her dad had once worked for the CIA and trusted he knew what he was talking about. Of course, what else could she do? She couldn't contact Travelocity to make reservations on a US Naval Base, now could she?

"Okay. I'll plot it out and enter the data into the nav system. I have lots of school work to catch up on after wasting all that time in Cape Town."

Dan laughed, "Yeah. That stop was such a waste of time. No fun. Didn't meet anyone interesting. No excitement. A really boring stop. By the way, has Darius contacted you yet?"

"Dad, it has only been a little over a day. Come on. The rules say that the guy has to wait at least two days before contacting a girl."

"Yes, well, I'll bet that rule was invented by guys so they could check out other options."

Willa struck a pose and demurely looked at her dad, "Well, look at me. Do you really think a guy would want to look around after meeting me?" She batted her eyelids.

Dan shook his head and said, "What have I done? I have turned my daughter into a tart!"

"Oh yes, that's me. By the way, has Amy contacted you? Girls' rules say she must wait at least three days or even longer depending on the guy. But, I don't know if the rules still apply to old people."

He couldn't help it. He burst out laughing. "Yes, we old people need to get on with it quickly before we get too old to recognize who the other person is. And, to answer your question, no she has not contacted me, so maybe the rules still apply to us old folks."

"Well, you better not wait too long. She's a hottie and a good catch for a guy like you."

Dan put on a hurt face and suddenly Willa thought that she had gone too far with this little tete-a-tete.

She scrambled over to her father, hugged him and said, "I didn't mean that dad. You know I think you are wonderful, handsome, kind and you would be a great catch for Amy or any woman."

Dan was going to say 'gotcha', but Willa's sincerity touched him and he gently patted her back telling her, "I know honey. Don't worry, I wasn't really hurt and I do know and appreciate you looking out for your dear old dad."

"Okay. Well, I better get down below and start on my homework. Man this is a lot of work. I do love doing the math and science stuff, maybe because it's so easy. I like the English assignments too, but they just take so long. My least favorite assignments are the history assignments. It just seems so boring writing out stuff which is already in most history books and available online. I mean, I try to relate each assignment to what I am actually seeing or experiencing at our stops, but that's tedious too. Arrgh, I guess I had better stop complaining and get to work. The sooner I get this done, the better."

XXXXX

The following day, they encountered some pretty rough weather and the sea swells were getting higher. Willa was at the helm and Dan was trying to get everything tied down and secured.

The storm struck at dawn as they were eating breakfast. They had felt the increased rolling of the boat and heard the winds pick up, which wasn't unusual out on the open sea. Then, suddenly, they were thrown to the side and everything on the table and cabin went flying.

They knew what to do. Willa ran up top and took over the helm. Dan immediately started grabbing boxes, supplies and loose items and stowing them in various secure compartments. He came up to the deck and saw that they had already lost several items that had been on the deck.

The storm had been tossing them around for about an hour at this point and did not seem to be getting any weaker but, luckily, it wasn't getting any worse. Dan secured all of the remaining items above and below then started checking the ropes, tie downs and sails, which seemed to be secure and holding.

He went to the helm. Willa was standing firm and handling the wheel easily. The floor was wet and she slipped a little several times as the boat was tossed in one direction or another.

Dan yelled, "Are you okay? Do you want me to take the helm?"

Willa shook her head and yelled, "I got it. Is everything secured and tight?"

Dan almost smiled. She sounded like the true captain of the ship, which at this point, she was. He responded, "Aye, aye. Everything is secured and tight. Orders for me?"

"No carry on. Good work, seaman."

If Dan could have seen her face, he would have seen a smile. He turned and went back to the work of checking sails, ropes, ties and supplies.

The storm began to weaken after about three hours. At five hours, the seas were pretty calm again and the skies were clear with bright sunshine. It had also warmed up considerably. Dan had taken the helm about an hour ago when Willa ordered him to. Her arms were really beat and she knew that trying to continue would only endanger them in the rough waters. It is always better to be safe than to try to be 'tough'.

Willa spent the last hour doing what Dan had been doing for the first four hours. She also started to take stock of what was lost, what was damaged beyond repair and what was left, especially food and water.

The food and water stocks were fine. Dan had been smart to get them secured first. They would have been absolutely necessary for survival had they been swamped and marooned. However, they did lose some of the spare replacement parts they had bought in Cape Town. The boat seemed in good shape, but they would need to buy more backup spares in Mauritius.

They also lost all of their deck chairs and tables and several items of clothes that had been set out to dry from the first day or so of the trip. The painting that she had given to her dad had, luckily, been stored in a water proof bag and well back inside one of the secure storage compartments. However, one of the bathing suits and one of the sundresses her dad had given her were now gone, but those could be replaced.

While Willa was checking on their stuff and once the seas had calmed, Dan relaxed and took inventory of the items in his pockets and around the helm. The equipment seemed to be functioning well and in good working order. Everything in the pilot house was, by necessity, waterproof and well secured.

The good thing was that on a boat in the open sea, you really didn't need to keep much, if anything, in your pockets. These items were usually stored in waterproof containers in a locker below. As he checked, the only thing he found was his phone. He couldn't think why he had forgotten about it, but he had.

He pulled it out, switched it on and glanced at the screen. He had one missed call and one text message. He went to the missed call and found a voice message. He listened and all it said was, "You must contact me soon. Please. It is imperative we talk."

Well, that sounded pretty important. He didn't recognize the number or voice and knew it wasn't anyone from his office. He pulled up the text message and it read, "Must talk. Vital info about family death. Ans next call."

Okay, this was getting creepy and seemed more serious than he had originally thought. I mean a death? What could that mean?

Just then, Willa said, "It has to be about mom and Peter." Dan was startled and almost dropped his phone. She explained, "I came up behind you just as you read the text. I guess I was pretty quiet. Dad, you have to take that call!"

He nodded and told her about the text he had gotten as they left Cape Town. He also told her about the voice mail message.

"You have to take the next call and I want to hear it too."

"Don't worry. As soon as it comes in, I'll find you and we'll listen together."

Willa wandered off and Dan turned back to the task of getting them to Mauritius. They were both disturbed by the message and needed time to individually process what this could mean. Olivia and Peter were not dead? No. That was impossible. Her body was found and identified with DNA and dental records but Peter had never been found.

Was the accident not an accident? That had to be it. But why wasn't it an accident? And, if it wasn't, then it was done on purpose, which meant murder. No. Why would someone go to the trouble of murdering Olivia and Peter. Peter was a boy and Olivia was a librarian turned mom. This did not make any sense.

At this point, he couldn't wait to get that next phone call.

17. Change and More Change

Eight more days passed and there had still not been a call. They arrived in Mauritius and pulled into the Port Louis harbor. They were led to a moorage area by the harbor master, paid the appropriate fees and signed the required documents.

They had talked a little off and on about what the phone call and texts must mean, but generally they kept their thoughts to themselves. A day out of Port Louis they had to get busy and take inventory. There were stocks to re-supply, spare parts that were needed and repairs which had to be done. They planned to stay for three days in order to complete all of it.

Dan left to find a shop to buy the spare parts and while Dan was gone, Willa worked on the navigation and communications equipment. She had been pretty good with that stuff before the trip, which is why she had taken that role on the trip. But, over the past few months, she had become quite the expert. She could now dismantle most of the equipment, make repairs and reassemble them. She found that the nav system was fine, but the communications equipment needed some work.

She reassembled the nav system and began examining the satellite uplink for the internet, which seemed to have the main problem. She found that water had made its way into one of the small components. As she examined it, she determined the component was beyond repair since salt water had corroded several key connections. The rest of it looked okay and only needed cleaning. She also decided all of the seals would need to be replaced in order to prevent any future leaks.

Dan came back to the boat after a couple of hours and asked "How's it going?" as he handed her items from the dock which she stowed anywhere there was room.

"I need to find an electronics store. Did you see one while you were out frolicking about?"

He smiled. "Actually, I did. There is at least one about half a mile away from here. To get there, go along the Port Access Rd then follow the Marine Rd. Once you cross a large intersection, continue on Military Rd. There appear to be several shops there as well as down a couple of side streets. What do you need?"

Willa explained that everything seemed to be okay with the nav system, but the comm system needed some work. She needed new seals and an internet uplink component.

Dan nodded. "Take your phone in case …."

Before he could finish, Willa flashed her smartphone at him and said, "Come on dad. Have you ever known me, or any teenage girl, to go anywhere without her smartphone?"

He could only smile and roll the palms of his hands over and up. He mouthed sorry!

Willa gave him a comforting smile and headed out to get the component and seals. She wandered along Marine Rd, passed the large intersection and headed up Military. She glanced left and right to find a store.

As she did, she began to wish they had more time here. It seemed like an interesting area and the people seemed quite diverse. There were African, European and Arab influences in the architecture she saw and the languages she heard. The main language here seemed to be French. It was accented, but it was easily understood.

As she scanned to the right, she saw a shop which should work. The sign was in both English and French and said that they sold parts and service for all types of electronic equipment.

She went to the shop and walked in. She looked around and immediately noticed the various packages of seals. That was good, one down, one to go.

She walked to the counter and asked the elderly gentleman in French, "Do you have internet uplink components for ocean communications systems?"

He must have wondered why this obviously young girl was looking for something so intricate. He finally shrugged and responded in French as well, "Yes, we have a variety of systems components. What exactly do you need?"

She handed him the component. She noticed his hesitation and instinctively knew why. But, she was used to people underestimating her.

He examined it then wandered into the back of the store. As he left, she moved over to the shelves with the seals she needed. She found the right ones and grabbed two of each type. She wandered the store and grabbed a few more items she figured they might need in the future. The rule was, better safe than sorry.

As she wandered the store, the gentleman came out from the back room and came over to her. He showed her several components he thought might satisfy her needs. As she examined them, she figured out what he was trying to do. He had brought out four components, but only one would work for her. He wanted to know if she really knew what she was doing.

She pretended to be confused and asked him, "Well, I am not sure. Which one do you think will work?"

He looked at her, realized what she was now doing and smiled at her cleverness. She smiled back.

"This one will work best, but I think you knew that all along. Yes?"

"Yes, I knew. Thank you for helping me. Do you have another one I could have just in case?"

"Of course, mademoiselle, I will be back quickly." He went into the back again.

Within in a minute, he was back with another component. "Merci, monsieur. How much do I owe you?"

Willa paid and thanked the man before she left the store.

As she headed back to the harbor and passed Municipality Street, she glanced left since she had to cross the street. That's when she saw him, the bum from Malta, Tenerife and Cape Town. He was standing about 100 meters away in a doorway and looked to be trying to hide. *What the hell is going on?* She thought. *Who is he? Why is he following me?* Then she had a new thought. *Maybe it has something to do with the calls and texts.*

She decided to continue on to the boat as though she had not seen him. However, she did quicken her step a bit. She wanted to tell her dad.

She arrived at the boat and saw her dad sitting quietly staring at his phone. He looked up as she came onto the boat and she hurriedly walked to him. She knew something was wrong. "What's happened? What's going on?"

He turned to her and said, "Look at this. I received this about ten minutes ago."

He found the text and showed it to her. She saw that the text was from the same person. It said, "Will call soon."

"Has he called?"

Dan shook his head 'no'! But, just then his phone buzzed. He immediately answered and put it on speaker.

"Hello."

Man, "I am glad you decided to answer this time. You need to hear what I have to say and we do not have much time."

"Go ahead. I'm listening."

"What you think happened to Olivia and Peter is not true. And, who you think Olivia was is also not true."

"Wait, what are you talking about? They found her body. There was a storm. She and I met years ago while she was working in a library. She is the mother of my children. I know her. Are you trying to get money out of me? I can guarantee that will not happen."

"Dan, please believe me, I know how you must feel. I knew Olivia and she was a wonderful person. The last thing I want is money or to add more stress to you and Willa's lives. But, I think we must meet. There is too much to talk about and phones are not secure, as you probably know."

"So, what do you suggest?"

"You are planning to head to Singapore, but you must abandon those plans. We need to meet face-to-face. This is too important. Please believe me, I would not ask unless this was a matter of life and death."

Dan stuttered, "What? Wait. Whose life? Whose death? You had better not mean Willa!"

"Rest assured, I mean no harm to Willa or you. I want to prevent harm to you both. That is my one and only goal and I pray that you will let me. It may be the last thing I ever do."

Dan paused, trying to gather his thoughts, "Okay, what do you suggest?"

"Can you meet me in Lima in two weeks? That should give you enough time to get to a port and arrange travel to Lima."

"We can do that. Send a text with the exact contact information."

At that, the call ended. Dan looked at Willa and saw that she was staring intently at the phone. He waited.

"We must go as soon as possible. Dad, we have to go. We have to know what this man knows and why he is bringing this to us now."

"I agree. We will leave tomorrow for Diego. We'll use that as our last stop before making our way to Australia, perhaps Perth or Darwin, to settle up on the boat and get a flight to Lima. Let's get everything finished up and head out tomorrow morning."

Willa decided not to mention the bum. Instead, she headed to the dismembered communication system and began to work. Dan got back to work on repairs and cleaning up the stocks.

They would be ready to sail for Diego the following morning.

18. The Rescue

After reassembling the communication system, Willa started plotting their way to Diego and subsequently to Perth or Darwin. As she examined her navigation charts, calculated distances and times, she started to realize they were going to be cutting it pretty close to be able to arrive in Lima in two weeks. It would probably take two weeks just to get to either of the Australian cities, and that is only if everything went perfectly. She decided to check on other options. After about an hour, she felt she had a solution so she went to find her dad.

Dan was just finishing up bringing the last of their new supplies on board when Willa came to him.

"Dad, I think we should change our plans."

"Okay. What are you thinking?"

"Come, let me show you."

Dan followed Willa to the charts that she had neatly arranged on the counter. He saw she had laid out a new route on the map and clearly marked times and distances along the way.

"I started looking at distances and times for our original routes to Perth or Darwin through Diego and quickly realized we would probably eat up the entire two weeks just getting to those locations and that's if weather and other problems remain neutral. We would still need time to dispose of the boat and fly to Lima."

"I figured maybe there was a better way. So, I started looking at other options. Continuing east was not an option since the distances are so great, so I looked backwards toward the west. Madagascar is an option since it is so close, but options for disposing of the boat and getting suitable flights to Lima are a bit limited."

"Since we have two weeks, I decided to look a little farther for a better option and I think we should head for Durban, South Africa. We can probably make it there in about a week since the weather should be good and we will not be passing through the passage off the Cape of Good Hope. Plus, Durban is the largest and busiest port in Africa. Its size is second only to Johannesburg and it has excellent international flight options. What do you think?"

Dan thought for a few seconds then turned to Willa. "I think you are brilliant. This makes so much more sense. It also means we will probably get into Lima a few days before we are to meet the man which will give us time to get a feel for the area. Let's make our plans for Durban. What are your orders for me captain?" and he gave her a crisp salute.

"My orders are, to get your butt in gear and get those remaining items stowed. We still have lots to do, so get to work or I'll have you flogged."

Dan smiled, saluted, turned and started grabbing the rest of their gear.

Willa went to the computer and began checking flights from Durban to Lima. There were lots of them. There were no non-stop flights, but there were many flights with one or two stops. They ranged in price quite a bit but no matter what they decided, they could be in Lima at least two to three days ahead of schedule.

They sailed out the following morning and followed Willa's new route to Durban. The winds and weather held nicely for them and they made good progress. At the end of the day, they were about 500 kilometers south of the island of Reunion, off the coast of Madagascar, and looked to make it to Durban with plenty of time to spare.

The next day while Willa was checking the charts and Dan was at the helm, they received a May-Day call over the radio. Dan responded. He said he was 'The Olivia' and gave their location. Willa had heard the call and came up to stand next to him.

The caller said his boat was sinking and needed rescuing and gave his approximate location. Willa ran back to her charts to map the location, check how far away they were from them and how long it would take for them to get there.

Dan told the man he would stay on the radio while they made ready to help.

Willa came back a couple of minutes later and told Dan they were only thirty minutes away. They needed to head northwest and gave him the coordinates.

He passed this on to the caller and told him they were heading to him now and asked if he had heard from anyone closer. The caller said no.

Dan looked at Willa and she looked back at him questioningly. He told the man to hold on and he would be right back to him. He switched the radio off.

Willa asked, "What are you doing? We need to stay on with him."

"Willa, this could delay us significantly. We may not even get to Lima for several weeks, depending on what we find."

Willa said, "Dad, I know. Believe me, I know. But, we cannot ignore this. We must go to him."

Dan nodded, "Right." He switched the radio back on and told the man they had the course plotted and would be there in approximately twenty to twenty-five minutes. He asked if they could hold on till they arrived. The man said they could, but they would likely be in the water. They had life jackets and there was enough debris around to hold onto. He told Dan to be careful as they approached. He would try to have some type of signal for them to see their location. Dan asked the man to tell him when they were about to go into the water.

Dan stayed on the radio and Willa took the helm. They both kept their eyes peeled for any sign of the wreck ahead of them. When they were about five minutes away, the radio came alive and the man quickly said they were going into the water. Before Dan could respond, the radio went quiet.

They approached the plotted location slowly and carefully scanned the water all around them. After a couple of minutes, Dan pointed and said, "There!"

Willa looked where he was pointing and saw what he had seen. There was something or someone in the water. It or he was holding up a stick of some type with a red piece of cloth tied to it. They headed for it.

Willa left the helm to Dan and ran to the starboard side of the boat as they approached the red flag. As they slowly closed in on it, Willa saw what appeared to be a man holding onto a piece of debris and waving another smaller piece of debris with a red t-shirt hanging from it. She also saw a woman hanging onto a piece of debris in the water a few yards away from the man. They both had their life jackets on.

Dan quickly ran to lower the sails and slowed the boat to a halt. As he did that, Willa tossed two of their life preservers to the couple. They each found and held on to one. Willa then threw a rope ladder over the side and climbed down into the water to help them.

Dan also came to the side to help. Willa was as far down on the ladder as possible and reached out to the first person they came to. It was the man. She grabbed his hand, pulled him over to the ladder and he grabbed onto the lowest rung.

Willa yelled at him, "Get up now or we won't be able to get the woman. He nodded and quickly started to climb. Willa hung onto the side of the ladder as the man climbed around her pulled himself into the boat. Willa moved and hung off the lowest rung and reached for the woman. As she grabbed her hand, Willa noticed that the lady was strong. Good! Willa held on as tight as she could and the woman slowly moved to the ladder and grabbed it with her other hand.

As the woman slowly emerged from the water, Willa saw that she was naked from the waist up. The life jacket covered some of the area but not all of it. Willa quickly moved up the ladder, ran into the small cabin, grabbed a towel and handed it to the woman as she climbed to the top of the ladder. The woman draped the towel over herself, it wasn't perfect, but it covered the important parts. The woman gave her a look of thanks and pulled herself onto the deck.

Once everyone was on deck, Dan set about getting back under sail and took the helm. Willa grabbed two blankets for the couple and they gratefully wrapped them around themselves. Willa then went to the galley and brought up cups of hot coffee, which they gratefully took and began taking small sips.

Once the boat was back underway toward Durban, Dan put it on autopilot and went over to the couple to ask about what had happened. Willa came over as well.

The man started. "First, thanks so much for coming to our call." Dan and Willa smiled, nodded and waited.

"My name is Butch Elliot and this is my wife Kendra. We were on a short sailing excursion off the coast of Reunion after renting the sailboat in Saint-Pierre. We hadn't planned to go far and only expected to be out a few days. We were actually due back this evening."

He paused to collect his thoughts then continued, "We were doing fine until I noticed early this morning that we were too far out in open water and I could no longer see any land. We have sailed before, but never out in open waters and in sea lanes. An hour later, we struck an object floating in the water but I don't know what it was. Maybe it was an old piece of debris or, well, I just don't know."

"But, I do know that it must have been big or at least hard because it damaged the hull below the water line. It wasn't a large hole, but I had no materials or experience to plug it. I tried pushing whatever I could find into it, but nothing worked, so we decided to turn back. Unfortunately, after a couple of hours, we still could not see any land. We were obviously lost."

"About an hour ago, a large cargo ship came toward us. I tried to call and signal, but they seemed not to see or hear us and they came close enough to almost swamp us completely. As it was, their wake simply washed over us and dumped a large amount of water into the boat, which was enough to force the stern into the water. We couldn't bail fast enough which is when I started making the May-Day call. Thank God you heard me because no one else seemed to be around and I have no idea how long we would have survived way out here."

Dan looked over at Willa then turned back to Butch. "I can't tell you why the ship didn't hear you. Maybe there wasn't anyone in the pilot house at the time you first called, but that doesn't explain them ignoring your May-Day. Anyway, you are here now and are safe."

Dan continued, "We are headed for Durban. We will be disposing of our boat there and heading on from there by air. We have room, although it will be a little tight, and plenty of food and water for all of us. We should make port in a little less than a week and you can use our communications system to contact anyone on Reunion or elsewhere, if you need to. Willa can show you how to do that."

Then he quickly added, "Sorry, I guess I should introduce myself. I am Dan Watson and this is my daughter Willa. We have been on an extended vacation sailing around the world. Feel free to use any of our facilities and, if you have any questions, either Willa or I can help you."

Kendra spoke for the first time, "Well, I want to also thank you guys for helping us. As Butch said, we had no idea how long we could have survived had you not come along. We would love to thank you in a more practical way."

Dan smiled, "Thanks, but that will not be necessary. The rules of the sea say that all available of craft anywhere near a May-Day must respond and may not accept any compensation for the rescue effort. So thanks, but no thanks."

Kendra smiled and said, "Well, thanks again. Maybe we can buy you dinner in Durban, if that is acceptable."

Dan smiled, "Sure. We would love that. Anyway, let me get Butch some dry clothes and maybe Willa can find something that will work for you, Kendra. Butch, please follow me, if you are ready?"

Butch followed Dan to the cabin area. Willa came to Kendra and sat next to her. "What happened to your shirt?"

Kendra smiled, "Well, the t-shirt Butch was waving is mine. It was red and we figured it would be easier to see. He had a dull gray shirt on, which probably would not have been easily seen even if you were only a few feet away. Men have no knack for color selection." She smiled.

"Yeah. I practically have to dress my dad when we go someplace nice. By the way, I am not sure I have much that will fit you, especially when it comes to underwear and bras. I do have some shorts you could substitute for underwear, but I am positive none of my bras will fit. I am a bit small there." And she smiled shyly.

Kendra squeezed her shoulder and rose. "Don't worry. We girls can be pretty inventive." Kendra followed Willa to her store of clothes.

19. Explanations

Over the next 24 hours, everyone sorted out their tasks and places on the small craft. Willa and Kendra were given the cabin area, while Dan and Butch slept on the deck while everyone took turns with the shower and head. Kendra insisted on taking over the meal preparations, while Butch took over cleaning up after the meals and the common areas. This freed up Dan and Willa to focus on navigation, weather and piloting.

On the second day together, they were all sitting on the deck eating a nice spaghetti meal that Kendra had fixed. Willa looked over at Kendra and said, "This is delicious. It is much better than dad or I have ever made."

"Thanks. I just used a few spices I found and ground in some old cheese that was about to be tossed."

Willa took this opportunity to ask, "So, were you guys gone long? Where in the states are you from? I would guess the upper northwest of the US, probably somewhere between Portland and Seattle, but my guess would be Seattle. However, I think you both started somewhere on the east coast."

Kendra looked at Willa, then at Butch, who stared at Willa and then at Dan, who simply shrugged.

"Wow. That is exactly true. We are from Seattle now, but I grew up near Lancaster, Pennsylvania and Butch just north of Cincinnati, Ohio. How do you do that?"

Willa smiled, "I don't really have a technique. I'm just pretty good with languages and accents and it seems to come naturally, I guess. I probably get it from my mom. She was really good with languages too." At that, Willa looked away.

The use of the past tense told Kendra what that meant. "I'm sorry, Willa."

Willa turned back to her. "It's okay. It happened a long time ago. Ten years ago my mom and brother died in a boating accident but we are fine now. As a matter of fact, it is sort of why we are on this trip. My mom had wanted the whole family to make a sailing trip around the world. After she was gone, we put it off until we were ready, which was only a few months ago. So far, it has been a wonderful experience for dad and me, right dad?"

Dan smiled. "Yes. I have enjoyed spending this time with Willa. As you can see, she is an extraordinary young lady. As a matter of fact, so far on this trip, she has won an archery medal on Malta and a running medal on Tenerife. She is quite the accomplished athlete."

"Dad, come on. They don't want to hear all that."

"Well done, Willa," commented Butch. "I am also impressed with your ability to do so much on the boat. I mean you didn't have to be told what to do during the rescue and you're the one who handles all of the navigation and you can even handle the helm. I think it's great you can do so much."

"Thanks, but it is really because my mom and dad were such patient teachers."

"So, what do you guys do way up there in Seattle?" Dan asked to help the focus move off of Willa, who was getting quite fidgety. She glanced at him with relief and smiled.

"Well, as I said, I started out in Cincinnati many years ago and attended Ohio State University. Kendra attended Penn State and we were both recruited into the FBI after graduation where we spent 4 years working on domestic terrorism cases. We met while working on a case and married about a year later. We both eventually decided to leave the FBI and start our own detective agency. We focus on high-end clients, which could include requests to investigate business espionage, hostage rescue and internal criminal activities in a business."

"We also figured the best place to do that would be in Seattle since they have so many high profile people and companies there. We started slow, but with help from some friends in high places, we began getting some excellent leads on possible clients. We are now very successful, have a staff of a dozen investigators and a nice house on Mercer Island."

"This trip is sort of a gift to ourselves for having such a successful first five years in business. Our plan was to tour some of the Asian areas we've always wanted to see so we started in Japan, then China, then Thailand and were going to head to Australia before going home. But, then a couple we met in Pattaya, Thailand at the hotel bar, suggested we take a look at some of the islands in the Indian Ocean before heading to Perth for the start of our Australian segment."

"So, we started in Madagascar then flew to Reunion a week ago. We had done some sailing, as I said, so we thought we'd take a short trip out before heading to Perth. Well, you know how that little adventure turned out."

Kendra looked over at Dan, "I won't even try to do what Willa just did. I'll simply ask where you guys are from and what keeps you busy when you are not sailing around the world with Willa?"

"Well, like you guys, I decided to go out on my own after working for the CIA as a research analyst. It was interesting work, but I couldn't see myself doing it for the rest of my life. So, I started a business investigating insurance and business fraud. It became a successful company and that is how we are able to leave it for a year to make this trip. Willa's school was very accommodating and allowed her to be gone for a year in order to make the trip. However, she does have assignments to complete relating to the trip and a few courses online."

Willa smiled and harrumphed, "Which reminds me. I need to get to work on a couple of assignments that will be late if I don't finish them before we get to Durban."

"When did you start this grand adventure?" asked Kendra.

Willa answered, "We left in June after I finished school. We started in Greece, went to Istanbul, then Malta, Gibraltar, Tenerife and Cape Town. Mauritius was our last stop."

"So, why are you going backwards toward South Africa again?"

Willa looked at Dan. He glanced aside then turned to face Butch and Kendra. He wasn't sure what to say so he looked back at Willa, who was still staring at him. He sighed and told them the story.

He related the accident that took Olivia and Peter. He told them about deciding to make this trip. He told them about the man following Willa and the man who contacted him on the phone. He finally told them about their change of plans to go to Lima to meet the man.

Kendra jumped in before Butch could open his mouth to say more. "I am sorry, but I am going to be blunt here. You should not do this. You do not know what might be waiting for you in Lima. You don't know who the man is or what he might really want. You don't know if it is the same guy who has been stalking Willa, or if they may be working together. You don't really know anything about what is going on!" Her voice was rising and Butch held up his hand to her. She was breathing hard.

Dan quickly said, "I know all of that, but we have to follow this through. If the accident which took my wife and son was not an accident, then we need to know. And, we need to find out why and who would do such a thing!" Now his voice was rising.

Butch jumped in before things got too hot. "Let's calm down here. Everything both of you said is true. You don't know much about what you are getting into. And, yes, you do need to find out what the truth is, if the accident is not the truth. But, please consider your safety and, especially, the safety of Willa. I am sure that you do not want anything to happen to her and I am equally sure she does not want anything to happen to you."

Dan took a deep breath. "Okay, I agree that we are going into this pretty blind, but I have a feeling we are not in danger at this point. If it gets to the point where danger is imminent, then we will back off and get the authorities involved."

Willa relaxed and was happy her dad had said that. She still wanted to continue, but she kept remembering the violent scene she had witnessed on the street in Cape Town.

"Good. I suggest," Butch explained. "Meet this man in Lima, but make sure it is in a very public place with lots of people around and it is during the day. If it goes well and you find out the truth and do not sense any danger, then good. However, if at any point along the way danger presents itself to you, then consider calling us. This is the kind of thing we do and have done at the Bureau."

Dan pondered his offer and looked at Willa, who nodded. "I like your plan and will do what you suggest in Lima. If things do not go well and I feel we are in danger, then I will call you. Okay?"

"Good. Thank you." Kendra looked at Willa and took her hand in hers. Willa smiled thinly.

20. Durban

The final days sailing to Durban were spent pleasantly. The weather held and it remained sunny and warm. The running of the boat became a simple routine and everyone got along nicely. Butch was a fast learner and started taking his turn at the helm. He also learned how to read and use navigation charts from Willa.

Kendra watched the interactions between Willa and Butch and felt a little melancholy. They had wanted children from the day they had started dating, but it seemed that it was not to be. She came from a small family and only had a brother whom she rarely saw. Butch had come from a large family with 6 kids and lots of extended relatives. Whenever they were able to attend Butch's family get-togethers, it was like being at an amusement park. The ages varied from little babies to folks in their eighties. There were lots of people and fun and food with a game of some sort going on all day while the adults smoothly shared supervision of the kids.

She knew Butch was disappointed they had not had any children yet, so they had gone to doctors and fertility centers, but there did not seem to be an answer to their lack of fertility. They finally decided to simply take things as they were and leave it up to God or fate or whatever.

"Hey. Why so quiet?"

Kendra turned and saw Dan. She smiled, "Oh I was just thinking how much fun we are all having. I will be sad to part with you guys and I know Butch will be too. He has definitely taken a liking to Willa. She is so, genuinely fun!"

Dan glanced over at Butch and Willa laughing and pointing at something on a chart. "Have you guys thought of having kids?" As the words left his mouth, he regretted it. "I am sorry, that is none of my business."

Kendra smiled, "Don't worry. All of our friends and family have asked it at one time or another over the years. We have tried, but it doesn't seem to be in the cards for us. We're happy together and have lots of nieces and nephews to spoil."

Dan looked away from Butch and Willa. "Well, I'm sorry for bringing it up." He paused then continued, "I think we'll miss you guys too. Although, with what's coming, I'm afraid we may not be having much fun for the foreseeable future."

"You must promise me you will adhere to the plan we talked about a few days ago. Please do not endanger yourselves and let us help."

Dan looked at Kendra, "Of course, I will call if we need your help. You made me realize how much danger I could be exposing Willa to by doing this."

XXXXX

As they sat around on the deck for the last evening meal, Dan spoke up, "We will be in Durban tomorrow at around noon." He looked at Willa for confirmation and she nodded. "When we dock and take care of the paperwork requirements, we will go with you to the US Consulate in order to make your report. Once that is done, we can head to our hotel, The Protea Hotel Edward. Willa has made our reservations. She and I will only be there for two nights at the most, but you can stay as long as you like. Willa made sure there was future availability."

"Thanks for doing that," remarked Kendra.

Butch raised his glass of water and said, "Here's to our last day on the water! And I mean that literally. I think that Kendra and I might not be destined to be sailors."

Kendra quietly mumbled, "Here, here."

They all touched their glasses together.

After a moment, Butch suddenly rose. He seemed deep in thought and he moved away a little, looked back at them then away and finally said, "We have a problem!"

Then he explained what he meant. "We cannot be seen together. Dan and Willa are being followed so, if Kendra and I are to help you guys in the future, then we can't seem to be connected to you in any way."

They all stared at him when he finished. Of course, he was right. They could not be seen together in Durban or anywhere from now on until this is all resolved or Dan asked for their help. Now, what do they do?

Kendra looked at Willa and motioned for her to follow. When they got to the nav charts, Kendra asked, "We need to be put ashore before we get to Durban. Can you determine a suitable spot using the charts? It should be at least ten kilometers away, but also a place where we can easily get to land and transportation."

Willa pulled out additional charts, opened her laptop and began to search. Dan and Butch came over and watched as she searched various spots along the coastline north of Durban. If she found a location with suitable currents and depth for the boat, she would then open Google Earth to examine the nature of the potential landing point for buildings and other structures as well as possible transportation options.

She finally located a spot of deserted beach that should work. It was about twelve kilometers north, there were no structures close by and but there was a road a kilometer away that they could get to.

Dan agreed on the location and went to the helm. Butch and Kendra began preparing for their trek in the water and on land. Willa plotted the course then went to Dan to show him the route.

An hour later, they discussed the plan. Butch and Kendra would make their way to the road and begin walking to Durban. Their story would be that they were swamped and rescued by a fisherman. They were then passed off to two more fishing boats before being deposited up the coast. Once in Durban they would head to the US Consulate to make their statements. By that time, Dan and Willa would already be on their way to Lima, so their paths should not cross.

XXXXX

The following morning was spent finalizing the packing and organizing of their possessions for their arrival. There wasn't much conversation, just quiet efficiency.

Two hours later, Butch and Kendra were dropped off in about a meter of water and began moving to the beach.

Dan and Willa continued to the Port of Durban and moved into their designated docking area. Their berth had been assigned after Dan had contacted the port official the day before. After completing the paperwork, they checked into the Hotel Edward and entered their room.

XXXXX

Butch and Kendra made it to the road an hour after entering the water and headed toward the city. They were given a couple of rides along the way and the last driver dropped them outside of the US Consulate. They went in and related their story to the officials.

After several phone calls to the states, the consulate officials were satisfied they were who they said they were. The consulate let Butch use the office phone to call their bank and ask for a transfer of a sum of money to a local bank in Durban. The bank agreed and would wait until Butch called with the account number and bank name. The consulate officer lent them the equivalent of $100 in Rand to get started. They were also issued temporary documents noting the loss of their passports.

They were then escorted to a maritime official and a police station to report the accident. Once all of this was completed, they were taken to a bank the consulate office recommended. They opened an account with the $100 the consular official lent them then used his phone to call their bank. At this point, the official left them while they waited for the money to arrive. When it did, they withdrew the equivalent of $1000 in Rand.

They left the bank, secured a room at a nearby hotel then went shopping for some clothes and other items. Once that was done, they went back to the hotel, showered, changed and ate at a nearby restaurant. They had been told to stay in town for a couple of days, just in case there were more questions. The consulate also needed a day to create documents that would allow them to travel back to the states. When they picked those documents up, they would pay back the official his $100.

XXXXX

Dan and Willa spent the day getting the boat into a consignment agreement with a boat dealer, cleaning it and collecting the rest of their possessions. They left most of the food and water stock, plus the spare parts they had accumulated. They also booked their flight to Lima for the following day and would arrive one day ahead of the agreed schedule.

On their way back to the hotel, Dan's phone buzzed. It was a text message. They were only 100 meters from the hotel so they hurried to their room in order to read it.

They entered the room and tossed their stuff on the floor then sat at a little hotel room table. Dan pulled out his phone while Willa quickly grabbed a pencil and piece of paper. Dan nodded and she said "Ready".

He opened the text message. It said, "Mak reserv SM Hotel on Av Patriotas. Wil mt at Parq Chicama Pucala few blocks back of hotel. 1 pm 2 days. I find you."

"That's it. What do you think?" Dan asked.

"Sounds simple."

"I agree."

After a few moments, Dan continued. "By the way, you and Kendra seem to have become pretty good buddies, which I am happy about. I think you have long needed a woman's touch." He looked away.

Willa knew exactly what he meant. She also knew even as he said it, he was thinking of Olivia and how she should have been that woman.

She decided to simply agree and move on. "Thanks dad. Yes, I do like Kendra. She's pretty cool and seems to know a lot of stuff I could benefit from. Well, I mean girl stuff." She looked at Dan, smiled and asked, "Have you ever been to Lima?" He said no so Willa grabbed her laptop. "Okay, let's check it out."

"Let's be sure to check out the meeting area and what is around it. Are there large buildings and dead end streets? If we have to get away, we can hide in large buildings and get help, but we will be trapped in dead end streets," Dan prompted.

Willa looked a Dan, "Yes, I remember what Kendra told us. She also suggested that, since we'll be there a day ahead, we should take a physical look at the area and spend at least an hour in the meeting area observing the people who seem to come and go. This will help us to identify people who do not seem to belong there when we meet with this man."

"We also need to observe everyone we see or meet at the various airports and the hotel in case they may be following us. Do we see them again at our hotel? Do we see them again at the meeting, along the street, or when we eat at restaurants?"

"Wow!" Dan said, "Looks like we will be even busier than we have been so far."

XXXXX

"What? Durban? What are they doing in Durban? Where are they headed now?" There was a pause and the man said Lima.

"Lima. I should have known. He'll be there. Get someone there as soon as possible."

After the call, he dialed a new number. Once connected, he said, "They are now flying to Lima." Pause. "Yes." Pause. "Yes, we have someone on the way." Pause. "Yes, I think backup would be helpful." Pause. "Okay." He ended the call, sat back and rubbed his eyes.

21. Lima

Dan and Willa arrived at the airport in Durban shortly after 5 am and made their way to the counter to check in for their flight. They took Butch and Kendra's advice and scanned the crowds of people. Of course, since many around them were checking in for the same flight, they expected to see them again at the gate, on the flight, at the stopovers and maybe even in Lima.

Their itinerary took them to Johannesburg, then London, then Lima. It would be a long trip, so Dan tried to get all seats in First or Business class, but only managed to find seats for First class on the London to Lima flight, which was fine. It was the last flight and the longest, so it allowed them lots of rest before arriving.

They arrived in Lima relaxed and rested. The local time was 10 am which they felt that would give them plenty of time to get to the hotel and to check out the park before tomorrow's meeting. They proceeded to the taxi queue and hailed a taxi. They still hadn't noticed anyone seemingly trying to follow them. They arrived at the hotel thirty minutes later and, since their room was ready, they went to it right away, changed and headed to the park.

The Parque Chicama was only three blocks behind the hotel. It was noon, so they stopped at a nearby minimart and bought sodas before wandering into the park. They found an empty bench, sat, chatted quietly and pretended to be enjoying the day and the nice weather. They noticed children running around and mothers pushing a variety of conveyances, such as strollers, carriages and coaches.

The men they saw usually passed through and rarely stopped. The few who did, chatted with someone they appeared to know then moved on. If they did stay, they were usually older men who either came with or met a friend and then sat for a while smoking and talking.

After two hours, they felt they knew the clientele of the park, so they decided to walk down to the beach area a few blocks farther on.

The beach area was rather trashy. There were large piles of trash along with trash tossed around randomly. They walked along Av Costanera which paralleled the beach for half a kilometer and found a small green park with benches. It was bordered by Circuito de Playas on the city side and the beach on the water side. They sat there for another hour before making their way back to the hotel. On the way to and from the parque and beach, they noted the buildings and streets they might use if trouble arose.

Later that evening, they ate at a restaurant called Rodizo only a few blocks from the hotel. Once back at the hotel they talked about what they saw and felt about the meeting spot.

"Well, what do you think?" asked Dan.

"The area looks safe, a little run down, but not dangerous as far as I can tell. I also haven't noticed anyone following us. That is, I do not remember seeing anyone that we saw at the various airports also hanging around us near the hotel or as we walked or at the restaurant."

"I agree. I don't remember anyone familiar either. Let's check emails to see if there is any news for us".

Willa powered up her laptop, signed in and checked her mailbox. "Nothing new. I guess we're on for tomorrow as planned."

They watched a little TV, then slept.

XXXXX

The hotel had a complimentary breakfast so they ate at 8 am then hung around the lounge and reading room for a couple of hours chatting and watching guests and staff come and go. They finally went back to their room at 10 and waited. The next 2 hours were excruciating.

Finally, at 12:30 pm they made their way to the park, found a bench and sat.

A little after 1 pm they heard someone behind them quietly say, "I know what happened."

They quickly turned and saw a man who was maybe in his 60s. He was dressed in slacks, an open dress shirt and black loafers with no socks. He was a little chunky and stood around five and a half feet tall. He moved to their bench and sat next to Dan.

He started without introduction or preamble. "I knew Olivia very well many years ago. She was smart, lovely and very clever. I was very sorry, disturbed and angry when I heard of her death so I finally decided I couldn't let them get away with it, which is why I contacted you."

He paused long enough for Dan to jump in. "What the hell are you talking about? How do you know Olivia? Who are 'them'?"

"I know this is all going to be very confusing and a lot to take in, but I assure you, it is all true. As I said, I knew Olivia well. I worked with her. She was a wonderful person and a proud American."

Why had he emphasized American thought Willa.

He saw the confusion and quickly continued. "You see, she did some work for the US government as well as the Russian government so some would say she was a spy. But, that doesn't really tell the whole story." Before they could interrupt, he continued. "Look, we can't stay here long and I need to get this out."

He quickly continued. "She grew up in Russia and was recruited by them when she was only sixteen. She was trained in Dresden, Germany by the German Secret Police and, after two years, she was sent to the United States to live with a couple who were designated as her relatives. Of course, they were not her relatives."

"They eventually made their way to Omaha and Olivia attended Creighton Dental School on an early admission. She graduated at 22 and became a staff dentist at a local dentist's office near Offutt Air Base, the home of the Strategic Air Command Headquarters. Her assignment was to seek out and become friendly with military men at Offutt. Specifically, she was asked to cozy up to Strategic Air Command officers and gain access to the base and the officer's club with one of them, which she did."

He could see that both Dan and Willa were having a great deal of difficulty taking this all in, so he decided to move along more quickly. "She did this until the age of twenty-four with no real reservations. But, as she learned more and more about what she was being asked to do and the people involved, she decided to get out. After some careful planning on her part, she stole a great deal of money and some files from her fake relatives then headed out of town, eventually ending up in Chicago. She used some of the money she stole to change her hair, have some minor facial surgery and to get a new identity."

"But, her conscience began troubling her more and more, so not long after she arrived in Chicago, she walked into the FBI office in Chicago and told them a little of what she had been doing. She told them she wanted to hide which is when I was assigned to her case. I worked with her to determine what she knew and once we verified what we could and felt she had been telling the truth, we asked if she would work for 'us'. She reluctantly agreed and even went to our training center in Virginia."

"However, after a couple of trial jobs, she wanted out. Her handler agreed that she was just not suited to the type of work they wanted her to do, so she was put into the witness protection program and into hiding. All along, she kept telling me that she just wanted to live a normal life and have a family. Luckily, she always felt she could trust me so we kept in touch after she was in the hiding."

"Not long after going into witness protection, she told me she wasn't sure if she was as protected as they felt she was. She was really scared. She told me she knew some things she thought might make her a target. I think the files she stole were what she was talking about. She told me about them but never showed them to me or said what was in them. She said she felt that someone was watching her."

"I believed her so I helped her to disappear again. I knew someone who could 'produce' different identities and documentation. Once she was ready, I set her up in San Francisco with her new identity and papers. She had a couple of cosmetic procedures to change her physical features even more, got a job as a librarian and settled into her new life. We had only little contact after that. The Chicago office decided she was no risk to the US and stopped keeping tabs on her."

"This is where you, Dan, met her and finally made her life complete and wonderful. You need to remember that. She was suddenly the happiest she had ever been in her whole life. She loved it, especially her new family."

"It wasn't often but she and I had ways to contact each other in case she ever got into trouble or if I sensed trouble coming her way and needed to warn her."

Willa couldn't take this any longer. "Wait. Stop. What you are saying can't be true. My mom was not a spy. She was my mother and Peter's mother and my dad's wife. That's all. You need to stop making up this story and scaring us. Go away."

Dan hugged Willa pulling her close which calmed her a little.

The man waited patiently.

Dan looked at him and thought about what the man had said. The guy seemed sincere and appeared to believe what he was telling them. Dan had to think about this logically and not emotionally. *What had Olivia told him about her past? Well, truthfully, not a great deal. As a matter of fact, according to Olivia, all of her family relations were either dead or no longer available for contact. That seemed pretty convenient, maybe too convenient.*

What did she say about her childhood and school and growing up? Again, not much. She said her childhood was typical. She rarely ever mentioned friends she had had or places she had been. If she did, she would say, Oh, I forgot their name. Or, I don't remember the name of the little town. It was so long ago. School or college? Again she couldn't quite remember names. She did tell him about Creighton and being a dentist for a few years. But, she had said she really did not like that line of work, so she left and ended up in San Francisco. Again, all of it very convenient.

Dan finally asked, "Can you tell me who you are?"

The man hesitated then shrugged and said, "My name is Dennis Metcalf. I retired right after Olivia's death and was actually at the funeral, but watching from a distance. I had wished at the time I could have approached you and told you how sorry I was and how wonderful she was. But, that would have opened a Pandora's Box that I wasn't sure should be opened, especially at the time and because I did not know if a threat remained for you."

"Then, why now," sighed Willa. "Why are you hurting us now with this? Why not five years ago? Or last year? Or, or whenever?"

"Because there was no danger," and he paused, "not until now. You were not in danger five years ago or even one year ago. My information indicates that your decision to make this trip stirred up old fears about what you might be seeking to find out and, again, I think it has to do with what was in the files she took. Those with an interest in you, kept tabs on you for a couple of years after Olivia's death but, when they saw that you seemed to settle into a routine life, they backed off. I suspect they had only kept limited surveillance on you after that."

"But then, when you flew to Europe, bought a boat, made travel plans, and started showing up at various foreign places, some of the places Olivia, and others, had been to, this seemed to get their attention."

"What about you? Do you have someone following us? Is he the bum I have seen along the way at each of our stops?" Willa demanded.

Dennis shook his head and said, "I don't know about a bum, but yes, I have had someone on you during your trip but he stays well back in the shadows and you will likely never see him."

Willa described the bum to him and Dennis' eyes moved left then right then centered and he shook his head. "I really can't say for sure if it is him. As I said, he could look like anyone. But, I assure you, others will have had people on you as well and I guarantee there are people in certain organizations watching you and their people are reporting your activities back to them. My information only indicates they are out there, but I have no idea where they are or who they are. And, who knows, there may even be others out there interested in you."

Willa became thoughtful while Dan got up and walked a short distance away. He looked around the park then turned to Dennis, "You mean that someone, right now, could be watching us and even listening to our conversation?"

Dennis shrugged and said, "Yes." He didn't look around because he knew, if they were out there, and he figured they were, they wouldn't be seen.

Willa rushed right to the point. "What do we do now? What is the danger? Did they kill my mom and brother? Will they kill us?" Her voice was breaking as she realized what her mother had probably gone through all those years in that job and then trying to hide her past from them.

Dan quickly came back over, sat with her and held her hands.

Dennis sighed. "I really do not have the answers to your questions." He quickly looked around. "We also need to get moving. We've already been here too long. Before we meet again, I will try to find out more information for you. Let's meet again tomorrow at about 10 am. There is a small park a short way up along the beach."

Dan nodded, "We know where it was."

"Do not talk to anyone about what we have discussed here. You cannot be sure about anyone's true relationship with you and your family. And I mean anyone. This means co-workers, school officials, fellow students and all of their families."

"Wait, wait. What are you talking about? I know those people. They are trusted friends. None of them would do anything to harm us." Dan protested.

Dennis looked at Dan and Willa. He took a deep breath and said, "Think about this, Dan. You didn't know about any of this. Most, if not all, of what she told you about her life before she met you is probably a lie or a half-truth. What makes you think that the various friends you have acquired over the years, before and after Olivia's passing, didn't enter your lives for reasons that they would never reveal?"

Willa was silent, then "This is so hard to take in. I am struggling to believe any of it, but I actually think you are telling the truth. Dad, we need to take what Dennis says seriously. We need to be careful. I do not want anything to happen to you," and before he could say, "nor to me."

Dan sighed, smiled and looked at Willa. "Yes, we need to take this in and think about it." He looked at Dennis, "Okay, we'll be careful and we will not discuss this with anyone. At least, until after we talk to you tomorrow and we learn exactly what we might be up against."

"Good. I will see what I can find out. You should leave here a few minutes after I do. I cannot emphasize how important it is for you to show care and caution from now on because they surely know we have talked. I would suggest you not communicate anything about this over the phone or internet. Continue to communicate as before, things about your trip, places you've seen, and people you've met but, of course, not me. And, you'll need to come up with an explanation for this change of plans in your itinerary."

"Okay, we'll do as you suggest."

"You may also need to keep your conversations normal in the hotel and your room. While you have been out, someone could have bugged it."

"What?" Willa exclaimed. "I can't believe this. People are listening to our conversations in our room? This really sucks. I hate it."

Dan turned to her, "I know, but we need to take the precautions that he has suggested. Willa, think about what we started out to do here. We wanted to find out what happened to mom and Peter, right? And, that is what we are doing. We certainly didn't expect this, but do we stop? Do we go back to our trip like nothing has changed? Do we just go home and get back to our former lives?"

Willa was quiet a moment. Finally, she took a deep breath, straightened up and said, "No. We continue and we find out what happened to mom and Peter. We have to do this for them even more so after what Dennis has told us. Someone has to be held accountable for their deaths." She looked at Dennis, "We'll do exactly as you say and will meet you at the park tomorrow at ten."

"Good. Till then." At that, Dennis got up and left.

Dan and Willa sat for a few minutes, then rose and walked slowly out of the park. As they walked around, they didn't talk, nor did they really make conscious choices about where they were going. After about an hour, they found a small café and had some coffee and a pastry while sitting quietly.

It was getting close to five so Willa suggested they head back to the room to change then go to a different restaurant for dinner. "Let's take a taxi to the central plaza in Lima to find a place there."

"Good idea."

They went back to the hotel, changed and asked the hotel to call them a taxi. The taxi arrived within a few minutes and they headed to the central plaza. Once there they walked down a couple of side streets until they found a small, nice little restaurant that wasn't too crowded with tourists.

After they ate, they caught a taxi back to the hotel. They had eaten their meal as though it was simply a duty. Once at the hotel, they made their way to their room watched some TV, and slept fitfully.

XXXXX

They ate breakfast the following morning and, afterwards, Dan read for a while and Willa checked emails. Finally, at 9:30, they left for the meeting. As they approached the small park, they noticed a crowd of people gathered around a bench near the beach side of the grassy area. They also heard sirens in the distance.

Dan wasn't feeling very good about this. As he glanced at Willa, she looked up at him with a worried look on her face.

They arrived at the edge of the crowd and moved to a point where they could see what everyone was looking at.

And, they stopped dead in their tracks. They saw a man slumped slightly to his side in the center of the bench. He was dressed in dirty, worn clothes, one foot was uncovered and the other had an old shoe but no sock. His face was dirty and looked like it had a day's growth of hair. It was Dennis Metcalf and he was dead.

Dan gently took Willa's arm and led her away. He didn't say anything but simply had her walk with him along the beach side of the road away from the gathering. After walking about three or four kilometers, they found themselves in the Miraflores area of Lima, which was much more upscale than San Miguel. They found a coffee shop that was almost deserted, bought a coffee and sat as far away as possible from the two other customers.

After sitting for a minute or so, Willa looked at her dad and asked, "What do we do now?"

It was a great question and he did not know the answer, so he said nothing and continued to stare into his coffee cup, possibly hoping the answer would magically appear there.

XXXXX

Homer yelled into the phone, "What the hell is going on there? Who killed him? Look, I want answers and I want them soon!"

XXXXX

Dimitri could not believe what was last reported to him. His minion in Lima sent him a report by secure line that told him a man was dead and that Dan and Willa were present right after it happened. This was a mess. The whole thing was becoming a big screw-up.

22. D&W and B&K

Willa and Dan eventually made their way back to their room. They were so paranoid about the room being bugged that they said nothing. Willa pulled out her laptop and started searching for any references to Dennis Metcalf, but she didn't expect to find any and didn't. Dan thought about checking with one of his former colleagues at the CIA, but then remembered Dennis' warning.

This was so frustrating. They wanted to share this information, but could not. They couldn't contact anyone.

Almost simultaneously, Willa and Dan turned to face each other. They didn't have to say anything. They were both thinking the same thing – Butch and Kendra.

They also knew they couldn't call from Lima. They had to leave. They had to go home. They couldn't risk going directly to Seattle or using their phones or email accounts. They had to pretend that they had decided to go home and be done with the trip.

Dan went online and booked their return flight to New York City for the next day. Once done, they left to go for a walk and to talk. They headed for the beach.

"We need to contact Butch and Kendra when we get back." Willa said softly. She looked thoughtful and Dan noticed.

"What's up? You look, I don't know, troubled?"

"Maybe we should wait a couple of weeks until we think whoever might be following us has backed off." Willa said it as though it was a statement, but she also meant it as a question.

Dan was quiet then sighed, "You're right. If what Dennis said is true, then I do not want to put them in harm's way too. Maybe we can tell everyone we decided that we needed to cut the trip short. We can say we kept having trouble with the boat, which was increasing our expenses and the stress levels were becoming too much for us to deal with. We can also say that we can pick up where we left off sometime in the future, if we wanted to."

Willa shrugged, "Sounds good to me. I can always add that the pressure of helping with the boat and trying to keep up with all of the school assignments was too much for me to handle and I began to enjoy the trip less and less."

"Good. Maybe after a month or so, one of us can secretly buy a burner phone then use it to call Butch and Kendra from some secluded spot."

They now had a plan and felt better.

XXXXX

They arrived back in Scarsdale, Dan went back to work and Willa went back to school.

School had only started a month before, so there wasn't much catching up to do, especially since most of the assignments she had been doing during the past few months were meant to be work for this current school year, thus, essentially, Willa was ahead of the rest of the class.

Dan's partners and staff were glad to have him back and had lots of questions about the trip. Dan responded to them with enthusiasm, stuck with the story they had concocted and, after a few days, everything settled into a normal routine.

School went much the same for Willa. There was lots of interest at first, especially from the girls who wanted to know all about the boys she had met. The counselors and teachers seemed to accept the reasons she gave for coming back early and didn't probe. The teachers she had been working with asked if she might be willing to give presentations in class about the work she had submitted and the trip in general. They were sure the other students would love to hear about her experiences. She wasn't as sure about that, but she happily agreed.

XXXXX

A month later, Dan and Willa were enjoying a relaxing walk in a nearby park. The leaves had all started to change colors and the fall air was crisp. People had started to put up Halloween displays and set out pumpkins, cornstalks and other fall scenes. Normally, Willa loved this time of year but now she hardly noticed the decorations.

"We need to get a burner phone." Dan glanced nervously around the park.

"I think I know how we can do it. I can ask one of the girls to get one for me. I'll choose a girl who has heard about my trip and about Darius. I'll tell her that I want to call him, but I do not want to let you know about it. I am sure she'll agree."

"I like it." And he smiled at Willa.

"We need to find someplace to call them from. Here seems good, but what do you think?"

"Here is good, although maybe we can wander a little farther away from houses and people when we do." He glanced around again.

"I'll let you know when I have the phone, but it should only take a day or two."

XXXXX

Two days later, Dan and Willa were out on a walk again in the park. They had been doing these walks almost every day since they'd been back hoping to make anyone watching them believe that this was just something they regularly did, that it was normal.

They were near the end of the park well away from people and homes and couldn't see anyone around. Dan had the phone in his pocket. He performed one last sweep, took out the phone and dialed the number Butch had given him. It was around 9 pm their time, so it would be 6 pm in Seattle. He hoped they were around.

The phone rang three times and Dan started to worry, then, "Hello. Butch here."

Dan almost didn't say anything, but then he stammered, "Butch, this is Dan. We need your help."

XXXXX

Dimitri asked, "What have they been doing?"

"As far as we can tell, they have settled into their former life. He goes to work, handles cases, then comes home. She goes to school, has archery and cross-country practice after school then comes home. They don't seem to do much else. They take walks in the park when the weather permits. Sometimes they go into the city for dinner or a show."

Dimitri told the agent to keep watch and to call if anything changes.

He sat back and thought about making another call. He finally picked up the phone and entered the number. When the call was answered, he quickly asked, "Was that your guy in Lima?"

"No. This means that someone else is involved. Any ideas?"

Dimitri thought a moment then finally said, "I might, but let me get back to you. I have to check out a few things first."

"Don't take too long. We need to find out and neutralize the threat."

XXXXX

Butch had to take a moment because he knew if they needed their help, then it probably had to do with the Lima meet. "Are you on a secure phone or burner? Is Willa with you?"

"Yes to both questions and she knows everything I'm going to tell you, so I am going to put you on speaker."

"Okay. What's up?"

Dan told him everything that had happened from the time they had parted in Durban. When he finished, he asked "So, what do you think we should do?"

Butch didn't hesitate. "Nothing. Continue life as usual. I am in the middle of a case right now, so I can't come, but Kendra can be there tomorrow. I'll have her fly into New York and take a room in town. Is there someplace where you think you guys can meet? Remember, someone is likely watching both of you, so it cannot be a place where they will become suspicious."

Dan thought a minute, shrugged and looked over at Willa. "I can't think of anyplace I go to normally. Can you?"

Willa looked thoughtful then asked, "Does Kendra know how to handle a bow?"

"I don't know for sure, but she probably can. She's pretty good with most guns and can handle knives as well. What are you thinking?"

"There is an open archery tournament this coming weekend in Greenwich, Connecticut. I was planning to compete and since it is an open tournament, anyone can enter. I have already qualified based on my second place finish in Malta. If Kendra can arrive tomorrow, then she will have three days to practice."

"I like it and will check with her today. Let's assume she will be there. What do you propose?"

"Well, as the tournament progresses, we could just casually start to chat and I'll make sure we have one or two other competitors with us. After the tournament, we can have something to eat in public and she can slip information to me somehow. Then, we can proceed from that point."

Butch couldn't think of any flaws, so he agreed and told them he'd be in touch.

Two days later, there was a knock on the door as Willa and Dan finished cleaning the dinner dishes. Dan went to the door, opened it and found a man dressed in a neatly fitting suit, looking very official. "Yes?"

The man smiled and asked, "Are you Daniel Watson?"

"What is this about?"

The man smiled again, "My name is Frank Young. I work with the FBI." He showed Dan his credentials then asked again, "Are you Daniel Watson?"

Dan looked at the credentials and nodded. "Yes, I am Daniel Watson. What can I do for you?"

"Is Willa here too?"

"Yes." Dan stepped aside, showed Frank into the living room and invited him to sit. Frank sat in a chair and Dan sat across from him on the sofa. He asked again, "What is this about?"

"I understand that you and Willa were at the scene of the murder of an American citizen in Lima, a Mr. Dennis Metcalf. I would like to ask you and Willa a few questions about the incident. As you can imagine we take the murder of American citizens seriously. Is Willa available?" He asked again.

"Quite some time has passed since we were there, so I am not sure what we could tell you."

"I apologize for our late involvement, but paperwork, permissions and agreements took some time to arrange. It would just help to hear what you and your daughter can remember and we would really appreciate your cooperation."

Dan sighed, "Please wait a moment. I'll see if she is finished." He walked into the kitchen as Willa was putting the last few dishes away.

"Who was at the door?"

Dan came close and quietly said, "Someone from the FBI is here and wants to talk about anything we might know about what we saw in Lima regarding Dennis' death. Let me do the talking and just agree with what I say. Okay?"

"Sure. I don't want to talk to the guy anyway."

They walked into the living room and Frank stood as they came in. He introduced himself to Willa and offered his hand. "Thank you for taking the time to talk to me."

Willa smiled, shook his hand and sat next to Dan. Once they were all settled, Frank started.

He asked them what they saw, did they know Dennis, why were they in Lima, why were they at that particular park and did they meet anyone else while in Lima.

Dan told Frank what they saw as they walked to the park, he said they did not know Dennis, were in Lima as part of their trip, were walking along the beach, ended up at the park and, finally, they met no one else in Lima other than various service providers. Willa agreed with everything Dan said or simply parroted it back to Frank if he persisted.

Frank asked a few follow-up questions as he took notes and Dan answered them in much the same way as he had the first time. And Willa nodded.

Frank finally closed his notebook, thanked them for their cooperation and left.

Dan and Willa retreated into the kitchen but did not discuss the meeting. They would wait until their walk in the park that evening. They had actually started switching their walks between three parks in order to make it harder to monitor them.

They left on their walk about an hour later and, once in the remotest part of the park, Willa asked, "What do you think that was about?"

"I really don't know. Maybe it was genuine or maybe they were probing us for something. I just don't know. He could even have been a fake and was sent by whoever is following us."

"I will be seeing Kendra in two days and will pass a note to her about this meeting sometime during the breaks in the tournament."

Dan nodded. As they continued their walk, he looked at Willa and noticed she seemed to be taking this harder than he had realized. He had felt that she was strong enough to handle anything, but he may have been wrong. She was certainly strong, but she was still a sixteen year old girl trying to deal with normal school stuff along with all of this secrecy and danger.

Dan moved to her and put his hands on shoulders. When she looked up at him, he smiled and told her, "I love you so much and I am so sorry all of this is happening to you. You should be going to dances and movies and other activities with your friends. I wish I could protect you from all of this, but that's impossible now. If you get to the point where you want to back off, then we will and never look back."

"Thanks dad. It is a pain in the butt to have to mess with people like Frank and to have the memories of Dennis on the bench stuck in my head. But, I want to know the truth. I have to know the truth and I do not want to stop until I do." She smiled at him and finished with, "I am fine and I am looking forward to seeing Kendra. She is great and we'll have fun catching up."

They continued their walk and after a few minutes she turned to Dan, "I noticed among the things you listed that I was missing at school as a teenage girl, you did not include dating and having a boyfriend."

Dan glanced at her as they walked. He was about to say something when she smiled and said, "I'm just kidding. I'm not ready for all of the drama that surrounds having boyfriends."

Dan seemed to relax, but then she continued, "But dating, now that's an interesting idea." If Dan could have seen her face, he would have seen a huge grin.

23. Greenwich

Willa was still working on getting her driver's permit, so Dan needed to drive her to places when there were no friends available. However, in this case, he was glad to be the one to take her to the archery tournament. This would allow him to see what she was facing regarding the meeting with Kendra. He only planned to stay long enough to watch the first round then he'd come back at the end of the tournament when Willa called.

Willa competed in the female under twenty-one age group and Kendra in the over thirty group. After the first round, the archers had a thirty minute break and Willa wandered over to the snack kiosks with one of the other archers in her group. They knew each other from school competitions. As Willa passed Kendra, they smiled but didn't talk.

Both of them made it past the first and second rounds and the contestants now had an hour and a half to have some lunch and/or practice. Willa and a couple of girls bought some light lunch items and found an area of grass to sit and eat. Willa could see Kendra wandering around holding her sack of food and a soft drink. She eventually came to where the girls were and asked if she could sit with them. They all shrugged and said sure.

"I hope you girls don't mind having someone join your group. I am from Seattle and don't know anyone here. So, I took a chance that you guys wouldn't mind me joining the group. My name is Kendra." She smiled at them.

They all smiled, nodded and introduced themselves. They also said things like "No problem.", "Glad to meet you.", "Wow, Seattle looks so cool."

Willa finally asked, "What made you come so far for a tournament."

Kendra thought it was a smart question to ask. If anyone were listening nearby, they would also want to know why.

"Oh, I don't know. I haven't competed in a long time and I didn't know how well I would do. I guess I figured it might be better to compete somewhere where, if I did poorly, none of my friends would know." Kendra smiled shyly. They all smiled back and nodded in understanding.

As they were picking up their stuff and getting ready to head back, Kendra thanked the girls and said, "Well, I need to head to the restroom before we begin again."

Willa got the hint and turned to Kendra, "Hey, I'll take your stuff and toss it away with mine, if you like."

"Great, thanks." Kendra handed her stuff to Willa and glanced down at the bag. "Good luck everyone!" She moved off to the restroom.

Willa followed the other girls to the trash bins. There was a little crowd around the bins as competitors prepared to get back to the third round. Willa moved until she was surrounded by girls and boys tossing away their lunch trash. She inserted her hand in the bag Kendra gave to her and found the carefully folded piece of paper. She slid it out just as she tossed all of the stuff in the bin then put her hands in her pockets.

Both Kendra and Willa made it into the final round. Willa finished first in her group and Kendra finished second to last.

As the contestants started moving to the exit, Kendra found her way slowly toward Willa. Willa felt her coming and slowed then stopped with a girl she knew from school competitions. They were laughing at something when Kendra came over to them.

"Hey guys. Willa, you did really great. Congratulations."

"Thanks. You did well making it into the finals, especially since you hadn't competed in a long time."

The other girl jumped in quickly and said, "Well, we all had high expectations for Willa since she is actually an international champion." She knuckled Willa's shoulder.

"Really?" asked Kendra.

"No. I competed in a competition in Malta last summer, but only finished second."

"Yeah, but it was second against women with lots of international experience. Anyway, I gotta get going. My mom is waiting. Nice to see you again Willa and you too, Kendra. Bye!"

Both Willa and Kendra said bye. "Do you need a ride, Willa?"

"Oh, no thank you. My dad is picking me up."

"Oh, okay. Well, it was great meeting you. My husband and I sometimes come to New York on business. I know we'd really love to meet your dad and maybe have dinner together."

"I'd love that too and I'm sure that my dad would be happy to meet you guys. Let me give you our phone number, so you can call when you have a trip here." Willa pulled out a piece of paper from her pocket and wrote their phone number on it. She folded it and handed it to Kendra.

"I'll talk to my husband when I get home and see what our schedule looks like. Take care." Kendra leaned in and gave Willa a little hug. She moved off and disappeared into the crowd.

Willa pulled out her phone and called her dad. The venue was only about thirty minutes from home, so she would probably only have to wait about ten minutes for him once she gathered her stuff and made her way to the parking area.

Dan arrived about five minutes after she called, so he had to wait for her. After she put her stuff in the trunk, she jumped into the passenger seat.

"Sorry you had to wait. I didn't expect you to get here so fast."

"I decided to drive over at about the time I figured the tournament would be over and wait at a coffee shop a few miles away. I didn't wait long. How did it go?"

"Great." Willa held up her first place ribbon. She also smiled mischievously.

And Dan knew what that meant.

XXXXX

During their walk that evening, Willa retrieved Kendra's note from her pocket. She read through it and turned to Dan. "Kendra gave us her phone number and it is different from the one Butch gave us. Her note is short and blunt. She says to not do anything out of the ordinary for 6 months. If all goes well at the tournament, then Kendra will contact me in about a month to set up a meeting."

Dan asked, "Did you tell her about the FBI?"

"Yes, I passed her a note and wrote my phone number on it."

They walked quietly for a little while, then Dan said, "I guess we live life as usual, if what we are doing can be considered 'life as usual'."

XXXXX

Kendra called a month after the tournament. They talked about the tournament, what Willa had been up to at school, what Kendra had been doing and then Kendra said, "Hey, Butch and I need to be in NY for a case we are working on. We could stay over a couple of days next weekend, if you are around?"

"Yeah, that would be great. I don't think we have anything planned, but hold on a sec and let me ask my dad." She turned, looked at Dan, asked, he said okay and then she got back on the phone with Kendra. "My dad said that would be great." They chatted a bit more then said their goodbyes.

XXXXX

The following weekend, Dan and Willa took the train into the city and met Kendra and Butch at Penn Station. They introduced each other as though the men had never met the others and made their way outside.

It was a nice fall day, so they walked the few blocks to Central Park. As they walked along, they chatted about nothing much. Dan moved next to Butch, and Willa walked with Kendra. They entered the park and wandered past the Tavern on the Green toward The Lake. They stopped near The Lake and started pointing and smiling. They also talked quietly.

121

Kendra started, "Frank doesn't seem to be who he said he is. None of my contacts could find him in any FBI data bases but I am guessing this is not a surprise to you."

"No, I was suspicious after a few minutes with him. His questions were too general and he didn't ask for any detail. What happens next?" Dan asked.

"Nothing. We need to build our relationship first. We need to act normal and pretend we are just enjoying each other's company."

Willa smiled, "Well, I don't have to pretend any of that. I already like you guys and have a lot of fun when we get together."

The adults smiled sheepishly. Dan put his arm around Willa's shoulder and gave her a little hug.

They had lunch at the Tavern on the Green then headed back to the train station, promising to keep in touch.

XXXXX

"Have you found out the identity of the guy who visited them at their home, yet?" Homer was very concerned about that surprising development.

"No." the guy on the other end said. "Have you found out who that couple is that they met in the city?"

"Yes. They own an investigation agency in Seattle. The woman met Willa at the archery tournament and they kept in touch. Dan's investigation business obviously gives him some affinity with them and I also suppose the woman presents a mother, or at least older sister, role model for Willa."

"Okay, you keep looking into the guy who visited them and we'll watch the couple."

XXXXX

Dan, Willa, Butch and Kendra kept in touch two or three times a month using open lines and once every two weeks using burners while Dan and Willa were on their walks. Butch told them at one point that they will quietly try to find out more about Dennis and Frank but, he still insisted Dan stay out of it for now.

Dan and Willa spent a week in Seattle over the New Year holiday, and Willa and Kendra attended another archery tournament in Phoenix in March.

In May, over Memorial Day weekend, Butch and Kendra visited Dan and Willa staying at their home in Scarsdale for a couple of days before they all drove north to the Berkshires. They booked two rooms at a B&B just west of Pittsfield on Onota Lake.

After they got there and as they started to settle into the rooms, the girls told the boys that they were going to room together, so the guys were going to have to stay in the other room. Butch and Dan shrugged and headed into the other room, while Kendra and Willa smiled as they moved off.

Once in the room, Willa and Kendra laughed and giggled about the boys having to room together. But, if they had been in the other room, they would have heard a sigh of relief from both guys as they sorted their stuff out.

The next day was warm and sunny, so after breakfast, they decided to go out on the lake. There was a boat rental place a short walk from the B&B so they rented a twenty-five foot Cuddy Cabin, drove to the small store nearby, bought some drinks, pre-made sandwiches, chips, ice and a cooler. They packed all of this, loaded it onto the boat, changed into swimsuits with shorts and t-shirts then headed out onto the lake.

After about an hour of puttering around, they cut the engine and pulled out drinks and sandwiches.

Butch started, "Okay, I think we are good here. Let's make sure we smile and appear to be just chatting about the day and what might come later, in case anyone is watching. First, we still cannot identify Frank. He is obviously a worry. Second, we obtained the police reports on the accident and the autopsy report on Olivia. I hope you guys are okay talking about this?"

Dan looked and Willa and she nodded. "We are."

Kendra took over, "Good. The autopsy report showed no evidence of foul play and nothing on the toxicology screen. However, there were photos included which I examined closely. Olivia had some bruising and injuries which were certainly indicative of being scuttled in a boating accident. But, there was one injury that could go either way. She had an indentation in the back of her head that could certainly have been made by being thrown against the side or another hard structure. But, it could also have easily been caused by a blow from a hard object. The direction of the blow was slightly downward and the indentation seemed regular, not randomly administered by banging into something."

She paused to give them time to absorb this and Butch continued, "The police reports didn't deviate from what we already know, but one thing stood out to me. They found a life jacket stuck up in a small cove on Nova Scotia near Yarmouth. As I looked at it, it seemed to be tied in a way to fit someone smaller than Olivia. She did not have a life jacket on when they found her and the report merely suggested that the life jacket simply washed ashore when the boat went down."

He paused to see what they did with this piece of information. Suddenly Dan looked over and said, "Peter. Peter could have survived."

Willa looked at him, then Butch, then Kendra, then back at Dan. She had to keep it together. She couldn't show emotions, other than, well, she could show happiness, right? Kendra saw what she wanted to do and nodded. Willa smiled. Granted, this was more hope than reality, but still, it felt good to her.

Butch and Dan moved to the cooler and each grabbed a beer. They also gave Willa and Kendra sodas. Once they sat, Dan asked, "Okay, what next?"

"First, let me remind you that Peter may have only tried the jacket on, but was not wearing it when the boat went down. We cannot assume, simply based on this, that he is alive. Okay?"

Dan and Willa nodded reluctantly.

"I have a friend in the office who is a very experienced sailor and have asked him to check to see if he is able to pin-point the location of the boat based on the current information. He may or may not be able to do this, but it is worth a shot."

Kendra continued. "We will also continue to check into Dennis and the bum. You might want to start building a family history. Talk about it and do it openly. It has been ten years, so it will simply appear that you are finally ready to try to trace your family history. Maybe you will uncover links or people who might help us to find out what may have happened. Do not do anything about what you find, just record it and continue. We can look at it together later." Willa and Dan nodded.

They spent the rest of the day swimming, sunning and chatting like normal vacationers. When they returned to shore, they decided to rent the same boat for the next day. They changed and had dinner at a nearby restaurant.

The next day, Butch and Dan went fishing early and the girls decided to go into Pittsfield to check out the shops and have lunch. They all met later and had dinner at the same restaurant.

They left the next day.

24. Dennis and Olivia

Dimitri couldn't believe they finally had something on this guy. "Who was he?"

The special agent continued, "His real name was Malcolm DeShawn. He worked for the CIA during the same time that Olivia worked for them. It appears that he had some contact with her, but I can't guarantee it. It doesn't appear he has any living relatives, or ever had, at least that we can identify. It also seems that he retired from the CIA shortly after she died. We think he lived in Belize for a time, then St Petersburg, Florida and, possibly, Omaha, Nebraska. That's all we have at this point."

"Okay. This is good, but we need more. We especially need to know who he was working for."

Dimitri ended the call and called another number. "Here's what we know about Dennis." And, he relayed what he'd just heard.

XXXXX

"It appears that everything Olivia told us about her family is true. Her mom was Tatiana, her dad Antoines, her sister was Ludmilya and his sisters were Celine and Anna. We couldn't find anything different in any of the genealogy sites we used." Dan looked at Willa and she nodded.

"Okay, that's good. It confirms what we know, which is always good."

Dan and Willa had flown to Seattle for a visit in June, a month after the trip to Pittsfield. They stayed at Butch and Kendra's for two days then drove to Ocean Shores, Washington along the Pacific coast. They were staying at the Morning Glory Hotel, Resorts and Suites and were now having lunch at the Galway Irish Pub and Restaurant.

Butch relayed what they had found out about Dennis. "His real name is Malcolm DeShawn. He appears to have worked with Olivia at the CIA, or at least at the same time as she. He does not appear to have any family and we couldn't find out anything about him before the CIA."

"We did find out that he had an inoperable brain tumor. He would have been dead about 6 months after you met him. We also tried to see the official police report and autopsy in Lima, but were unsuccessful."

Butch continued, "We also found some places where he has lived. They include Belize, St Petersburg, Florida and Omaha, Nebraska." He looked at Dan, "So, Dan, any plans for a vacation? How'd you like to go to Florida?"

Dan looked at Willa, shrugged and said, "Sure. But, wouldn't that look suspicious?"

"It might normally look that way but, I actually have a case there that involves insurance fraud. You could be going along with me as a consultant. It makes sense since we have now developed a verifiable friendship."

"When do we go?"

"Let's plan to head there next Thursday."

Willa started to say something, but Kendra jumped in and said, "And, Willa and I will be heading to Omaha. Our cover will be that Willa wanted to go to see where her mom had lived and went to school as part of a school project she chose to do for a fall class." She looked at Dan. "And, since you will be gone, you asked me to accompany her. We'll leave on the same day. Do you have enough stuff to just leave from here?"

Dan looked at Willa and she nodded. "Sure. We are good to go."

They spent another couple of days at the shore then headed back to Butch and Kendra's house on Mercer Island. They all left for SeaTac Airport on Thursday morning to catch their flights.

25. Another Other Man

"Malcolm was going to die anyway. We just helped him along."

"Why?"

"Because he was following them and decided to warn them of the danger they faced. He probably told them a good bit about Olivia's past as well and I didn't think you'd want him to tell them even more. So, we followed him and eliminated the threat." The man standing in front of the large ornate desk waited.

"Okay, I want you to head back and keep me informed."

After the man left his office, the man behind the desk sat back in his chair and closed his eyes. After a few minutes, he placed a call and, when it was answered, he said, "We may need to tie this all off soon."

26. Omaha and St Petersburg

Kendra and Willa exited the terminal and went to pick up their rental car. They were planning to stay in Bellevue, a small community on the southern edge of the city of Omaha and very close to Offutt Air Force Base. It is where Olivia had lived with her fake relatives.

They had a reservation at the Holiday Inn Express and their plan was to check with neighbors in Bellevue to see if anyone remembered Olivia. They were also planning to visit Creighton Dental School and the dentist's office where she had worked.

They checked into the hotel and headed to a nearby Famous Dave's Bar-B-Q Restaurant to eat.

After they placed their order, Kendra suddenly asked Willa, "Oh my gosh, I forgot to ask if you brought the address of your mom's house where she lived while here."

Willa smiled and pointed to her head. "Yes, I brought it with me. I have everything we need from my mom's records right here."

"Right. I forgot about your incredible memory. Okay, tomorrow we'll ride over to the house and start knocking on neighbors' doors to see if we can find someone who remembers Olivia."

"What exactly do we want to find out?"

"Anything actually. But, it would be great if we could find out who the guy was that she met at Offutt Air Base. If he is still there, then we might be able to learn more about where she came from and something about her fake parents."

XXXXX

The following morning they drove to Lincoln St and parked. Kendra turned to Willa as they stood at the curb and said, "This is one of the very annoying parts of investigative work. We simply knock on doors, act polite, and ask if people remember Olivia and her parents. It would be nice to have a picture, but we don't, so we'll just have to do the best we can when describing her. We could hit more doors if we split up, but I think we'll get more cooperation if they see you with me. Besides, you can describe her to a 'T'. Ready?"

Willa nodded and they headed for the houses that lined the street closest to where Olivia had lived. What they were finding was that many of the people were new to the neighborhood and others simply didn't remember or know her or her parents. They found a few people who remembered them, but couldn't provide much information about them.

They took a break for lunch and as they ate, Willa asked, "Maybe we should try the dental office where she worked."

Kendra smiled. "Good idea. I don't think we are going to get very far in her neighborhood. It's likely they may not have interacted with their neighbors."

Willa gave Kendra the address of the dental office and Kendra entered it into their GPS and it showed that they were only two miles from the office. After parking, they walked in and approached the receptionist, "Hello. My name is Kendra and this is Willa. Willa is working on a school project to investigate her family history and her mother worked here about thirty years ago. Is there anyone working here now who might remember Olivia Tissot?"

The receptionist was probably in her mid-thirties and said, "Dr. Fisher might. I think he worked here back then. He is probably just finishing with a patient so, if you'll have a seat, I will tell him that you are waiting."

"Thanks." Willa and Kendra turned and sat in the small waiting area.

About fifteen minutes later, an elderly gentleman came over, "Hello. I understand you are asking about Olivia."

Kendra and Willa stood. Before Kendra could say anything, Willa immediately extended her hand to the doctor and said, "Yes. I am Olivia's daughter and this is my friend Kendra. I have been working on writing my family's history for a school project and I'd like to find out about my mom's time here in Bellevue and at Creighton. Can you help me?" She gave the doctor a sweet smile.

And, of course, he would help Willa. He smiled and said, "Please follow me to my office. We'll be more comfortable there."

They wandered into a nicely decorated office with a number of what looked like family pictures, diplomas and other certificates on the walls. After they entered, the doctor closed the door and asked if they would like some refreshments. They both said no.

The doctor sat and started. "I was only out of Creighton about three years when Olivia started here."

XXXXX

Dan and Butch had been in St. Petersburg for a couple of days trying to find someone who might know about Malcolm. They had a sketch Butch had done with Willa and a sketch artist at his office but, so far, they had found no one who knew him. St. Petersburg was spread out, so they had tried to narrow their search to places where someone like him, given his line of business, might live and hang out. Since they were both investigators, they figured they'd be pretty good at this.

But, apparently, not that good. On the fourth day of their visit, as they walked through the Placido Bayou area of the city, Dan nudged Butch and suggested they check out the Lutheran Church they were just passing. Butch moved in that direction, but was unsure as to why Dan was suggesting it.

As they entered the church, Dan led Butch to a side area, near a small chapel. As they moved close to the front of the chapel, Dan whispered, "We are being followed by the bum."

Butch simply gave a slight nod and continued to move around the inside of the church. As they slowly proceeded, Dan described what he was wearing. Butch listened then led them to the front door, stood back and gave a slight 'out the door' nod to Dan, so he left the church by himself.

Dan continued to walk in the original direction away from the church and Butch watched through one of the windows facing the street. He didn't see anyone so he moved toward the back of the church. An elderly lady walked out of a small office and Butch asked if there was a back exit. If she thought his request strange, she kept it inside and simply pointed to a door in the back to the right.

Butch exited and made his way around the side of the church until he could see the street. He saw no one. He walked slowly to the street and headed in the direction Dan had taken. He hoped the bum had continued to follow Dan.

Butch finally saw Dan well ahead of him and, walking about a hundred yards behind Dan, was the bum. Butch stayed well behind Dan and the man while observing the various people coming and going on both sides of the street. They were heading away from the water along a fairly residential street and, after about half a mile, Dan turned left with the man close behind. The man was on the opposite side of the street now and needed to cross at two lights to keep up with Dan. He jay-walked and ran through the second light. Butch kept back and eventually crossed to the same side as the man.

Butch was slowly getting closer to the bum but, since they were still on residential streets, he couldn't risk doing anything just yet. Dan made a right and as Butch got closer he could see where Dan was heading. There was an open area or park just behind the houses to the left. *Good idea!* He thought.

Dan then made a left and walked into the park. He headed for a small group of trees just behind the parking area and disappeared from view. The bum slowly walked to the right side of the parking lot and hesitated. He finally made his way just slightly onto the edge of a tennis court near the trees Dan had entered, moved behind the nearest tree and waited.

Butch made his way around the far left side of the park, moving from tree to tree. When he moved into an open area, he walked casually and acted like he was just out for a nice walk-in-the-park. He eventually made his way to the edge of the tennis court and began moving slowly along the tree line toward the bum.

He finally saw him waiting behind a tree looking intently where Dan had entered. Soon, Dan appeared at the edge of the trees and stopped. The bum turned his back on Butch and kept his attention on Dan. Butch made his move.

He rushed at the bum's back and tackled him. The bum was a fighter, but Butch was bigger and stronger and eventually pinned the bum's arms behind his back. Dan also came over and Butch asked him for his belt then used it to tie the bum's arms behind his back. He also took off his own belt and tied it around the bum's ankles. Once done, he stood next to Dan who was desperately holding onto his pants.

Butch looked at Dan, who smiled. "I lost some weight over the past six months worrying about all this stuff." He shrugged.

Butch leaned down to the right side of the bum. "Who are you and why are you following Dan and Willa?"

XXXXX

Willa and Kendra left the dentist's office about a half hour after entering. They didn't know a lot more, but they now had a very important lead and Dr. Fisher said he'd help smooth the way for them.

Dr. Fisher told them that he didn't know Olivia well, but he did know that she was very good friends with another young graduate of Creighton. Her name was Dr. Sharon Michaels and she now taught at Creighton Dental School. Dr. Fisher called her, but was told that it was her day off. He then called her home number but she was out, so he left a message for her to call him back. Kendra gave him their number and he said he would call as soon as Sharon called him.

Kendra and Willa drove to Famous Dave's for lunch. As they sat eating, Kendra's phone buzzed. She answered, said 'yes' and 'okay' a few times, then grabbed a pen from her pocket and wrote on the kids menu that was stuck in a stand on the table. She finally said 'thanks' and put her phone away.

"Okay. We will be meeting with Sharon tomorrow morning at ten. She has classes in the afternoon, but none in the morning. There is a McDonalds nearby where she will meet us. Let's go back to the room. We need to discuss how we will approach her about the issue of the meetings with that Offutt officer. Are you comfortable with that line of questioning? I'll certainly ask the questions, and you can excuse yourself if you think you might feel uncomfortable."

"I will be fine and I can ask the questions. She might feel uncomfortable if you are asking and I'm sitting there looking all passive. She might be reluctant to say things out of respect for my feelings. But, if I am asking the questions, then I will be looking her in the eyes, letting her know I need to know everything about my mom that she might know."

"Good. I was hoping you'd say that."

XXXXX

They now knew the bum's name. His name is Devon Daniels.

Dan asked, "So, Devon, why are you following Willa and I?"

"I was paid to follow you two from the time you left Greece. I was called by a guy I had worked for over the past few years and told to call a number he gave me for a job that would set me up for a long time so, of course, I called the number. The guy's voice was scrambled but he told me that there was a package waiting for me if I agreed to do this job. When I asked what the job was, he said it was simply to follow you and your daughter wherever you went. I was to provide updates each week, or when I thought something significant had happened."

"I was told that if the two of you ever split up and went to totally separate locations, as you did in Malta, but you both stayed in the same general location, then I was to decide whether to follow you or Willa. If you travelled well away from each other then I should follow you."

"Why? What was the reason?" Dan asked.

"I don't know. When I asked, I was told I didn't need to know. The job was simple and that is all I needed to know. I asked how I was supposed to pay for all of this. He told me that the package would contain money and a credit card. But, I was told, if I agreed, then tried to skip out on the deal, they would know and would find me no matter how long it took."

"I was told to go to a particular UPS store and ask for the package. The store would check my ID then give it to me. Once I opened it and checked the contents, I was to call the same number again. I went, got the package and inside was an American Express credit card and $5,000 in hundred dollar bills. I called the number again, told the man I had the package and he asked if I was satisfied. I said yes. He said I would receive the same amount when the job was over. I was also reminded what would happen should I back out of the agreement. So, that has been what I have been doing. I assure you I had no instructions to do harm to either of you. I was only to follow you. Besides, I am not a killer for hire, so if that had been the job, then I would have turned it down."

Butch undid Devon's ankles and helped him to stand. "What is your plan now, Devon?"

"Well, I don't know. Now that you know who I am and what I am doing, I guess I can't hide any longer."

Dan motioned for Butch to step aside with him. Butch reminded Devon to stay and not move.

After moving off to a spot to talk and still watch Devon, Dan said, "You know, Butch, now that we know who he is, what he is planning and that he means no harm, maybe we can use him to our advantage. We can tell him to continue doing what he is doing and posting his reports. But, he could also send the link he uses to us and maybe we can get someone to trace it."

After a moment, Butch said, "I like the idea. Even if we don't get a hit the first time, or ever, we at least can monitor his movements and actions."

They moved over to Devon, untied his hands and Dan quickly secured his pants.

Butch explained their plan to Devon, who agreed and looked at Dan, "I am really sorry about this. I needed the money and it didn't sound all that dangerous to you, your daughter, or me, so I felt it would all go just fine. I didn't think about how traumatic it could be to your daughter and, of course, to you. I hope you can forgive me and I promise I will cooperate with you on this."

Dan shrugged. "Okay. I just hope our plan will work and we'll be done with this."

Butch suggested, "Devon, you exit first and move down the street a little so you can watch us as we come out of the tree-line."

Devon rubbed his wrists and said sorry again as he walked away. He got to the middle of the parking lot and turned his head slightly toward the street as he walked that way.

There was a sound like a 'phht', Devon seemed to stand still then he slowly fell onto his back.

Butch pulled Dan into the trees and whispered, "Sniper. Stay down."

Butch slowly crawled to the edge of the trees and glanced out at Devon. His head was a mess. He was gone. By the sound and the way Devon fell, the shot must have come from somewhere to the left of their position. Butch scooted back to Dan. "I'm going to move out to Devon. You call 911 and stay down."

Butch slowly made his way to the edge of the trees. He moved quickly in a crouch to Devon and lay next to his right side opposite the line of the shot. He glanced in that direction and saw that there were residential homes, a large wooded area past the homes and then, farther away, some large white storage tanks. The shot could have come from any one of those areas.

As he felt for a pulse on Devon's neck, which he knew he wouldn't find, his other hand found Devon's phone. He slowly retrieved it and slid it into his pocket and, at that point, heard the sirens. As the first police vehicle pulled into the parking lot, Butch slowly stood.

XXXXX

Kendra and Willa were sitting in the McDonalds having a coffee when they saw a woman walk through the door and start to scan the customers. Kendra caught her eye and Dr. Michaels made her way to their table. As she walked to it, she asked, "Are you Kendra?"

Kendra stood and approached Sharon. "Yes, I am Kendra and this is Willa. Thank you for coming to meet us. Can I get you something?"

"That's okay, well, maybe a coffee, black, please." She sat and Kendra went to the counter. As she walked away, she glanced at Willa and indicated for her to start without her.

Sharon was short and a little chunky with brown hair cut short. She had brown eyes and wore very little makeup, if any. Once Sharon sat they looked at each other and smiled.

Willa started, "Thanks for coming to talk to us. I really appreciate it."

Before Willa could continue, Sharon spoke, "Frankly, I am not sure why I am here. Dr. Fisher said it was important and that you were doing some family research. But I really don't know what I can tell you. I only knew Olivia for a few years while we both worked together at Dr. Fisher's office."

Willa noticed that she continually rubbed her hands together and would not look Willa directly in the eyes for long, if at all. She seemed worried about what she should say. Willa figured that she would have to be very careful in how she asked her questions and reacted to what Sharon said.

Willa smiled. "Well, I am still very happy to meet you. My mom was very special to me but, after the accident that took her life," at this Willa looked away then back, "I have felt like I really didn't know her well. I was only five at the time. But now, I am really, really interested in learning more about her life. My dad has told me some things from the time that they met, but even he doesn't know much about my mom's life before that."

"He knew she lived here in Omaha, graduated from Creighton and worked at Dr. Fisher's office but, we know nothing about her friends and her time at school or at work. Those are the kinds of things that would give me a really good idea who my mother really was." At this point she looked Sharon directly in the eyes. Sharon looked at her with sympathy then turned away.

Just then Kendra returned and set Sharon's coffee in front of her. Kendra didn't sit, but said she wanted to get Sharon a stir stick. As she moved off, Willa told Sharon she needed to use the restroom. As she passed Kendra, she whispered, "She's holding back, probably doesn't want to tell me about the officer." She continued to the restroom.

Kendra went back to the table, sat and smiled at Sharon. She glanced toward the restroom then back at Sharon. She pulled her lips tight and looked at the restroom again.

She finally looked at Sharon and started with, "Willa doesn't know about the affair with the officer. I am a long-time friend of the family and her dad told me about it many years ago. When Willa got this school assignment, he really worried about what she would hear. However, he knew he couldn't stop her from taking the project on with 'gusto'." Kendra smiled and looked at the restroom again. She was still smiling when she turned to Sharon, "Willa is a sweet girl, but she is a little willful at times. When she decided to come here, her dad planned to come along. You know, to monitor what she learned."

"But, an urgent business trip came up, so he asked me if I could come with her." Kendra glanced at the door then back at Sharon. "Look, if you could tell me all about the affair, then I can talk to her dad about it when we get back. This way, he can decide when and how to tell her before someone else tells her about it at school or later in life. These things seem to have a way of seeing the light of day. Do you know what I mean?" She paused.

Sharon looked back and forth between Kendra and the restroom and finally started. "Look, I don't want to hurt Willa, but I do think you are right. It is better if her dad tells her, so it is better that he know all of the details so Willa doesn't start digging into it based on what she thinks might be a lie told to her by someone."

Sharon looked around again. Kendra assured her that she would let her know if Willa started to return.

"Okay. Here goes. Olivia was a beautiful girl and we had so much fun when we went out in the evening. All the guys hit on her. Oh, she flirted a little, but never went any farther than that with them. The only ones she seemed to be attracted toward were the men from the base, especially the officers.

When I asked her about it, she would always smile and say something like *well a girl's gotta look after her future you know.* One evening, we were at a bar across the river in Council Bluffs and she met Major Erickson. I think his first name was Tom."

Kendra smiled and nodded for her to continue. "At first they would only meet at the bar and he always left her with me at the end of the evening. Then, she started meeting him without me and when I asked about those, she would say it was a movie, a show or something like that. I knew these were lies, but I had my own boyfriend issues to worry about, so I didn't question her."

"But, then a few times, she would be gone for the entire weekend. I knew then that she was having an affair with a married man. We knew he was married because he once showed us pictures of his wife and kids."

"After a year or so, he got reassigned somewhere and that was it. Shortly after that, she left and then, shortly after she left, her family moved back to Russia. I think to St Petersburg, but I am not sure. Please don't tell Willa this. Her mom was a great friend and, once she was away from the night stuff and her parents, she was really sweet."

Kendra asked, "Do you remember what the foster parent's names were? Willa never learned them."

"I think their last name was Reinhardt." She was thoughtful and then said, "Lilly and Jake? No, Lisa and, I don't know. His name was something like Jake or Jack or Jim. I just remember that it started with a 'J'."

"Okay, that's great. Do you remember anything else about Olivia?"

"She would sometimes come to my house for a sleepover. I know, we were a little old for that, but they were fun for us. She always helped around the house and would even do some light cleaning if I was busy. I really missed her after she left."

Kendra looked at the restroom door and Willa finally came out and headed for their table. Kendra quietly told Sharon she was coming so they sat quietly while Willa arrived and sat down.

Willa started right away, "I'm sorry for taking so long. Would you believe it, I met a girl who moved a couple of years ago from my school. It was so fun to see her and, well, we got to talking and just lost track of time. Anyway, so, where were we?"

Sharon talked about her mom's time at the school and at the office. She mentioned how sweet she was and how she helped around Sharon's house when she visited. She talked about what a good student Olivia was, how helpful she was at the office and how she had a wonderful way with the patients, especially the children. Sharon never mentioned the affair and Willa never asked. She seemed to be relieved that she was done with it after talking to Kendra.

They talked for an hour or so then Sharon apologized and said she had to get to the school for her classes. Willa and Kendra thanked her for all of her help and she left.

After Sharon left, Willa turned to Kendra and asked, "Did she talk?"

"Yes, but how did you know she wouldn't talk to you?"

"She was so nervous while we sat here just talking casually. I figured she would definitely not want to talk to me about an affair my mom had twenty plus years ago. So, I figured I'd leave and let you handle it."

Kendra nodded. "Well, it worked. Let's head back to the room and figure out what to do next. I'll also contact Butch to see what the boys are up to."

27. What Now?

Homer was beside himself. There was another dead body and this one was in the US. That's never good. Now, there will be local cops, local detectives and maybe the FBI involved.

XXXXX

Dimitri yelled into the phone, "I don't care what you have to do. I want you to find out who is behind all of this."

XXXXX

"Yes, Mr. Daniels finally broke his promise, but it was really only a matter of time. He was just our eyes and we only needed him to let us know where they were so that we could decide what to do, if anything."

"I agree." said the man behind the desk. "But, this will bring the local US authorities into this and they can't be dismissed as easily as those in Lima and Russia. A little bundle of dollars or euros always did the trick with them. But, never rubles. No one wants rubles. Okay, you can go."

After the man left, the desk man called his boss. When the call was answered, he said, "I think we need to end this now."

"I agree. Do what is necessary. Get rid of those two annoying investigators, but bring the dad and the girl to me. We need to get those files back."

XXXXX

Butch finally picked up on the third ring. "Hey honey."

"Honey? Did I interrupt something? What's going on there?"

Butch looked over at Dan who was sitting on one of those hard, metal chairs that the police love to make people sit on. "We have a problem." He thought quickly and continued, "Remember the guy I mentioned that we met here? Well he's dead." Pause. "I know. It was so sudden. I mean he was heading back to his hotel and we were planning to meet up later for a beer and then 'poof' he was dead and lying on the ground." Pause. "I don't know what happened. The police are talking to Dan and me trying to figure this mess out." Pause. "Okay. I will as soon as I can. Love you, too." He ended the call and thanked the officer for letting him answer his wife's call.

Kendra slowly placed her phone back on the table. She hadn't said a thing after her first comment when Butch called her honey, which he never did. She and Willa were at the hotel sitting at a table in their room going over what they had found out from Sharon. Willa looked over at Kendra and saw that something was bothering her.

"What's wrong? Are Butch and my dad okay?" She said nervously.

"He's dead." Kendra immediately corrected herself when she saw Willa's distraught look. "No, no. I don't mean your dad or Butch. The bum is dead. I don't know any details. Butch will call later and fill me in."

Willa was stunned. "Dead! Really?"

"Yeah. I wish we knew more, but we don't. It appears they are pretending to have been friends with him for the benefit of the police investigation. If that's the case, then they must have actually met with the guy."

Willa calmed, but she was still worried. "Will they be okay? Should we go to them? Can I call my dad?"

Kendra smiled. "I am sure they will be okay. They are both smart and Butch has done this sort of thing before. I don't think it would help to go there, but I do think you can give your dad a call."

Just as Willa reached for her phone, it buzzed. She immediately answered when she looked at the screen. "Hey, dad. Are you okay?" Pause. "Good. I was worried." Pause. "Okay, I won't worry, but do you want me to come there?" Pause. "Well, okay, we have lots to do here anyway. I'll just wait until you call me again. Love you!" Pause. "Bye."

Willa was quiet for a bit and Kendra sat patiently. She took a sip of her wine.

Finally, Willa sighed and started, "Okay, let's see what we have learned."

Kendra summarized the basics of what they knew. "It appears that Olivia's foster parents returned to St Petersburg, Russia not long after Olivia took off. There has to be something there that will help us."

Willa was thoughtful for a moment. "You know, it was also around the same time the major left. I wonder if those events are related."

"They could be. Let me contact a friend of mine. She retired from the Air Force last year and worked in personnel. Maybe she can help us find the major. By the way, did you ever go back to the friends you were visiting on the day of the accident to ask them what they remember?"

"No, at least I didn't. Maybe my dad did. Should I call and ask him?" Kendra nodded, so Willa grabbed her phone and tapped out the number."

"I'll call my friend." Kendra moved to the other side of the room.

After Kendra finished talking to her friend, she went back to the table. Willa was already finished and waiting for her.

"What did your dad say?"

"He told me that after we left about two months after the accident, he never talked to them, but assumed the police did. The only thing he remembers hearing was that they had moved away and were probably divorced or getting divorced. He gave me the last phone number he had for them."

"Well, give it a try, while we wait for my friend to call back."

Willa keyed the numbers and waited. She finally heard a recording that told her the number was no longer in service and told Kendra.

"Okay, let's get something to eat and continue later."

"Sure, but let me try something first. I'm going to post a request on Facebook. I'll say that I would like to contact my long-lost friends, Susie and Eden Buchard. They would be around my age now, so I would bet they are on Facebook." She quickly posted her message then they left for their favorite eatery, Famous Dave's.

XXXXX

"I think we need to combine our resources. The murder of Daniels here in the US could raise unwanted interest in our mutual concerns."

Dimitri didn't say anything for several seconds then sighed. "Okay. How do you want to deal with this?"

After a brief pause, Homer sighed and said, "We can probably control the situation here by calling it some kind of drug hit. We can have drugs and money planted in Daniels' room and insist that Watson and Elliot stay available in the states for further questioning. But, my guess is the women will figure out that they need to go to Russia sooner or later. Can you deal with that?"

Dimitri frowned but realized this was the kind of thing he was supposed to be able to handle, so he said, "Yes, we can take care of them while they are here. I'll put a couple of my best people on them. Let me know when you learn they are heading over."

"I will. And, Dimitri, we have to protect the girl. We couldn't protect her mother, so I don't want to lose her too. Call me a sentimental old fool, but when I retire in a couple of years, I don't want to have to remember the death of a sixteen year old girl for the rest of my life."

"Don't worry old man. I don't either. We'll protect her. You have my word." He slid the phone to the middle of the table and stared at it for several seconds. Cases like this caused him to hate his job sometimes.

XXXXX

Kendra and Willa were eating breakfast in the room the following morning when Willa's phone pinged. Willa grumbled, looked at the message and put the phone back down. "I am beginning to regret including my hash tag and email address in my Facebook post. Both are accounts that my dad's techy guy set up for me. They can't be traced and they are not linked to any personal information but still, I have been getting all kinds of responses to the post and some of them are pretty disgusting. Yuck!"

Kendra smiled, "Well, you know, using social media …"

Willa interrupted her with a "Yeah, yeah, blah, blah. Man, you old people drive me nuts." She smiled at Kendra, who harrumphed. Just then, Kendra's phone buzzed.

"Hey, thanks for getting back to me so quickly. Were you able to find anything?" Pause. "Oh, really?" Pause. She turned to look back at Willa, but Willa had her head down and was madly typing on her phone's small keypad.

"He did? When was that exactly?" Pause. "Okay. Thanks again." Pause. "Yeah, that would be great. Maybe I'll have a job in your area and we can have dinner. I'd love to see you again." Pause. "Okay. Bye."

Kendra looked at Willa and saw that she was still typing. She started to ask something, but Willa waved a hand at her. She waited.

Willa finally looked up and smiled. She could also see that Kendra was smiling too. Suddenly, they both said, "We're going to Russia!"

Kendra, still smiling, asked, "What did you find out?"

"Susie sent me a tweet and told me to check my emails. When I opened the account, I found an email from her. She started out by telling me she sent the email because she didn't want to post all of her information on Facebook."

"Susie told me her whole family moved to St Petersburg, Russia about three or four months after the accident. She said her parents eventually divorced and she hasn't seen her dad in over eight years. Her sister, Eden, died of leukemia about five years ago and she now lives with her mom in an apartment on the outskirts of the city. She gave me her address in case I ever wanted to visit."

"I wrote back, told her I was sorry about Eden and the divorce then asked her if her parents had ever mentioned the accident. She just responded and said they did not. But, she does remember hearing them arguing one time and it sounded like they were arguing over something to do with the accident. But, since they argued all of the time, Susie said she often just tried to shut them out. But, this particular time she listened a little more intently because she heard Peter's name early on during the argument, but she remembers the rest of the argument being the usual yelling and name calling."

Kendra nodded and said, "My friend found out that the good major was actually court-marshaled and kicked out of the military. He apparently lied about having a family and was ordered to pay back all of the money he had collected over the years, along with some hefty fines. He didn't receive jail time because of a plea agreement."

"The total was over $200,000 and he was somehow able to pay all of the money back in three months. Of course, authorities started asking him where he had gotten all of that money but, before they got a definitive answer, he left the country. Guess where he went!"

Willa smiled. "Maybe St Petersburg?"

"You are one smart kid. Okay, I think that is our next lead. I mean, first the foster parents, then the major and then the Buchards all head to the same city in Russia shortly after the accident! It can't be a coincidence. I think we need to go there if we want to find out what all of this means."

"What about Butch and my dad?"

"They can follow along after they get their role in Daniels' death cleared up with the local authorities. I'll call Butch and you should call your dad." She grabbed her phone.

Willa picked up her phone and stared at it. She thought. *What is my dad going to say about me heading to Russia? He will probably say no.* She resolved to be firm and to make him understand that she needed to go. These leads were too important. She called.

"Hey dad." Pause. "I'm good. How's it going there?" Pause. "Oh, a few more days, huh? Sorry. Um, hey dad, um Kendra and I have uncovered some really fantastic leads." Pause. "Yes, it is exciting. The parents and the Buchards all ended up moving back to St Petersburg, Russia." Pause. "I know. That's what we think. There is no way those moves are just a coincidence." Pause. "Um, yeah. Anyway. Here's the thing. We need to go there. I mean Kendra and I need to go there." Pause. "No, I don't think it is a good idea to wait for you and Butch. Besides, you guys can be there a few days after we get there, so we'll be fine and we can reserve a room for you at the same hotel."

Willa and her dad went back and forth about the merits of waiting versus the merits of her and Kendra going there now. Willa glanced at Kendra. She had long finished her conversation with Butch. Willa rolled her eyes. Kendra smiled at her and gave her a 'thumbs up'.

Willa finally finished. "Yes, dad. I'll be careful. I love you too. Bye."

"So, it sounds like your dad finally gave in."

"Yeah, he did, but I think he will kill you if anything happens to me and then he'll kill me for going. Anyway, what now?"

28. Russia (Part One – Shots Fired)

"As we figured, they are all heading to Russia. The girls are headed there now and the guys will likely follow."

Dimitri asked, "Homer, do you know if they found out anything?"

"We are still digging into it, but based on phone calls, emails and social media posts we think they learned about the connections to St Petersburg. They know that the Reinhardts moved there based on Olivia's friend's comment. Kendra found out from a friend of hers that Erickson moved there shortly after the Reinhardts. Willa tried to contact the daughters of the Buchards and we know that one of them responded, but we can't get into the email account she used."

"Okay, I'll post several people in St Petersburg to shadow them when they arrive. Let me know their flight data once you have it."

XXXXX

The man contacted the big man behind the desk, who then contacted the boss. The boss said, "Well, how very sweet of the girls to come to us. Let's prepare a very warm welcome for them. And, by the way, do we have a very special event planned for the men?" Pause. "Good. Let me know when it is completed."

XXXXX

After exiting the terminal, Willa and Kendra took a taxi to their hotel. As they entered their hotel room, the bellhop placed their luggage on separate luggage stands and pointed out where everything was located. He also showed them into the bedroom next to theirs and left after Kendra gave him a tip. Willa started to say something, but Kendra gave her a brief side-to-side head nod, meaning 'not here'.

They unpacked, changed into jeans and t-shirts then went for a walk. They were staying at the Hotel Pribaltiyskaya, which is located on one of the larger of several islands that are part of the city. Kendra had noticed a park about a half kilometer from the hotel on the taxi ride from the airport and they walked there now.

They chatted amiably on the way to the park, talking about the flight, the food, and the sights around them. As they entered the park, they moved to a group of trees and began weaving in and out of them. Willa finally said, "I am sure we were followed from the airport."

"I am not surprised. I would bet we are being followed by several people."

Willa asked, "How are we going to communicate with my dad and Butch? I mean, if we are constantly under visual surveillance, I'm sure all of our communications are being monitored too. I could use the email account I have, which is heavily encrypted, if that might help."

Kendra said, "Actually, I don't think we will need to worry. Butch and I developed a secret cipher code years ago that only we know."

Willa knew that cipher codes have been around for a long time and that they were used by spies to transmit messages only they could read. A couple of the more famous ones were the Beale cipher and the Paoli cipher.

"We can use it whenever we want to communicate sensitive information back to the boys. It is a simple cipher we developed using our wedding vows. We never said our vows at our wedding and they have never been written down. We said our vows to each other the evening after we had our traditional wedding. We each memorized the other's vows and have used them ever since to pass coded messages back and forth. They include more than enough letters and symbols to communicate any messages we may need to send."

"Wow, that's such a clever way to create a cipher."

Kendra smiled, "Tonight, I will send a coded message to Butch to inform him that we think we are being followed and our room is probably wired. That way, when we call to exchange routine pleasantries, the guys will know not to say anything that should not be overheard."

Willa frowned thoughtfully and asked, "Do you think they have cameras in the room too?"

Kendra shook her head no, "But, I'll check when we get back."

It was getting late, so they wandered back to the hotel and went to its restaurant. Several of the male guests introduced themselves to the girls. Kendra and Willa were polite, hinted they were not interested but still had to refuse a lot of drinks.

As they entered the room, Kendra wandered around as though she were checking out things to make sure they worked or just to see what they had, like the coffee maker, clock radio and temperature control. She finally wandered to the desk and wrote on a notepad. She showed it to Willa. It read 'No Cameras.'

The following day, Butch read Kendra's cipher, smiled and told Dan what the message said.

XXXXX

Dan and Butch flew back to Seattle, went into Butch's house and flopped onto chairs in the living room. "Man, what a mess."

Butch agreed. "Want a beer?"

"Oh, yeah. I'm bushed. I can't believe they made us stay in St Pete for three full days. It was ridiculous. It was almost as though they were just doing it to be mean."

Butch went to the fridge, pulled out a couple of Rainier beers and handed one to Dan. "Let's sit out on the deck, since it's such a nice day. We don't let those go to waste out here in the Emerald City."

Once they settled down on the deck, they each took a swig of their beer. Dan glanced at Butch and noticed he seemed preoccupied. "What are you thinking, Butch?"

Butch was quiet for a few seconds then said, "You know, it almost seemed like someone didn't want us to leave St Pete for as long as possible. They probably had to let us go eventually because we didn't give them any more chances to create new excuses. I am wondering why someone would want to delay us, and from what?"

"My guess is someone didn't want us to follow the girls to Russia. I mean, that is the only thing we planned to do as soon as possible, right? But, how would they know we were going to go there?"

Butch now looked at Dan with real concern on his face. "Because, they already know Kendra and Willa are there and that we will follow them. Dan, someone is involved in this in a big way. I think this someone also knows what it is we are trying to find out. I think they know why Olivia and Peter were killed and who did it."

"Well, if you are right, then you and I know exactly who could know all of that and I am guessing it is either the United States or Russian governments."

"Or, both. Think about it Dan, we know someone asked Daniels to follow us and he said there were probably others. We also know that DeShawn was following you and he also said there were probably others. The thing I don't know is whether they might be working together or separately and, more importantly, whether they mean to harm or help you."

Dan quickly added, "We need to get to Russia as soon as possible. Willa and Kendra are undoubtedly in danger."

Once back into the living room, Butch opened his laptop and started checking flights to St Petersburg. He went back and forth between websites and airlines and, while he did that, Dan called a travel agency he found on a smartphone search.

Dan paused in his call, looked at Butch and told him tomorrow was the earliest they could depart. Butch nodded and Dan got back on his phone to book the flights.

"We leave tomorrow morning at 9 am and arrive the following day at 9 pm. We go through New York City, London and Moscow before arriving in St Petersburg."

"Okay, I'll send a message to Kendra to tell her our plans and I'll relay our thoughts on the American and Russian governments' suspected involvement. I also need to go into the office to check on a few things so how about if you come along and we can have some dinner in downtown Kirkland, near my office?"

"Sounds good to me. I'm ready when you are."

XXXXX

Kendra passed on to Willa what Butch had told her while she and Willa were walking around the grounds of the Cathedral of Saints Peter and Paul located within what is called the Fortress of Saints Peter and Paul. The entire complex sits on a small island.

As they wandered the complex, they frequently reviewed a travel brochure of the Fortress grounds they had picked up at the hotel. They would point and smile and sit every now and then. They noticed they seemed to have at least two 'buddies' who were taking the tour with them. After a couple of hours, they wandered across the bridge that spans the Neva to explore the Church of the Resurrection. As they crossed the park in front of the church they pretended to point out various sites but were actually quietly discussing what they had learned. At one point, Kendra whispered to Willa, "I hope our 'buddies' are enjoying our guided tour."

"Susie sent me another email this morning and told me she could meet me one day while we are here if I wanted to talk more about her parents and sister. She also wants to just say hi and to catch up on what Peter and I have been doing, which may mean she does not know what happened to my mom and Peter. What do you think?"

"I don't know. If she is an innocent in all of this, then we could be putting her in danger. Let's hold off agreeing to meet her. I think I am going to have to contact someone from my past to get more information about Erickson and the Reinhardts. They have probably changed their names and maybe even their appearances. My friend may not find any information, but unless we try, I am afraid we may not find out anything on our own by just wandering around."

Willa thought a moment, "What if I meet with Susie then ask to go to her house to meet her mom and that you'd like to come along with me too? If she is innocent, then she shouldn't mind having you along. Right?"

They were now approaching the entrance to the Hermitage Museum so they paid the entrance fee and started following the floor plan to see the various objects. They especially wanted to see the Faberge Eggs. As they moved into the next exhibit room, Kendra quietly told Willa to contact Susie and agree to meet her and her mom.

XXXXX

Butch introduced Dan to the various staff and then they went into his office. While Butch was busy in his office, Dan sat and called his office.

Butch talked with a couple of investigators about various assignments they were working on. At six, Butch sat back in his chair and looked at Dan who was reading something on his smartphone. "Are you hungry yet?"

Dan looked at him and smiled, "Oh, yeah. Just a second and I'll be ready to head out."

Butch's office was located in the Park Place Office complex only a five minute walk from downtown Kirkland. It was a beautiful sunny evening so there were lots of people out enjoying the shops, cafes, bars and restaurants. Butch led Dan to the Wilde Rover Irish Pub and Restaurant. It was just off of Central Way and had an outside deck area with no smoking. It overlooked a park and a beach where numerous kids were out playing and making various sand buildings or animals on the beach. There were also teens swimming and sunning. They ordered a Harp beer and Guinness Lamb Stew and watched the various activities.

They didn't talk about the Olivia case since they were feeling even more paranoid than before. However, they did talk about Butch and Kendra's travels and how they ended up in Seattle and what kinds of things they liked to do when not working. Butch also mentioned they had been trying to have kids, but it just didn't seem to be in the cards to have any.

It was around 8:30 pm when a light rain shower moved over the area and chased most people off of the beach and the deck. Dan and Butch went inside and took two seats at one end of the bar. They ordered one more beer and planned to leave after finishing it. It was a short walk back to Butch's car and a fifteen minute drive to his house.

There was a small band playing in the corner called Palmer Junction. They played blues music and both Butch and Dan thought, *they are really good*. They especially enjoyed the lead singer whose name was Jenny Lee. Her voice was gritty and smooth and soothing. It was a hard combination for any singer to get right, but she did.

They were almost finished with their beers when Butch noticed a commotion near the door of the restaurant. There were a good many people left in the bar because of the band but none of them had yet noticed the trouble at the door. As he watched, he saw a waitress trying to get a man to leave who was swearing and shouting at her. Butch sighed and went over to the waitress. "Hey mister, maybe you should head home now. Better yet, let me call you a cab."

By then, Dan had wandered over too and shielded the waitress from the guy in case he got belligerent. The guy started cursing and yelling again and, just as it looked like things were going from bad to worse, a guy came up behind him and said, "Come on Joe, let's go. You've had enough. Your wife is going to kill me if I don't get you home."

He then turned to Butch and Dan and said, "I'm so sorry about this. We were across the street and when I went to the toilet, he wandered over here." He peeked around at the waitress and told her, "I am really sorry miss. I'll get him home right away."

Jen, the waitress, nodded as he pulled the man out to the sidewalk and headed around the corner to the parking lot.

Dan and Butch went back into the bar, finished their beer, paid and left. They walked back to Butch's car and headed to the interstate highway to make their way to Butch's house. Traffic was light, so they should be at the house quickly.

They were almost to the Mercer Island exit and, as they approached the interchange to head there, a car suddenly came up on the driver's side of the car. Butch glanced quickly across and immediately yelled, "Gun!"

He swerved right and hit the brakes just as the passenger in the other vehicle fired off three quick rounds. One bullet hit the rear window and shattered it. Butch did not know where the other two shots went.

Butch yelled for Dan to pull a box out from under his seat. Once he did Butch told him to dial 4477 into the coded lock. When the case opened, Dan lifted out the gun, a 38, checked that the safety was off and that it was loaded then handed it to Butch. He then leaned back heavily in the seat and groaned.

Butch yelled again and told Dan to get into the back and down on the floor. Dan obeyed and, with some difficulty, climbed over the seat.

Butch maneuvered and sped up toward the other car as they were crossing a short bridge. They would be exiting in a couple of miles and Butch didn't want to carry this battle into the residential neighborhoods.

The other driver was using those few cars on the highway to create havoc. He was bumping other vehicles and causing them to swerve into barriers and other cars. None of the accidents seemed to be too serious, but that didn't mean they wouldn't start to turn deadly.

Butch stepped on the gas and quickly sped up to the rear of the other car. He moved his gun to his left hand and put his arm out of the window. He fired off two quick shots and the other car began to swerve to avoid the shots. As the other car moved to his right to get out of his line of fire, Butch hit the gas again.

He aimed for the other car's left rear bumper, hit it and caused the car's back-end to swerve sharply to the right. It suddenly went completely out of control and flipped over. The car tumbled at least five or six times before smashing into the wall that split the main highway from the exit lane.

Butch jammed on his brakes and pulled to a stop about twenty feet behind the smashed vehicle. "Stay here," he yelled to Dan.

Butch held his gun at the ready as he approached the upside down vehicle. He slowly approached the passenger side and saw that the passenger was the drunk at the bar. He also saw that he was dead. Then, he heard the sirens. He cautiously approached the driver's side, recognized the driver as the guy who hauled the drunk away and that he was also dead, or close to it.

The first state police vehicle pulled up behind Butch's car and, when he saw the gun, yelled for Butch to put it down and to get down on his knees with his hands behind his head. Butch complied. The trooper saw Dan crawl out of the car and told him to do the same. Dan tried, but, after a few moments, he fell over on his side. He had been hit in the shoulder by one of the shots from the other car.

At about this time, three more police vehicles arrived and Butch, yelled at one of the troopers to check Dan. As the trooper moved toward Dan, Butch was thinking that they weren't going to Russia any time soon.

29. Russia (Part Two – Seattle)

"Something is wrong." Kendra said as she put her phone back in her purse.

"What do you mean?"

"Every time I call Butch, it goes to voice mail. I have left two messages already, but he still hasn't called back. Try calling your dad."

Willa called, waited then put her phone in her pocket. "It went to voice mail, too. What could be going on?"

"I don't know, but I am sure they are okay. They are probably at some location where they can't use their phones."

"Or, they are out on dates and don't want to be interrupted." Willa smiled at Kendra.

Kendra didn't miss a beat. She smiled then looked thoughtful. "You could be right. This is just the chance I have been waiting for to kill Butch and inherit his rather large insurance policy which, of course, I bought for him without his knowledge."

Willa cracked up. Once she stopped laughing, she asked "Okay, what do we do while the boys are out having fun?"

XXXXX

Homer sat patiently and listened to the report he was being given by the agent in front of him. When the agent finished, Homer rolled his shoulders. He was getting too old for this. "Okay, David, I want you to go to Seattle. I am going to authorize you to take over the investigation as a matter of National Security. Tell them we know that the two dead men were agents of a foreign government and that they were trying to kill Dan and Butch in order to stop them from investigating a security issue assigned to them by me. Make sure you give Butch my personal number and tell him to call me immediately."

"Will do."

After the agent left, Homer thought a moment then called Dimitri. When Demitri answered, Homer said, "Did you hear what happened in Seattle?" Pause. "Yes, this is getting very critical. You need to get security on Willa and Kendra." Pause. "I know. I'm not an idiot. I know they don't know anything and that they are not a threat. But, I still don't want another American life wasted on this mess. Do you hear me? I don't want another death!" He was yelling, which he rarely ever did. "Thanks, Dimitri. I am getting too old and grouchy for this." He chuckled. "Well, you're just a tough old bird, but I am still grateful. Call me. You have my number."

XXXXX

Butch was telling the same story again for the, well, he didn't remember how many times. "No. they didn't know the men." "Yes, he fired back at them." "Yes, he had a license to carry." "Yes, he was a private investigator, as was Dan." "No, he couldn't think of a reason why they were after them." "Yes, he had seen them at the Wilde Rover." Butch thought. *How many times do I have to say the same thing?*

He also kept asking when he could see Dan. He already knew he would be fine since they had told him that much. Dan had taken a bullet in his left shoulder but the bullet had passed through and, luckily, hadn't hit anything serious as it did. He was at Harborview Hospital in downtown Seattle.

He had also asked several times if he could call his wife. He explained that she and Dan's daughter were traveling on a short vacation and would be very worried if they couldn't get in touch with them. Finally, a detective Butch knew from earlier work, came into the room.

"Hey Butch! Man, what a mess you've created. Why can't you just stick with simple divorce surveillance cases?"

"Are you kidding me, Jim? You, of all people, ought to know that divorce and domestic cases are the most dangerous. This was just a couple of idiots taking pot shots at another car for some reason. People in domestic cases always favor severe bodily harm."

Jim smiled, "Yeah, I know. Anyway, you can go and see your friend. He is in Harborview as you know. I'll have an officer drop you off. Can you get home from there?"

"Thanks. Yeah, I'll take a taxi home. Do you have any more information on those guys? IDs? Anything?"

"No, they weren't carrying anything that could identify them. The car was apparently stolen and we are trying to track down the owner. We have taken their prints and DNA and sent them to the FBI office, but I haven't heard anything, yet and probably won't because, and here is the big news, the investigation is being taken over because of National Security." Jim smiled. "Any thoughts on that, Butch?"

Butch looked at him, thought a minute, and then smiled. "Hey, I'm really sorry. If I could have said anything about it, then I would have. But, you know, National Security and all that."

"Oh yeah, I know. Anyway, a government agent will be here tomorrow to talk to you. I'll send him to your home and, by the way, you will need, at least for the time being, to stay in the local area." It looked like he was done, but then, "Unless, of course, some National Security issue comes up. Well, then you gotta do your job, right?"

Butch smiled, "Yeah, my job. Thanks, Jim."

"Sure, call Kendra on the way to the hospital and, be careful." He looked very seriously at Butch.

"Will do."

They shook hands and Butch exited the police station. There was a cruiser parked at the curb and the officer waited while Butch got in then drove to the hospital. As they drove, Butch pulled out his phone and called Kendra. She didn't pick up right away, so he left a short, coded text message.

XXXXX

Kendra and Willa had been in the hotel lobby when her phone had first come alive. They had been talking to the concierge so she didn't hear it. They eventually left and were now strolling along the Neva River's walkway. She checked her phone and opened the message Butch had left. When she finished, she stopped and continued to stare at the phone.

Willa had continued for a few meters before noticing that Kendra had stopped. She saw the look on Kendra's face and quickly went to stand in front of her. "What's wrong? What is it?"

"Butch sent me a text. The message was short, so I do not know any details." She could see that Willa was getting anxious, so she decided to just relay the message to Willa.

"They were in an accident. There was gunfire and your dad was shot, but he is fine. He will call you soon. That's all it says."

Willa's eyes welled up right away. "I have to go." And, she started to hustle back to the hotel. Kendra ran to her.

"Willa, wait." Willa slowed and turned. She was crying.

"I can't lose my dad. It would be only me. Why is all this happening to me?" She suddenly began shaking, and crying, and finally collapsed to the pavement. Pedestrians simply veered around the two of them as though this was a normal occurrence.

Kendra ignored the people around them, sat down next to Willa, put her arm around her and gently pulled Willa to her. Willa resisted a little at first, but then gave in to Kendra's hug. She slowly crawled into Kendra's arms and sobbed. Kendra held her tight, gently brushed Willa's hair with her hand and quietly whispered things like, "Shhh. It will be okay. Your dad is strong. Butch said it wasn't serious. Your dad will call you soon."

On the third mention that he will call soon, Willa's phone buzzed. She quickly fumbled it out of her pocket and answered.

"Oh dad. Oh dad. I was so scared that you... Are you okay? Please tell me you are okay!" Pause. "Are you sure? Is that what the doctors say? Please tell me the truth!" Pause. Kendra could see a noticeable relaxation in Willa's shoulders and face. "Well, I am glad of that. What happened? Why was someone shooting at you?" Long pause. "Okay, I'll wait until you know more. How is Butch?" Pause. "Good, good. I am sure that Kendra will want to hear from him as soon as possible." Pause. "Okay. Please call again soon. I love you! Bye!"

Willa put the phone back into her pocket and slowly got to her feet. Kendra stood as well.

Willa finally took a deep breath, letting it out slowly. She turned to Kendra, smiled, and said, "Thanks for being here for me. It really, really helped me to hang on. Oh my gosh, I can't imagine what I would have done if…" She couldn't finish the sentence.

Kendra grabbed both of Willa's hands, turned to her and told her, "I am glad I was here for you too and I hope you know that I will always be there for you. Even when we are on our separate coasts, I am just a phone call or a quick flight away."

Willa came in to Kendra and they hugged. She finally moved back, looked at Kendra and said, "I want this to end. I want the people who are doing this. Let's get to work. What's next?"

XXXXX

David arrived at Butch's house the following afternoon. He had called when his flight took off, introduced himself to Butch and told him when he would arrive. He also gave him Homer's number and told him to call it.

Butch called Homer right after he hung up with David and Homer filled him in on what was going on. Homer told Butch that much of what they knew about Olivia's past was true, but not all of it. There were also some things he did not know and asked Butch to come to his office as soon as Dan was able to travel and he would explain everything in more detail.

Butch welcomed David when he arrived and they sat in his living room. After asking about something to drink, Butch went and retrieved cokes for them.

Once they were settled, David started. "I have information about your shooters."

Butch thought. *All business. Fine with me.* "So what do you know about them?"

"The finger prints didn't help, but we used facial recognition from the footage at the bar and got a hit on Interpol. Apparently, these two guys are 'thugs for hire'. They are British, but seem to roam the world doing jobs using lots of fake IDs. Their names, and these could also be fake are Jeremy King and Webster Smith. They had some evidence in their vehicle that we think they were going to plant on you or in your vehicle that would indicate a former client of yours was involved. It's all fake, of course. I'm sure Homer filled you in concerning our interest in this."

"He actually told me very little and asked that I come to see him once Dan is able to travel."

"Good. I'll stay here as long as it takes to calm the minds of the locals. You should prepare to head to Homer as soon as possible since he is anxious to get this situation resolved. If you don't have any questions for me that I can actually answer", he smiled, "I will head to Seattle to get to work solving the case."

"I'm good now. I am heading to Harborview to see Dan again and to talk to the doctor about when he can travel."

David left his coke almost full and headed to Seattle. Butch sat and finished his while he thought long and hard about what he had learned in the past twenty-four hours. He really needed to talk to Dan and to send Kendra a message.

He decided to head to the hospital first, since it was nighttime in Russia and the girls were probably asleep.

30. Russia (Part Three – Let's Party)

"Who were those idiots? Who hired them? If they weren't already dead, then they would be soon. Take care of the person who hired them. I don't want idiots working for me." The boss seemed to calm a little then continued, "I am guessing that the guys will head here as soon as they can. It is getting too hot in the states to attempt a hit there, so we'll wait until they are here in our own backyard."

"Yes, I am sure they will come here soon. Do you still want the girl and her dad?"

"Yes, even more now than before. But, please, don't disappoint me and hire idiots to do this. I want you in charge of this. Do you understand?"

"Yes, I do and I will not fail you."

"Whatever. Get out and do your job. By the way, if the dad can't be taken alive, so be it. If he knows about the files, then that knowledge will go away with him. But I want that girl alive. She might know about the files too. Besides, if she doesn't, she still needs to be punished for her mother's treachery." And at that, she turned and stared out the window.

XXXXX

Kendra set the phone on the table and looked at Willa. Willa looked back expectantly.

"Butch had a visit from an agent who represents someone high up in the CIA."

Willa scrunched her forehead and asked, "Um, why? What do they want?"

"Well, it seems they want to help us. Butch learned that much of what we know about Olivia is true, but there is more." Willa started to ask something, but Kendra held up her hand. "I don't know any of it and neither does Butch. Once Dan is ready to travel, which should be in a day or two, they are heading to Washington, DC to talk with this person. They'll learn more and pass it on to us."

"Will they come here?"

"I am sure of it. This is apparently where it all started and where the answers are."

Willa sighed, "Okay, what's next for us. I hate just sitting around doing nothing!"

Kendra grimaced, "Wow, what they say about teenage girls is really true. Fine, how is this for an idea. Let's go out this evening to check out the night life. I don't mean in the 'searching for dates' kind of night out. I mean 'searching for information' night out. I have found that people talk much more in the evening, especially when they have had a few drinks and when they are talking to a pretty girl."

Willa smiled. "Sounds like fun to me."

"No. You are not drinking and I wouldn't take you along, except that two are always better than one. You will be joined at my hip and I do not want you to ever be out of my sight. Understand?"

"Yes, I understand, Attila. Goodness. You are such a control freak." Although, secretly, she was glad that Kendra cared so much about watching out for her.

"Okay. As long as you understand, we're good. It's about 10 am now, so let's wander around the club area to scope out places where we might go."

There weren't many nightclubs around their hotel, especially Russian or local bars, which is what they wanted. Kendra figured that they'd get more information in a local Russian bar then in a western bar. Both Kendra and Willa could speak Russian fluently, so they could mingle pretty easily with the crowd. However, as they walked across the Neva and past the museum, Kendra pulled Willa aside.

"Have you spoken Russian much since here?"

Willa was surprised by the question, but said, "Well, I spoke Russian at the hotel to the staff and concierge. But, when we have been out, I really haven't thought I needed to. Why?"

"Well, for this excursion, I want you to speak English only, while I will speak Russian. Our story will be that I am your older cousin and have been living in Russia for the past five years. I went to school here and decided to take a job here. I'll think of a job later. But, you will be my young cousin from the states visiting with me."

"Cool, I can do that. So, I am guessing my job will be to pretend I don't understand anything that is being said around me. But, of course, I do and I'll listen carefully for information we can use."

Kendra smiled, "You might just become a great investigator someday. That is exactly what I want you to do."

Willa smiled as they continued walking along.

They crossed Fontanki Canal, found themselves on Nevsky Prospect Street and headed toward the Railroad Station. At this point, they started noticing many, at least what appeared to be, local Russian clubs. These were clubs that had all kinds of attractions for the customers, none of which was suitable for Willa, but that couldn't be helped. These were the bars they had to frequent if they were going to get any more information about who was behind what was happening.

Kendra suggested they enter one just to see what they might expect. They were dressed casually in jeans and shirts. Willa had on one for the Seattle Seahawks football team and Kendra had on a plain blue blouse. Kendra felt they would be safe pickup attempts.

Boy was she wrong. As they entered, she saw that the place was crowded with men, and it was not even noon. As soon as they walked in, they were noticed by several of the customers and invited to sit with them.

They continued to refuse and were about to leave, when a guy came over and told the rest of the guys to move away and leave the ladies alone. As they all moved away, he turned to Kendra and said, in English, "I am sorry for the terrible behavior of my fellow countrymen. They have no respect for ladies. If you would like, you can sit at my table." He pointed to a table with another guy who looked over and nodded. "I promise you that we are gentlemen and you will be able to sit, enjoy a drink and leave with no trouble."

Kendra smiled and responded in Russian, "That would be nice. I think we would enjoy sitting with you gentlemen."

The man looked at her with surprise then spoke in Russian, "You speak Russian extremely well. Please come with me."

They approached the table and the first man introduced himself. "I am Georgi and this is Ivan. Not, the 'terrible', he's Ivan the 'nice guy'."

Kendra smiled and said, "My name is Kendra. I went to school in Russia and now live here. This is my young cousin from the states, Willa. She does not speak Russian. She is visiting me for a short holiday and we are only in St Petersburg for a couple of days."

In English, Georgi said to Willa, "Well, I hope you are enjoying your visit to our beautiful city."

"Oh, I am, very much. The architecture is wonderful and the people have been so nice."

"Well, some are not so nice", and he glanced at the other men in the bar.

They talked for about ten minutes then Kendra suggested they had to leave.

Georgi and Ivan got up when Kendra and Willa stood to go and asked, "Would you like some company this afternoon? We will be wonderful tour guides for you."

"Thank you, Georgi, but I am very familiar with the city, so we should be fine. We are only planning to see one or two things this afternoon then head back to the hotel to rest."

"I understand. It can be tiring to walk around the city. There is so much to see." After a short pause, "I am wondering, would you like some company this evening? We would enjoy taking you to a really nice, authentic Russian restaurant."

Kendra paused, glanced at Willa, who shrugged, and then turned to Georgi. "Okay, that sounds nice. Where and what time shall we meet?"

"Oh, do not worry. We will pick you up at your hotel at 8:00 pm. Where are you staying?"

"Actually, Georgi, I'd prefer that we meet you at the restaurant."

"Well, if you prefer." He gave her a business card with the name and address of the restaurant.

After they had walked far enough away from the bar to not be overheard, Willa said, "They already knew who we are, didn't they? They seemed to suddenly appear in that bar after we had walked in."

"I agree. I can't be sure if they are the ones following us. There could be someone else and these guys are working with them. We are going to have to be on our toes this evening. If they are not the followers, then they are probably more interested in some fun, rather than a nice dinner. I'm not sure if you should be going. You should stay …"

Before Kendra could continue, Willa turned to face her, "No. You are not cutting me out of this. This all started as my mission and I will not bail out now. Especially, now that we are so close to finding out what happened to my mom. I am going with you tonight."

Kendra looked at Willa and could see that she'd have a real fight on her hands to try to stop her from going. She was also a bit uncomfortable with the idea of leaving her alone in the hotel room. The people following them would know she was alone which would make her vulnerable.

"Okay. We'll go together, but again, no alcohol and no wandering off on your own, especially with either of these guys."

Willa responded, "No, no, of course not. I won't drink and I will not leave your side with anyone. I promise! Okay?"

"Fine. Let's get back to the room. We need to select our dinner outfits."

"Can we stop along the way at a few shops? I really don't have anything I could wear to a nice dinner restaurant. I pretty much only brought a couple of pairs of jeans and some shirts."

"Good idea. I have a dress, but it's more suited to the beach. Also, it gets chilly here at night, so we'll need light jackets or coats."

XXXXX

They stopped at a couple of shops near the city center then another one near the hotel. They eventually made their way to the hotel and headed to the room.

Once in the room, Willa called her dad. He said he was getting better and could now travel. As a matter of fact, they had already booked their flights to Washington to talk to the CIA guy. Before they ended the call, Willa passed on what Susie had told her and that she and her mother wanted to meet with Willa and Kendra at their home.

Kendra and Willa rested most of the afternoon then at 6 pm, they began to get ready for their night out.

Willa and Kendra took turns getting dressed in the bathroom. As Kendra hung up the room phone, Willa came out of the bathroom with her cream colored light coat on. It was thin enough to not be bulky, but it covered Willa from neck to knees and would certainly protect her from the chilly air.

Kendra had bought a light jacket that stopped just past her waist. She was wearing a light blue flowing skirt that stopped an inch above her knees and a frilly, at least Willa thought it was frilly, white blouse with three-quarter length sleeves. Kendra had left the top two buttons open.

They went to the Lobby and asked the concierge to call them a taxi. It arrived a few minutes later and Kendra gave him the address. The taxi ride was around thirty minutes and they arrived shortly after 8:00 pm. They entered the restaurant and found the men sitting at the bar.

Georgi and Ivan were both dressed in casual slacks with open colored dress shirts and dinner jackets. Georgi was wearing gray slacks, a white shirt and a black jacket. Ivan was wearing black slacks, a light blue shirt and a dark blue jacket. They actually looked quite nice.

"You boys look very handsome." Kendra acknowledged as the guys approached them.

"And, you girls are very lovely."

Willa and Kendra smiled and said thanks.

The restaurant interior was reasonably fancy, but not garish. Ivan and Georgi offered their arms to each gal and they moved into the restaurant area where they found a coat check counter. They stepped to it and the girls removed their coats to check them.

Kendra removed her jacket and handed it to the girl behind the counter. She then stepped aside as Willa also removed her coat and handed it to the girl. As she did, Kendra stood rigid and stared at her. Willa was not wearing the dress Kendra had helped pick out for her. It had been a very pretty dress that ended just below Willa's knees.

Instead, Willa was wearing a form fitting white dress that stopped about five inches above her knees. It fit tight around her neck, had long sleeves and every part of the dress fit Willa's body tightly. But, what was really holding Kendra rigid was the fact that it was semi-sheer. Not the entire dress, but enough of it so that you could faintly see right through to Willa's skin just above her breasts, her entire waist and the bottom two inches of the dress. Willa looked stunning! Hot!

Ivan and Georgi were also staring, as well as several men in the area.

Willa turned, smiled and said, "I'm starving. Let's eat."

As they were shown to their table, many eyes, men and women's, followed the small group. Once at the table, Kendra smiled and said, "I think Willa and I need to use the ladies room. Right, Willa?"

Willa smiled and followed Kendra to the restroom. Once inside, Kendra turned to Willa and barked, "What do you think you're doing? You can't be wearing that. Your dad would kill me, if he knew I let you wear that thing. We need to leave now. Ivan and half the men in here want to paw you." She stopped and angrily turned away.

Willa touched Kendra's arm and turned her around. "Look, these guys are not interested in a travel dialogue. They want to be with two hot girls. I mean look at you. You certainly look hotter than I do. I figured if they were constantly distracted by how we look, they will not pay as much attention to what they say to us. Aren't we here for information? "

Kendra sighed. Willa had a point. She, herself, had primped for this night, so how could she blame Willa for thinking the same thing.

"Okay, okay. We need to get back out there. We can discuss this later but you are not to go anywhere, including the restroom, without me. Understand?"

Willa nodded. They walked back to the table and sat as both men held out their chairs.

31. Russia (Part Four – Trouble)

Dan checked out of the hospital early on the morning after he talked to Willa. Butch met him, drove to his house and they were now sitting in the kitchen drinking coffee. Dan got up quickly then, just as quickly, sat back down. He had become a little woozy.

"You can't do that, Dan. You're going to heal fine, but it will take some time. It's only been three days since you were shot. And you lost a good bit of blood, so I don't think you should suddenly start acting like nothing happened. If you need anything, let me know and I'll get it for you."

"I just can't stand not doing anything. The agent you talked to said he would handle things here, so we can go now."

"Dan, you are not cleared to fly. You know they will not let you on any flights, let alone through security, without the doctor's approval and that approval is for tomorrow, not today."

Dan sat motionless and Butch got up to start making some breakfast for them. Finally, Dan rose slowly and said, "I'm going to try to contact Susie to talk to her over the phone. It should be early evening there, so she is probably available."

Butch nodded and went back to laying the bacon into the pan.

Dan got his computer and sent an email to Susie using Willa's account. He asked her if he could call.

As they finished breakfast, Dan's computer sounded a soft bell indicating an email had arrived. Dan pulled it to him and saw that Susie had responded. He opened it and read, "Yes, please call. I'm worried. Here is my number."

Dan called and Susie answered after the third ring. "Hello."

"Hello. Susie, I am Dan, Willa's father. Do you remember me?" Pause. "Good. How are you?" Pause. "I was sorry to hear about your dad and sister. Listen, I'm calling because I was wondering if you'd mind talking to me about what you wanted to tell Willa?" Pause. "Well, I am sure she's okay. She is traveling with another woman, who is very smart and capable." He didn't know how else to describe Kendra. He listened for a long time, then said, "What exactly are you saying, Susie?" Pause. "I am finding this hard to believe. Is your mom available for me to talk to?" Pause. "Okay, I'll wait."

Butch was staring at him. When Dan glanced over, Butch looked at him questioningly. Dan waved Butch off for the moment.

"Yes, this is Dan. Hello Marilyn. Thank you for talking to me. Susie was saying something very disturbing to me earlier. Do you know anything about this?" Pause. "Probably. They are able to listen to almost all calls unless you are on an encrypted phone or line." Pause. "Okay, I look forward to hearing from you."

Dan pushed his phone aside and pulled the laptop to him. He quickly motioned for Butch to sit next to him. Just as Butch settled next to him, his laptop beeped again. He opened an email from Susie.

It read, "I am sending this, but my mom will be dictating it to me. Some of this I think I already know, but my mom said I needed to be prepared to hear some things that might shock me. Okay, she is ready."

"I worked for the KGB back when you knew us. Our daughters never knew because we kept them away from any of our work. We moved back to Russia soon after the boating accident and have lived here in St Petersburg ever since. Xavier ran off with another woman and I learned later that he was killed while out on a mission but I was never told where or why or how. We just knew that he was dead. Eden died of leukemia, as Susie has already told Willa."

"What Susie does not know, and neither do you, is that we knew there would be an accident that day and that Olivia and Peter were supposed to die. It had been arranged at KGB headquarters but we provided the place and boat. I am so sorry. This is exactly what caused the troubles between Xavier and me. Trading in secrets is one thing, but taking part in a cold blooded killing was something I never wanted to be a part of. Xavier called me a traitor, amongst other terrible things."

"The other thing we argued about was why Peter had to be a part of this. Xavier actually said that he didn't, but since he had gone with Olivia he now was a part of it. Once Olivia and Peter left and you left, I told Xavier I was not going to go through with it. He slapped me around a bit, but not in the face. He didn't want you to see it. Even so, I kept insisting that Peter had to be saved or I would call the authorities."

"He finally relented. He took his fishing boat out and rescued Peter from the water. Unfortunately, he had taken a nasty hit on the head, so he was unconscious. Xavier took Peter to an abandoned beach house about a mile away from us. I am not sure if you remember, but several times one of us would go off and we were actually taking care of Peter. We would always come up with some excuse about helping with the search or getting stuff from town or any one of a number of other bogus excuses."

"It took about a month for him to be well enough to move. Over that time, we kept telling him you would be coming soon but then we'd give him a sedative. We kept him this way for several months and then took him with us to Russia. We told him his mom had died in the accident and that you and Willa had died trying to rescue her. We told him that you and Olivia had always told us if anything happened to them, we should take care of him and we did."

"He went to school here and is now finishing his Engineering degree at the Moscow Institute of Physics and Technology. He has turned out to be very brilliant. I have felt guilty about this all of these years and wanted to contact you, but I was scared. I was scared about what the government's new secret service would do to me and scared of Susie and Peter finding out. But, when Willa contacted Susie and talked about coming here and indicated she had no idea what Susie was talking about when she mentioned Peter, I decided I had to tell the truth. Please believe me when I say that Susie had no idea about any of this. Even as I sit here dictating this to her, she is crying and has been since I said that I used to work for the KGB. I still work for the government, but at a desk job."

"I want to correct this. I don't expect forgiveness and I do expect punishment, but I don't care. My heart has been broken for so long over this, it is beyond caring anymore about me. Susie knows this next part. I am dying of breast cancer, so my punishment will probably come sooner rather than later. Please tell me what you want me to do."

Butch had no idea what to say to Dan, so he just sat quietly. Dan stood and walked over to the window that looked out toward Lake Washington. After, what seemed like an hour but was only a few minutes, he turned and looked at Butch.

"What do I do? What can I say to her? I don't know if I am angry or happy. I guess I am both. What am I going to tell Willa? Oh God, this is a nightmare wrapped in a silver lining. I mean, Peter is alive and well. I can't believe it. I am so very happy that Peter is alive and I know Willa will be too. But, Marilyn, a friend, participated in the killing of my wife. I can't forgive that. I can never forgive that."

Butch still had no idea what to say, so he stood and walked to the window where Dan was standing.

XXXXX

Kendra and Willa actually enjoyed the food and conversations with Ivan and Georgi. And, after a few shots of vodka, the men had become more talkative, so it was time for Willa to signal Kendra to leave for the restroom. She looked at Kendra and nodded slightly toward the restroom.

Kendra seemed reluctant at first to leave Willa alone with them, but then she relented, excused herself and left. She knew this was an important part of their plan, so she had to leave Willa alone with the men. The restaurant was crowded with customers and waiters, so Willa was probably safe. She walked away to the restroom and stopped where they couldn't see her but she could take quick peeks at the table.

Willa smiled at the men after Kendra left. Ivan asked her a couple of things about school in English that she answered politely. Georgi finally began to speak in Russian to Ivan. Willa glanced away nonchalantly but listened intently.

After about ten minutes, Kendra wandered back and the men immediately started to speak in English. They talked and laughed for another twenty minutes and, when the table was cleared of dishes, the men asked if the girls would like dessert. They both said yes, but when the men were about to order, Kendra suggested that she and Willa go to the dessert display to check them out first.

Before the men could argue or go with them, they were off. The men stood for a few seconds, then sat back down. However, they kept their eyes on the girls as they stood at the dessert display pointing and talking.

162

When they got to the display, Kendra smiled and said, "Oh that looks good."

Willa agreed and then spoke softly. "They started speaking in Russian shortly after you left."

They both kept smiling and pointing.

Willa continued. "Ivan asked Georgi if they were still on. He said yes. Ivan asked when. Georgi said at the club when he gave the signal. They were about to say more when you appeared, so they stopped. What do you think this means?"

"It means that these two guys have been given an assignment regarding us but we do not know what it is. It could be to kidnap us or get rid of us, so I want you to stay even closer to me. I think we have to play along for a bit longer to see if we can find out who is behind this."

"Willa, I can't emphasize this more, these are bad people and something bad is probably going to happen. If I say the word Alerion, then you run and run fast for the nearest exit. Okay?"

"Okay, I will. I promise."

They finally headed back to the table, sat and told the men what they wanted.

They finished dessert and as Ivan paid the bill, Georgi said that the night was still young and suggested they head upstairs to the club to check out the music.

Kendra smiled and said, "Sure. That sounds like fun! Don't you think so Willa?"

"Oh yeah. I love dancing and I'd really like to experience a Russian club. It will make a great story for my friends at school."

"Well ladies, then let's go and enjoy more of this lovely evening."

XXXXX

Dan finally turned to Butch. "I am going to write her back and tell her that I can't forgive her for Olivia, but I am grateful to have Peter back. I am going to tell her that we will be in St Petersburg in a few days and ask her to tell me where we can meet."

Butch nodded and they sat back down at the laptop. Dan typed his message and waited.

After a few minutes, the response from Susie arrived. It said, "I understand. Let's meet in the courtyard in front of the Cathedral of Saints Peter and Paul."

"Hi, this is Susie. I will be with my mom. I am very anxious to see Willa again. Will she be there too?"

Dan responded that he couldn't be sure. Willa was already there with a friend and they may be busy.

"Okay. I understand. Please contact me again via email when you arrive and know when we can meet at the cathedral."

Dan sat back in his chair. "Let's get a cup of coffee and sit on the deck. I need to think about all of this."

Butch grabbed two cups and followed Dan out the door.

XXXXX

Kendra, Willa and the men went up an elevator and exited onto the third floor where the club was located. The noise was very loud, so communication was difficult. They walked a short way, turned right and entered through a set of double doors. The music was now deafening. The bouncer at the door looked at Georgi, Ivan and the girls and nodded. They walked past the bar area and moved to the back right side of the room to an empty table. It was the only empty table there and there were two men standing close by. They obviously had kept others clear of the table just for them.

As they sat, Ivan went over to the bar and ordered drinks. When he started back, Kendra leaned next to Willa's ear and said, "Smile. Don't drink."

Willa laughed, as did Kendra. Georgi laughed too. "Some joke!"

"No, just girl talk! I told Willa that you guys are very handsome, so don't mess that up and get drunk." Kendra laughed again and poked Georgi in the side. She also leaned into him a little and brushed his cheek with her hand.

Georgi smiled and kissed her. He tried for her mouth, but she turned slightly at the last moment so he could kiss her cheek.

They sat watching the dancers. Willa and Kendra ignored their drinks and clapped a little to the music.

Kendra noticed Willa staring out at the crowd of dancers intently. Kendra nudged her and asked with her eyes. *What's up?*

"I need to use the restroom. Come on Kendra." They all rose and the men moved so that the girls could head to the restroom. Kendra saw that one of the table guards followed them, but stayed outside the door when they went into the restroom.

Kendra checked around, saw no one and they moved to the back of the restroom. "What's wrong?"

"I know one of the girls out there dancing. Her name is Francine and she was one of the French girls at the race in Tenerife. She stood out in the crowd of dancers because her hair is the color of orange with blue highlights through it. Why is she here?"

"She must be one of the people who have been following you. I think we are going to have to leave soon. I am very uncomfortable with all of the people around us who do not seem very friendly. I get the feeling the men are going to ask us to dance soon. We'll dance the one dance then tell them we need to leave. I'll tell them we will take a taxi, so they can stay and continue to enjoy themselves."

"Unfortunately, I think they will disagree and want to stay with us. If that is the case, then as soon as we get outside, we both start yelling help in Russian. Hopefully, that will get us some attention and maybe dissuade the men enough for us to get in a taxi. There is a taxi queue just to the left of the door so we'll head in that direction as we start yelling. Okay?"

"Okay." Willa was getting scared, but trusted Kendra.

They returned to the table and, after a couple of minutes the men asked them to dance. They moved to the dance floor and started moving to a weird, loud techno song from the 1980s.

The men kept the small group of four somewhat together, but Kendra noticed they were slowly moving toward a position in front of one of the doors that led out the back of the club. This is really bad.

Finally, she decided she couldn't let this continue. She moved as close to Willa as possible and shouted "Alerion, Alerion, Alerion."

Willa heard Kendra and didn't hesitate. She quickly started rushing toward the door they had come through but it was slow going with all of the people. Suddenly she felt hands on her arm. She looked and Francine was holding her arm tightly. Francine smiled and yelled, "Going somewhere?"

Kendra saw Francine grab Willa and started to head for her but got nowhere. Ivan and one of the table men grabbed her and pushed her through the back door into a hallway. She fought Ivan and brought him down with a knee to the groin. When the table man tried to grab her she hit him hard in the face, but he shrugged and punched her hard in the stomach.

Kendra went down next to Ivan. Table man came over and tried to kick her, but she squirmed behind Ivan at the last minute and Ivan took the kick for her. It was a vicious kick and Ivan groaned then went quiet. She looked quickly behind her then back at table man and saw him coming in for another shot at her. She started to move behind Ivan again, when she saw something sticking out of the back of Ivan's trousers.

It was the grip of a handgun. She grabbed it, rolled and fired at table man. He went down in a heap and she didn't wait. She stuffed the gun into the top of her skirt and pulled out her blouse to cover it. She kept one hand on it as she darted out into the dancers.

Kendra quickly searched the room, but saw no sign of Willa. She noticed that Georgi, the other table man and Francine were also nowhere in sight. She rushed past the bouncer who tried to grab her but missed and scrambled down the stairway.

She ran out of the front of the building and rushed to the parking garage. Just after she entered, she ran to a side exit and emerged facing Georgi's car as it careened out of the garage. She pulled the gun out of her skirt and fired at the tires and engine compartment.

The car never slowed and she had to jump aside at the last minute. She thought she might have hit the engine, but couldn't be sure. Soon she heard sirens, so she sat on the curb and watched as the first police vehicle pulled to a stop. The cop yelled for her to put the gun down and to lay on her stomach with her hands behind her. Two more police cars arrived.

At the same time, a man off to the left behind the crowd pulled out a phone and held it to his ear. And, across the street in the shadow of an entrance way, another man pulled out a phone and held it to his ear.

32. Russia (Part Five – The Team)

"Why didn't you stop them? I can't believe this. Why do I have such incompetent people working for me? Okay, stay with the woman. I'll make sure the evidence clears her in all of this." Dimitri put his phone down then his head into his hands.

XXXXX

"Wonderful! I am looking forward to meeting the offspring of the thief and traitor. Bring her to me right away. I need her to tell me where the files are before I kill her nice and slowly."

After hanging up, the boss leaned back and thought. *Those files contain names, dates and places of murders and other actions that could get a great many people, including me, in trouble; trouble like life in a gulag or a bullet or two in the head. Much of the information in the files had already been stolen from files in Moscow in order to have information on others that might protect them from the gulag or bullet. Then, Olivia had stolen them. They had to be found and destroyed, as well as anyone who has seen the information in them.*

XXXXX

Dan and Butch entered the hotel room they were told to go to by Homer's agent. As they entered they saw two men sitting at a small table near the only window in the room. The two men rose and approached.

"I am Homer and this is agent Tolliver. He is very familiar with this case. Please sit."

After everyone shook hands, Butch and Dan moved to two other chairs placed at the table. Once seated, Dan asked. "Case? This is a case for you? What does that mean?"

"First of all, Dan, I am very sorry about what happened to you in Seattle. I hope you are healing well."

"Thanks, but what is going on here? I contacted Marilyn Buchard and her daughter in Russia and she told us a story almost too strange to believe. Plus, the man who followed us around the world was assassinated in front of our eyes in St Petersburg, Florida. This is crazy stuff. Willa and Kendra are in Russia checking on any leads there, so my question is this. Are you helping or hindering us?"

Homer could see that Dan wasn't in the mood for beating around the bush. "I am hoping that we can help. Tolliver has been working on the details over the past few months, but let me give you the highlights."

"I was the agent in charge of Olivia's witness protection security when she decided to defect in Chicago. She had never really done any spying for the Russians. Sure, she got some bits and pieces of information from some of the officers at the base, but none of it was classified, so her foster parents

167

were getting frustrated with her. The man actually knocked her around a good deal for not making any progress."

Dan bristled when he heard this. Homer continued quickly, "She never had a love relationship with Major Erickson. It turned out that he was actually an agent for the soviets and was testing her since her results were so poor. He would pass information to her then check to see if it made it up to the men in charge back in Russia. It all did, but he could tell that she wasn't very good at this type work. After several months of this, Erickson's boss told him he would be returning to Russia soon."

"The men in charge in Russia also told Marilyn and Xavier they were to eliminate Olivia and head back to Russia. But, as you know, Olivia got out before they could take care of her. We don't know how she found out, but it makes no difference now. She must have saved, or stolen, a bunch of money because she was able to make her way to Chicago, change her looks and name, and then hide."

Dan interrupted, "That must have been the money she said she had inherited and used to start our business."

"You are probably right. Anyway, she eventually became scared and nervous, so she contacted the FBI. They contacted us and I was assigned to be her point-of-contact. She was in our program, but we also soon learned she was not cut out for it. We finally had Malcolm help her to get away and hide in San Francisco."

"When we heard about her death in the boating accident, we assigned Tolliver to look into it. He will continue from here."

Tolliver nodded and took over. "We investigated the accident and came to the same conclusions as everyone else did. I backed off, but kept poking around into it for the next seven years. I was reassigned elsewhere at that time, but couldn't let this go. Then, last year, when you started your sailing trip, an informant told me that someone in Russia had become interested in your adventure. He has dropped bits of information to us over the years and has always been reliable, so I took his warning seriously."

"I was now working in Homer's group so I got his permission to put someone on you to see what might be going on. He started reporting that someone else was also following you. Then, the incident in Lima when Malcolm was murdered raised this to Homer's desk."

Homer took back over. "I have also been working with someone very high up in the Russian security services. He is very concerned about this and has been helping us quite a bit." Just then, his phone buzzed. He pulled it out, looked at the screen, frowned and said, "I better get this."

"Hey Dimitri." Pause. "What? Wait, what are you talking about?" Pause. "Okay, okay. I'll be there as soon as I can." At that, Tolliver got up and moved to the other side of the room. He pulled out his phone and began hitting keys. "Yes, Dimitri, they are right here. I'll bring them too."

He set the phone down and looked at Dan. There was no easy way to say this. "Dan, Willa is missing. We think she has been kidnapped."

Dan started yelling at him as soon as he had said kidnapped. "What? What are you saying? Kidnapped? How? What's happening over there?"

Butch put a hand on his shoulder. Dan seemed to settle a little, but he was still shaking and finally rose to walk around the room. "I should not have pursued this. I should never have let Willa become involved in this. All of this is my fault."

When Dan calmed himself, Butch asked, "What about Kendra?"

"She's fine. She was attacked by two men but she shot one and disabled the other. We'll learn all of the particulars from Kendra when we get to Russia. We leave in a few hours."

As they began to ready themselves to go, Butch went to Dan and put his hand on Dan's shoulder. "Don't worry, we'll get Willa back. Look, Willa is smart, she's clever and she's a lot stronger than most people think. She'll survive. We will find her and bring her home."

33. Russia (Part Six – Old Debts)

Willa woke from whatever drug they used to knock her out and immediately saw that she was bouncing around inside the trunk of a car. She suspected that it was the car that Georgi had used to get to the restaurant for their dinner. Some dinner that turned out to be.

She had to think about escape. She wasn't tied up, so they must have thought she'd be out longer or, at least, that she couldn't get out of the trunk. She was still in her pretty dress, which wasn't very pretty anymore. It was torn in a couple of places and had lots of grease and dirt stains. There was also, what looked to be, blood stains. She couldn't see any injuries on her, so she figured it was blood from injuries suffered by Francine or one of the men.

She started to take inventory of what she had access to in the trunk.

XXXXX

Francine grumbled from the backseat of Georgi's car, "She scratched me. I'm going to pay her back once we get to the house."

"I'm guessing that you will not be permitted to do any such thing. That is what the boss wants to do. She is really mad because the girl's mom stole over $500,000 from her when she ran away all those years ago. She also stole something else that made the boss even angrier. And, since the mom is already dead, she wants to take her revenge out on the daughter and find out what she knows."

"But, that's none of our business. We should be at the house in about a couple of hours. It is her summer home on the north side of Novgorod and is very remote so they won't be disturbed."

XXXXX

Willa felt around the inside of the trunk. She could make out much of what was there by the feel of the objects. The spare tire was pretty obvious. She also found the tire iron. That would definitely be a handy item. She felt what seemed like a small tool bag, rooted around inside and found a screw driver.

She also found some rags, a hammer and some items that she could not quite make out. She next turned her attention to the trunk lock. She knew that most cars had mechanisms on the inside of the lock to allow escape if someone was trapped inside. Unfortunately, she didn't pay attention to that discussion in the driver's education class so she didn't know how it worked.

She touched, pushed and poked at the lock, but nothing seemed to make it pop open nor did anything even feel like an unlocking mechanism. She was becoming frustrated.

She stopped and lay quietly, thinking. Then, she remembered something that Kendra had told her. She had said, "There are times when you find yourself in a situation with many unknowns and no knowledge of what's happening or going on around you. It can be very scary but, the best thing to do as soon as that starts to happen, is to take action. Any action is better than taking no action at all."

Willa was going to take action. She was not going to just lie there and wait for them to do something, likely very bad, to her.

XXXXX

Dimitri called Heinrich. "Homer and the two men are coming to meet me tomorrow morning and I'd like you to be here."

After hanging up, Heinrich started making phone calls. One call was to someone he also worked for. "Homer, the dad and the detective are coming tomorrow to meet with Dimitri." Pause. "Okay. Before or after the meeting?" Pause. "Will do."

XXXXX

Willa had finally worked out what she would do. Her plan was pretty simple. Force the trunk open, escape and run away as hard and fast as she could. Wow, she liked it. Simple, yet something she could do. After all, she was an award winning runner!

She grabbed the screw driver and positioned it on the inside of the lock at a spot she figured would cause it to open. Just as she was about to start jamming it in, the car slowed, started swerving then began bouncing around and knocking her all over the trunk. *What in the world was going on now?*

XXXXX

Georgi felt the car suddenly seize then start jerking to the right. They were far out into the countryside surrounded by thick forest. The car swerved off the road, bounced up and over a shallow ditch then headed down a steep drop. At first they crushed or bounced over small trees and low shrubs. But then suddenly, they slammed into trees on both sides, barely wedging through.

They had been going at 100 km per hour on the highway, but even as the engine seized, the car only slowed to eighty kilometers per hour as it left the road. They were not stopping any time soon except when they finally hit something big and unmovable. Then, he saw that particular something coming straight at him. He quickly ducked down across the seat. Fortunately, he had his seatbelt on but neither the table man nor Francine did.

They hit the tree hard on the front passenger side. Table man went out through the windshield and Francine slammed up into the roof then into the side window. Her head made it out of the window but not the rest of her.

Georgi tried to rise from the seat, but stopped and shrieked in pain. His legs were jammed down by the dashboard, which had been pushed in and down onto them. He couldn't tell whether they

171

were broken, but figured they were. They hurt like crazy. He guessed that Kendra's shots must have connected with something important inside the engine compartment. Based on what happened, he surmised that she probably hit either the brake fluid reservoir or the oil filter or both. He moaned then he heard the trunk open.

XXXXX

Willa had been tossed around pretty good but, once they stopped bouncing around and the car stopped, she checked herself and felt she was fine. She could move her legs and arms easily, but she did get a good knock on her shoulder and her head. She couldn't hear anything coming from the men or Francine, so she jammed the screw driver into the trunk lock.

The crash must have weakened the mechanism because the trunk popped open with just one hit and twist. Willa could smell forest, smoke and dirt. The smoke worried her so she scrambled out and quickly looked around. She saw no movement in the vehicle and was inclined to run, but decided to check to see if the occupants would be coming after her anytime soon.

The first thing she saw was Francine's head sticking out of the rear window. Okay, she wasn't coming after her. Then, as she moved a little closer to the right side, she saw Table Man lying on the ground. And, by the look of him, he wasn't coming after her either. She continued along the right side and saw Georgi pinned under the dash. He wasn't moving.

There was nothing she could do for any of them so she headed toward the road but then stopped. She warily made her way back to the left side of the car, which was in relatively good shape, so she grabbed the door handle and slowly opened it.

Georgi moved a little, moaned and stopped. She gingerly reached into the vehicle and felt inside Georgi's pants' pockets for his phone. She found it and his gun and took them.

As she pulled her hand away, Georgi suddenly grabbed it. She screamed and tried to yank it away once, then twice then a third time. He groaned and let go on the third yank. Willa stepped quickly away from the car, breathing hard. Her heart was pounding, but she had to calm herself and get moving.

She moved cautiously to the back door and opened it. She kept one eye on the back of Georgi's head as she reached toward Francine. She felt horrible about doing this, but felt she had no choice. She pulled and tugged Francine's shoes and slacks off. She also grabbed Francine's jacket, which she had taken off and tossed onto the seat next to her. She checked all of the pockets and found Francine's phone and some money.

Finally, she moved to Table Man. He was a mess. She steeled herself, searched for his phone and found it in his back pocket. She grabbed it, some more money and headed back to the road.

She moved about ten meters from the vehicle, removed her pretty little party dress and put Francine's pants and jacket on, buttoning it up. She also put on Francine's shoes, which were a little tight, but they would have to do.

As Willa stood by the road, she had glanced back at Francine. She sighed and felt a little sad for the girl, but not much. I mean, Francine would have gladly harmed Willa if the accident hadn't happened. She finally shrugged, turned and faced away.

She turned on Georgi's phone and had no problem finding Russia's version of Google Maps. She had heard Georgi say they were going to Novgorod as they dragged her to the car and before they drugged her, so she entered it. She wasn't going there, nor would she head back to St Petersburg. She needed to find a better option.

She figured they had been on the main road to Novgorod and checked the map. She found the road that she figured was the main one to Novgorod and back-tracked to where she thought she was. She thought. *Heading west was better than east since east would take her deeper into Russia.* If she was right, then she was close to Torkovichi, which would put her about 200 kilometers from Estonia to the west.

Before heading north along the road, she pulled the battery and SIM card from Georgi's and Francine's phones. She buried her dress, the phones, batteries and SIM cards about one or two meters away from each other. She took Table Man's phone, but removed the battery and SIM card and placed them in her pockets along with the money and the gun. She looked back at the car, sighed then started north along the road.

After about fifteen minutes she heard an explosion and quickly turned back toward where the car was. There were smoke and flames shooting up into the sky. She wondered if Georgi had made it out, but decided not to check.

XXXXX

Homer and his entourage arrived at Sheremetyevo Airport in Moscow. They were directed to a special visitor arrivals area of the airfield. Dimitri's assistant met them inside the building and escorted them out to a limo sitting at curbside. They all piled in and headed off. The assistant informed them that Dimitri would meet them at his office.

They headed into the city and parked in a subterranean parking garage. They entered the elevator, exited on the fifth floor, walked a short distance and entered a large conference room. Dimitri stood and came forward. Butch took off and ran into Kendra's open arms.

"Are you okay? Let me see. Were you hurt? What happened? Oh, God, I was so worried."

Kendra held him tightly. She finally pulled back and said, "I am fine. I have a couple of bruises, but nothing serious." She smiled, but then frowned and moved toward Dan.

"I am so sorry, Dan. I am so very sorry. We stayed together, but then we moved to the dance floor. I was getting nervous about the situation, so I signaled for Willa that we were leaving. She was only a few feet away. Suddenly strong arms pulled me backwards and out a back door. I could see Willa struggling too. A girl she said she knew from a race in Tenerife had hold of her. There were also two other men around her."

"I was able to get free of the men and ran after Willa and her captors. I went to where the car was parked, but I was too late. They almost ran over me as they sped out and away. I am so sorry. I promise we will get her back."

Dan nodded. "Look, I don't blame you. I am sure you did all you could to protect her. I blame myself for letting her get involved in this mess."

"Dan, do you seriously think you could have stopped her? You know that if you didn't help her, she would have gone off on her own."

"I know, but still, I blame myself."

"Let's all sit down. I have some news that may or may not be good." Dimitri indicated the table and they all moved to it.

Once everyone was seated, Dimitri took a breath and said, "There was an accident reported just south of St Petersburg in the area of Tokovichi. A car apparently lost control and crashed into some trees then burst into flames. Based on the license plates and the vehicle identification number, we believe it was Georgi Ivanovich's car."

"He was one of the men with Willa and me."

Demitri sighed, steeled himself and continued, "There were two bodies in the car and one outside of it. The one outside went through the windshield and probably died instantly. The driver was pinned inside and did not survive the flames." He paused, then started again, "There was a passenger in the back seat that also did not survive the flames. It was a female around Willa's size. We will need either DNA or dental records to be sure."

Dan put his forehead on the table and mumbled, "My fault, my fault, oh God, why did I let her come here."

Kendra immediately went to him. "Dan, no. I am sure that it was not Willa. Remember, I said there was another girl there and she was one of the three who took her. They were around the same size, so it must be her." She looked at Dimitri pleading for him to agree.

"She could be right Dan. The trunk was open, so maybe she was in there. We'll know more as soon as forensics gets done with the scene."

There wasn't much else to say about the accident, so they moved on. Kendra explained what they had found out and gave them a fairly detailed account of what she and Willa had been doing since arriving.

Butch did the same over the same time period. He included what they had learned from Homer, who nodded when Butch started to talk for him.

Dimitri filled them in on things new to them. "Major Erickson did come here to pretend defection and work for the security services. He did so for a few years then he disappeared. He resurfaced a year later when an informant for the mob told us he was now working for them. We believe he is the one who ordered Malcolm and Daniels killed."

"We also know that Lisa, Olivia's fake mom, became involved with the mob soon after returning. Apparently, her husband, Jack, decided to start beating her when Olivia left. Lisa had hoped it would stop once they were back in Russia and he could take a few mistresses, but it did not."

"We think that after she became involved with the mob, she met and became involved with one of its bosses. She also started an affair with Erickson. We think she had Erickson kill Jack, but we have no proof since his body was never found. Anyway, apparently, her mafia boyfriend became the head of the St Petersburg mafia. And, fortunately for her, he was killed by a rival."

"She took over for him through ruthless negotiations and assassinations and is still in charge. It is our guess that she is behind all of this and wants revenge for Olivia stealing money from her many years before. It must have been quite a bit, but we don't really know how much. The mob does not take kindly to treason within its ranks and even a small amount stolen can sometimes lead to severe punishment. But, in this case, I think there has to be another reason we don't know about yet. Lisa has waited a long time and gone to a lot of trouble and expense to stop Willa and you, Dan."

They discussed more details and what should come next but after a couple of hours, they broke up and the Homer group went to their hotel for some much needed rest.

XXXXX

Later that evening, Dimitri was home reflecting on the meeting. It had gone well, considering the hard news he had to report about the accident. He could see that Dan was relieved when Kendra brought up the other girl and said she was sure the dead girl was the girl from Tenerife.

They had spent another hour discussing how best to find and rescue Willa. If she was alive, and everyone decided to assume she was, then she would probably try to contact Dan or Kendra at some point.

The plan was to meet again tomorrow morning when they would, hopefully, have the forensic report from the accident.

He fixed himself a glass of Vodka and moved to the living room to sit. It was still light out even though it was 8 pm. Moscow usually had almost eighteen hours of daylight this time of year.

He felt guilty that he had not told the whole sordid story of the history of Lisa, Erickson and Olivia. But, to be fair, he felt that this part of the truth would not add anything to what they were now planning to do, which was to find and rescue Willa. Besides, the admission would be too painful for all of them to hear and, more importantly, for him to say.

How could he tell them that it was he who had recruited Erickson and brought him to Russia? Worse, how could he tell them that it was he who had given the order to take Olivia out? He was, at least, glad that Peter was alive and well. It was a different time back then. He had had different bosses and they could be unforgiving and brutal. Olivia had been trained to spy, but she refused to provide anything of value then defected to the CIA and told them what she knew and disappeared again.

The order actually came from a lot higher than Dimitri, but he was the one who hired the people to do it. He found them in New York City and told them to make it look like an accident. He shook his head sadly. It was because of all of those earlier mistakes that he was trying to help to protect Willa. Besides, it was possible this case might also allow them to get Lisa and, as a bonus, Erickson.

He sighed and took a sip of Vodka. That is when the window shattered, Dimitri dropped his glass and then fell to the floor.

XXXXX

Heinrich quickly climbed down out of the tree and packed the rifle in its bag. The shot had been fired from 600 meters, which had not been a hard shot for him. He trotted to his car hidden in some trees about two kilometers away. When he got there, he was surprised to see Erickson.

He tossed the rifle in the trunk and asked, "Hey boss, what brings you out here?"

"Did you get him?"

"Yeah, it was a pretty easy shot."

"Good." Then Erickson quickly pulled his hand from behind his back, aimed the 45 handgun at Heinrich's chest and pulled the trigger twice in quick succession. It was fitted with a silencer, so only small pops escaped the muzzle. Before Erickson walked off he shot Heinrich one more time to make sure he was dead.

He went to his car half a kilometer away, got in and pulled out his phone. "It's done. Both of them are down."

Lisa smiled. "Okay, we are almost done. You take some men and go after the two men. I will take care of the girl myself." She pushed the phone aside and sat back in her chair thinking and smiling.

She finally leaned forward, pressed a button under her desk and a book cabinet slid aside. She moved to the heavy door behind it, unlocked it, opened the door, went in and smiled at the arsenal of weapons hanging on the walls and nestled in drawers.

She moved to one section of a wall and took two Glock 20–10mm Auto handguns. They weren't as powerful as other handguns she had, but their kick was much more manageable. She was excited about heading after the girl. This would be the first time in a long time she actually executed a hit on someone. Usually, she ordered others to do it.

She was only sixty and Willa was over 40 years younger. Lisa felt she kept in pretty good condition, but one never knows what one will encounter on a hit. She didn't smoke anymore, rarely drank and exercised in her private gymnasium almost every day.

She went into her bedroom and packed a small backpack, including the guns, both with full magazines. She looked around to make sure she had everything and went to her garage. She selected an old Volvo, which would not raise eyebrows in the rural areas where she was heading.

She knew where Willa was because she had several people following her from the time of the kidnapping. It wasn't that she didn't trust Georgi and his men, she just liked to be careful. When the accident was reported and Willa had survived, she told them to stay back, keep watch and report what they saw.

She already had several reports and knew Willa was heading west from Torkovichi. She figured that Willa would try to make it to Estonia, thinking she'd be safe there. She smiled and thought. *Kids. They always think they are smarter than adults.*

Lisa would never let her get to Estonia. She would have one of her people intercept her before she could cross the border and hold her until she got there.

34. Russia (Part Seven – Lost and Found)

Homer's phone woke him while it was still dark outside and he fumbled around on the nightstand until he had it. He looked at the screen and knew he had to answer. "Hello. What's up?"

The number displayed was Dimitri's, but the voice on the other end was not Dimitri. "Mr. Simpson, I need to ask you and your team to please come to Dimitri's office right away."

"What's happened? Have they found Willa? Is she okay?"

"Please, Mr. Simpson. Come to the office as soon as possible and you will be briefed." He ended the call.

Homer stared at his phone for almost a minute then started calling Dan, Butch and Tolliver.

The five of them eventually assembled in the hotel lobby then climbed into the waiting limo. The all asked Homer what all of this was about, but he said he didn't know.

They walked into the same room they had been in yesterday and started taking seats. They were still rubbing the sleep from their eyes and hoping that there would be some very strong coffee served.

As they moved to seats, Homer looked around the room and saw that Dimitri wasn't present, which seemed unusual. Just then a man he did not recognize came into the room. He stood at the head of the table, but did not take Dimitri's seat.

Once he felt he had everyone's attention, he started. "My name is Aleks Kristoff and I am sorry to inform you that Dimitri Visiliev was assassinated last night at his residence. We do not have all of the details, but we do believe we have the shooter. The problem is, he is dead too, and not from our efforts. He was found a short distance away lying next to his car. He had been shot three times with an unidentified handgun. We are now looking for that shooter."

Homer was stunned and simply looked at the Russian. Dan, Butch, Kendra and Tolliver looked at Homer, figuring this was his conversation to handle. Finally, Homer responded. "I wish to offer our condolences for the loss of Dimitri. He was a very good friend of mine and of the United States. He was also a great man to the Russian people. Please let me know if there is anything we can do."

Aleks shuffled his feet a bit and looked toward the door. Finally, he said, "It seems it might be appropriate for you and your people to leave and return to the US. We will mourn Dimitri and continue to search for the criminals who perpetuated this heinous act of treason."

This got Dan's attention. "I'm sorry about Dimitri, but I can't leave without my daughter. She is missing and is probably being pursued by dangerous criminals. Perhaps even the same people who killed Dimitri. If they were able to get to him so easily and quickly, they could, even now, be close to getting Willa. Please, I cannot leave without her. I won't leave without her!"

Homer jumped in before Dan got too angry and inadvertently said something to really anger Aleks. "Dan, please. Let's discuss this calmly. I am sure that Mr. Kristoff knows how important it is to find and safely return Willa to you." At this, he turned to Aleks, "You do see how much danger Willa is probably facing and how it is imperative she be found and rescued?"

"I do certainly sympathize with you and Mr. Watson. But, you are on Russian soil and under our protection."

Dan stirred and Butch put a restraining hand on his arm.

Homer continued, "We have good intel from your people already that could lead us to Willa soon. Please let us follow it while you search for the people behind this atrocity. Perhaps you could send someone along with us to make sure we stay within the law and that all information we find gets sent back to you immediately."

Aleks had known that it would come to this, so he had already developed a plan for handling it. He actually believed this would be helpful to him. If they find the killer and Willa, then he could take the credit. If they mess it up, then they could be blamed. It would work out in his favor no matter how it turned out.

Aleks sighed, nodded and said, "Okay. What do you propose?"

XXXXX

The day after the accident, a light rain started falling and didn't let up. That night, Willa crawled into the barn on a farm and slept quietly in the corner. She rose before dawn and slipped out. It was still raining.

The good thing was that the rain masked her tracks and gave her a certain amount of invisibility when in open areas between trees or on a road. However, she needed food and raingear. Since her clothes were Russian made in the current style and she spoke fluent Russian, she took a risk and entered a small store in the next town she passed through.

The Russian people are generally not very inquisitive so no one asked who she was or where she was going. She bought some toiletries, food and a light windbreaker but she couldn't find an umbrella or rainwear. She asked to have the items put in one large plastic bag, which they made her pay extra for. She used money she had found on Francine and Table Man, which wasn't much, maybe the equivalent of about $100.

She walked the short distance out of town always keeping in mind anyone she saw or dealt with in order to check for anyone following her. She suspected there was someone but wanted to have a face to put with the person.

She receded a little way into a forested area and sat under a tree that provided some cover from the rain. She ate her food, brushed her teeth as best she could then put on the windbreaker. When she started her trek again, she held the plastic bag above her head.

The next evening, Willa came across a hunting cabin. It was empty of people, but it seemed to be well stocked with the basic necessities. Perhaps, the hunters used it extensively during the hunting seasons but left it empty in the summer. She didn't know much about that sort of thing and didn't care. The door was locked, but she found a window in the back of the cabin that had not been secured. The locking mechanism had only been pushed a little way over the latch, so she jiggled and pushed the window until it opened.

She crawled in and found a bed, some clothes, kitchen items and a variety of old pieces of furniture. As she searched the cabin, she found some canned food, but no other food. While peeking under the bed, she noticed a large backpack and pulled it out. When she did that, she noticed a bow along with a quiver containing ten arrows and a hunting knife in a sheath behind it. She pulled those out. Next, she found a sturdy tarp in a closet that the hunters probably used as a ground-cloth.

She put all she had, including Georgi's gun, into the backpack with the knife and canned goods. She had Francine's jacket but only had her bra on underneath so she looked through the clothes she found. They were neatly folded and stacked on several shelves. She got close enough to them to sniff the sides of the piles. They didn't have any body odor or any other distinct smell so she figured they were okay to wear. They were all men's cloths but there were several t-shirts and tank tops that were only a little too large for her, maybe a teenager also used the cabin. She took three t-shirts and three tank tops and put them in the backpack as well.

As she headed to the window to climb out, she saw that the sun had come out and no rain clouds were in sight. She took the jacket off and windbreaker off, put on a tank top and then put the jacket back on figuring she could shed it if it got too warm. She stuffed the windbreaker, t-shirts and tank tops into the backpack, tossed the bow, quiver and backpack out of the window then climbed back out.

She slung the backpack on, hung the quiver over her right shoulder and picked up the bow. As she walked away from the cabin, she thought about the bow. She had figured when she started this escape to Estonia she might need a weapon. She had the gun that she took off of Georgi, but she had never shot one and knew very little about them. The only thing she did know was that, if she was going to shoot it, she had to make sure the safety was off, to point it at the target and then pull the trigger. She figured she'd never hit anything she aimed at, but maybe she might. At least, she might scare them off.

But, the bow was different. She knew how to use a bow and she could hit a target easily. She didn't want to shoot a person, but she did not want to die either. She hoped she would not have to cross that bridge but, well, she might have to.

She spent the night in a cluster of trees and, as she got ready to head out for the day's trek, she noticed that the temperature was quite warm so she removed the jacket and stuffed it in the backpack. As she approached another small village, she hid the backpack with the bow and arrows in some brushes a little back from the road. She wandered into the village, found a small store and purchased some food and a can opener since she hadn't found one in the cabin.

She walked back the way she had come and turned off of the road. As she strolled along, she saw the person following her. It was a woman and she had even tried disguising herself, but it was a sloppy job. Willa had seen right away that this was the same person she had seen previously. Willa also noticed she never followed Willa closely and tracked her movements from afar.

This bit of information told Willa that the followers were not going to take action against her. They were simply reporting her movements to someone else. She sighed as she picked up her pack, bow and arrows and placed the items she had just purchased into the pack.

She now knew that she would eventually need to shoot at a human target because the person would not want to let her get away, or likely, live. She sighed, turned and continued heading west. She began to think about what she could do to avoid the killer and, if that didn't work, what she could do to protect herself.

After about an hour, Willa stopped. As she stood just inside the tree line, she decided she needed to practice with the bow. As in Malta, she had never shot this bow and would need to get used to it if she hoped to hit a target.

She moved about 100 meters along the tree line until she found a relatively open area that was still well concealed from prying eyes. She picked a couple of trees located about 25 meters away and set the pack next to her. She picked up the bow and quiver of arrows. As she began to nock an arrow into the bow string, so noticed the tip of the arrow for the first time. It was a sharp, steel, barbed tip meant to kill a large animal.

She looked at the tip thinking about what she was intending to do with it. If things went the way she suspected they would, then she was going to put this killing object into another human being. She sighed, lifted the bow, took aim and let loose. She missed the tree. She continued practicing until she could hit the target nine out of ten times. Luckily, she was also able to recover all but two of the ten arrows. She finally packed up her stuff and continued her escape.

As she passed a farmhouse, she decided to risk using their landline phone, if they had one. She hid her pack, bow and arrows, moved up to the door and knocked. A woman answered the door and asked what she wanted in a gruff tone. Willa asked if she could use their phone to call her father. She told the woman that her phone stopped working and held up Georgi's to show her the dead screen.

The woman shrugged, let her in and led her to a landline phone. Willa thanked her and dialed Dan's number. She would have to speak English, since her dad did not understand Russian. If the woman asked later, then Willa would tell her that her dad is British and hadn't learned Russian yet.

Once he answered, Willa started talking, "Hello father." Pause. "Yes, I am okay, but my phone died." Pause. "Yes, I can get to auntie's house." Pause. "Okay, I just wanted to let you know. And, yes, I'll be careful. Cheers."

She thanked the woman who never asked about the shift in languages. She offered to pay, but after several "Nyets", she gave up. The woman even apologized for not being able to drive Willa to her auntie's house, but her husband had the car and was working a second job in Torkovichi.

XXXXX

Dan put the phone away and told Homer, Butch, Kendra, Tolliver and Lev, their Russian helper and spy, "That was Willa and she says she is okay. She didn't say where she was and said that her phone had died. I guess she took one off of someone at the accident. Anyway, she isn't coming here but, instead, she is going to her auntie's house."

"Does she have an auntie here?" asked Lev.

"No, but I think I know where she is going. When she was little, maybe three or four years old, she pretended that an old neighbor lady was her aunt. The woman was very kind to her and didn't seem to have any relatives around her or who were alive, I don't remember. But, I do remember that she was from Estonia. I would bet that is where she is going. It is only about 200 kilometers west of the crash site so she probably figures she can get help there and that Lisa will not be able to get to her once she crosses the border."

Lev wasn't known for his people skills and promptly said, "Well, Lisa can get her anywhere she goes, so she is wrong about that plan. Lisa will probably kill her soon, so we should get moving."

The last part was all Dan wanted to hear. He wanted to get moving. The other part of his speech was crap. Willa was not going to die at the hands of that crazy woman.

Homer seemed to agree. "Okay, let's get going right away. It is about 100 kilometers to the crash site, so it should take about an hour." He looked at Lev and said, "But, we could go faster if we had help." He smiled.

Lev understood. "Yes, we will have an escort and will make the trip in 45 minutes or less."

It was raining, so they didn't linger at the curb long. They loaded quickly into two large, black SUVs. Lev, Homer, Tolliver and a driver were in the first SUV and he told the driver to hit the lights. The second SUV followed with their lights flashing. Dan, Butch, Kendra and a driver were in that one.

XXXXX

There wasn't a great deal of traffic, but there was just enough so that neither vehicle noticed the 3 other vehicles on the highway following them. Erickson was in the first vehicle and he told the others to stay back and to not try to keep up. They were all to keep a steady speed and out of view.

Erickson figured they might stop at the crash site to do a quick search and analysis to compare to the forensic report. Their three vehicles would bypass the site and head to Torkovichi. There, based on Lisa's report, the Homer group would head west toward Estonia. Lisa guessed they probably knew by now where Willa was heading and if they didn't and headed in a different direction then Erickson would need to figure that out where on his own.

XXXXX

Homer and the others headed to the crash site. Dan was against it, but Butch told him it was the smart thing to do. They needed to make sure they had all the information they needed to get to Willa swiftly. Butch told him they'd only be there about ten to fifteen minutes since there were eight of them to inspect the site.

They arrived a short time later and perused the site for about ten minutes then, finding nothing new, they started heading back to the vehicles. Kendra, however, hadn't bothered to look around the scene of the crash. Instead, she walked around the perimeter a few meters away. The rain had stopped, so she could easily scrape her foot along the ground to see what might be there. After a couple of minutes she found Willa's dress. She didn't think it would help Dan to see the skimpy dress and the blood on it. She continued searching the area and found the phones, batteries and SIM cards.

Kendra called the others over and inserted the batteries and SIM cards into each phone then turned them on. She searched through calls and online searches and finally found a map search which seemed to h confirm that Willa had looked toward Estonia. She also saw that Georgi had made and received calls from Lisa and Erickson.

She handed the phone to Lev and said, "It is very likely that Erickson and his men are on our tail, while Lisa is probably following Willa."

35. Russia (Part Eight – Death)

Erickson and one of the other vehicles headed east at Torkovichi. The third vehicle proceeded south and reported that Homer and his team had stopped at the crash site. The leader in the car told Erickson he would circle back and follow them when they left the site.

Erickson told his driver, "Head west on the R39. About 500 meters past Zhivoy, there is a stand of trees to the north side of the road. Pull off a little to the right and block part of the road. Stay in the vehicle and act like the engine will not start." He told his car, "Pull off to the left into the short brush." He pointed to the driver, "You will go over to the first car and act like you are helping to get it started." He turned to the remaining two people in the car, "One of you will stay hidden inside while the other will come with me into the trees."

He then contacted the third car and told them to keep following, but to stay back until they got to Zhivoy. "When you get there, gradually pull up close behind them and block off any retreat. We will all be about 500 kilometers past there. Once they reach our point, everyone will open up on them." He had decided not to try to take Dan alive.

XXXXX

Willa approached Osmino and hid her stuff amongst the trees. As she entered the town and searched for a store, she noticed the follower on the other side of the street sitting on the stoop of a house. Willa didn't really need anything, but this was the only way to keep track of what she was faced with. She found a store, went in, wandered around the store and finally picked up some matches and chewing gum. She paid for the items and went out.

As Willa stepped out of the store, she saw that the woman was walking back toward the east talking on her phone. Willa sat on the steps of the store and opened the pack of gum. As she popped a stick in her mouth, she saw the woman disappear down a side street. She waited several minutes and was about to leave, when she saw the woman sitting in the passenger seat of a car with a driver. They came to the main street, turned and headed east away from Willa.

Willa rose and began walking back to where she had left her bag. As she thought of what had just happened, she realized the killer was now close. He may even have his own eyes on her right now. Willa didn't know for sure, but she just had the feeling someone was always standing right behind her. And, as she remembered what Kendra had told her, she decided to take action.

She went back to her stuff, grabbed it and headed into the woods. Once well into the trees, she stopped and opened the backpack. She pulled out the gun and knife. She stuffed the gun into her waistband at her back. She stuffed the knife and sheath into her front right pocket.

She started to drape the quiver and bow over her shoulders then hesitated. But, after a moment's thought, she slung them on and headed east to the killer.

XXXXX

As they approached Zhivoy, the driver started looking more frequently in the rearview mirror. Homer noticed this and asked what he was looking at. The driver in the trailing car was doing the same. He said that he thought they were being followed. Homer took a look back and saw a black vehicle about 100 meters back.

Homer's vehicle started to slow as they saw the two vehicles ahead. He told everyone to be alert. Both vehicles stopped about 50 meters from the road block. The third vehicle sped up and stopped about 25 meters behind them. There were two men in it. Homer got on comms and told everyone they were in a trap, as though they all didn't know it already. Lev told them their vehicles were armored and Homer countered that was great, until the bad guys decide to pull out heavier weapons and, knowing who was after them, they probably had them.

Suddenly, the attackers opened fire on them. Bullets pinged off of all sides of the vehicles like heavy hail on a tin roof. None of the rounds penetrated, but the staccato noise was certainly intimidating.

Homer suddenly yelled, "Here it comes!" And they saw one of the men in the vehicle on the left swung around it with a shoulder rocket. Homer opened his door and, staying behind it, began shooting back. Everyone in both vehicles did the same, while Butch and Kendra continued firing at the third vehicle behind them.

The man let loose with the rocket and everyone near the first vehicle ran for cover. The others jumped back into the second vehicle. The first car exploded an instant after they scrambled into ditches and into the second vehicle.

The second vehicle's front end was damaged, but no one inside was hurt. Before the smoke cleared, the driver of the vehicle climbed quickly in back and came up with his own rocket. He jumped out, took aim at the third vehicle and fired. The vehicle exploded in flames. That threat was now neutralized, so they all could focus forward.

Tolliver went down. The driver loaded the launcher with another round and was taking aim when he went down. Dan ran to him and grabbed the launcher. He got down on a knee, aimed and fired at the vehicle on the left side of the road just as their man was about to take aim at them. But, the bad guy was just a little too slow and the car exploded and men near it went flying up into the air.

There was a constant hail of bullets. The Erickson shooter with the launcher was down so one of the two men in the other vehicle was about take aim. Butch saw this and began firing a hail of shots at him until the man finally fell. Homer was limping and Lev had blood running down his arm.

Suddenly shots started ringing out from the woods and Butch went down. Homer, Lev and Kendra opened up on the area where the shots came from and, just as suddenly, they stopped.

Kendra took off into the woods because she had seen Erickson take off deeper into the woods. Butch didn't see her go, but Dan did and he headed after her.

Willa continued moving along well back of the road. After about two kilometers, she made her way back to the road. She brought the gun to her right pocket and moved the knife to her left. As she walked, she kept her right hand on the gun, swept the sides of the road and checked every car that came her way.

Five minutes into her stroll, she saw a vehicle approaching her. As the vehicle got closer she saw that the driver was a woman with blond hair and probably in her fifties or sixties. The vehicle was an average looking vehicle, nothing expensive or showy. This was it. Willa began to grip the handle of the gun tightly.

When the vehicle was about twenty meters away, the driver's side window opened and a hand came out. Suddenly, Willa heard loud bangs and bullets hitting the trees behind her. She turned and ran. Lisa had hoped to scare Willa into giving up. She didn't, so now Lisa had to give chase.

As Willa raced into the trees, she heard the car come to a screeching stop and the door bang open. She then heard someone rushing through the trees toward her, so she pushed deeper into the trees.

All of a sudden, bullets began pinging off of trees all around her. Willa decided to fire back. She aimed her hand at the sound of the shots, pushed the safety off and pulled the trigger. The gun began firing shot after shot. She couldn't count how many, but it didn't matter since she had no idea how many shots she had anyway. Suddenly, she heard a click and the gun stopped firing. Empty. She tossed it aside.

She ran harder into the dense growth. She had come by this area earlier before doubling back to face her killer and knew there was a small river running parallel to the road. She also knew there was a large open field across the river with several copses of trees in it. If she could get there and into those trees, then maybe she could get a shot at the killer since the woman would be exposed in order to cross the open field toward her.

Willa didn't hear the rustling of bushes and pounding feet behind her as loudly as before, so she took a chance and cut toward the river. She reached it but never slowed. She had had to cross it a couple of times before and knew it was fairly shallow. It was about a meter deep at most but that was only near the opposite bank which slowed her a little. But, once she reached the bank, she quickly scrambled up to the field and took off for the nearest group of trees.

Lisa was upset that Willa had not stopped with the first couple of bursts and this made her think the girl might be tougher than she originally thought. Be that as it may, she was confident she would get to her eventually. She had been surprised by the shots that came at her and started ducking and dodging, but then she noticed they were all hitting the tops of the trees around her so Lisa never slowed. Until now.

She wasn't used to the great outdoors, so she didn't see the clump of roots sticking up near a tree and twisted her ankle badly. She could walk with pain, but running was impossible. She now regretted not bringing help with her but it was too late for that now.

She made her way as best as she could and then heard Willa making noise to her right. She headed that way and, after a bit, didn't hear anything. When she came to the river and saw the field and the small groups of trees, she wasn't sure if Will had crossed or, if she had, where she might be now. However, logic told her that Willa had crossed and was hiding in the trees.

She yelled out, "Willa, if you come out now, then I will let your brother live. Yes, I know about him and have known about him since he came here with Marilyn. As a matter of fact, if you come out now, I will also let Susie live. I know you know her, so maybe you also care about her. But, dear, I am sorry to say that if you do not come out soon, then once you are dead, I will have both Peter and Susie killed too. So, what is it to be, your death only, or yours and theirs?"

Willa heard her quite clearly. She was hiding about three meters up in one of the trees in the first copse she had come to and had an unobstructed view across the field to the river. She estimated by the woman's voice that she was about fifty meters away and maybe ten meters left of a straight line in front of Willa. Willa shifted her position so that she was looking in that direction.

She didn't wonder if the woman spoke the truth, but she did figure that even if she came out, the woman would still go after Peter and Susie. She could not let that happen and knew what she had to do. She had crossed that bridge. She yelled at the woman.

XXXXX

Kendra had seen Erikson run into the woods, probably trying to get away and she couldn't let that happen. She was fast and was soon only about twenty meters behind Erickson. He had turned and fired at one point, but his shots were off. Kendra decided to put a little scare into him and fired off three quick shots. He cut sharply left and kept going. She stayed on the same line then decided to try to out flank him.

Dan was straining to keep up with Kendra. He could now barely hear them, but kept pushing forward toward the sounds.

Kendra suddenly stopped and listened. She couldn't hear anything at first, but then she heard someone behind her running toward her. She had no idea if it was one of the good guys or bad guys. She crouched low and waited. As the sound got closer she turned and saw that it was Dan. She was about to move to him, when she heard a noise behind her.

She quickly turned, but before she could do anything, she heard a gunshot. She stood and fired at the sound and the sound fired back. She kept firing until she was empty. At that she fell to the ground and began reloading. She noticed that she was having trouble holding the gun. She looked at her arm and saw blood, lots of it. She began to feel woozy and then it all went dark.

"Okay, okay, I'll come out. I dropped the gun, so I am unarmed. Please don't shoot."

Lisa yelled, "I know. I saw the gun as I came after you. Of course I won't shoot you, dear. I really don't want to do this here. I hope you understand that this must be done. Your mother betrayed me, her country and Erickson. She also stole from me. If Dimitri hadn't killed her, then I would have killed her and been satisfied. But he did, so I must get my revenge on you after you tell me where the files are."

Willa had no idea what she was talking about. She had never seen or heard of any files her mother had, but she couldn't think about that now. She saw the woman walking toward the river and Willa needed to concentrate on what would happen next. It would be a long shot, over fifty meters.

She yelled, "None of that is our fault. Why attack me, my dad and all the others?" She wanted the woman a little closer.

Lisa stepped into the river and began walking across. "The sins of the mother fall on you and your father. The others, well, they are just in the way." Lisa reached the bank and stepped to the top.

Willa fired. The arrow sailed smoothly across the field, entered Lisa's left shoulder and she fell.

Lisa screamed as the arrow penetrated her shoulder. But, she was tough and rolled to her side ignoring the pain. She began firing at the spot where she thought the arrow originated from. She emptied her weapon, tossed it aside then pulled another gun from behind her back and waited.

Willa had already dropped to the ground when the woman started firing into the tree. She estimated that the woman was now about five meters closer to Willa.

Lisa yelled, "You are going to die a horrible death and nothing you can do will stop me. I have men right now eliminating your father and the rest of them and they will be along in just a few minutes. When they get here, you will be badly mistreated by the men until you tell me about the files and then I will personally put a bullet in your brain."

Willa made her decision. She quickly stood, ran about ten meters across the field toward Lisa, stopped and fired her next arrow. Before the arrow was half-way to its target, she quickly took the next arrow from her mouth, nocked it, fired it then fell over and blacked out.

Lisa had started to shoot at Willa just as Willa emerged from the tree line. Lisa had seen the first arrow and had felt it strike. She had seen her shoot the second arrow, but had no idea what happened to it because everything suddenly turned dark.

Dan scrambled over to Kendra and saw that she had been shot in the side. He quickly took his shirt off and pressed it against the wound. He was fine, other than the bump on his head when he fell on his face as Erickson started firing. Kendra finally opened her eyes and asked, "Are you okay, Dan. I saw you go down. How is the rest of the team?"

"I am fine, but I don't know about the rest of the team. As soon as you took off, I ran after you."

"Is Erickson dead?"

"I don't know. I came straight to you. I haven't heard any more shots since his last burst and I also haven't heard any rustling in the trees."

Kendra nodded. "I am fine. Set me up against that tree and go check on Erickson. But, be careful. Go slowly and keep your gun aimed at him. If he moves, even a little, open fire on him. Don't hesitate. Understand?"

"Yeah, yeah." He propped her up and made his way slowly to Erickson. As he got close enough, he saw that he was bleeding from wounds to his stomach and head and lay perfectly still. Dan kicked his leg but he didn't budge. He also checked for a pulse and found none. He went back to Kendra. "I'm pretty sure he's dead. Can you walk or do you want me to run back and get help?"

"I can stand with your help. Let's go back to the group. I want to know if Butch is okay. Keep your gun ready and hand me mine. I can still shoot." He handed the gun to her, pulled her to her feet and they slowly made their way back the way they had come.

As they got closer, they could hear Homer yelling instructions to everyone. Some of his words were English and some were Russian. Kendra and Dan figured it was safe to come out. As they walked clear of the trees, Homer yelled. "There you are. We had no idea where you went." Then he saw the blood on Kendra.

"Are you okay? What happened?"

Dan started to tell him but Kendra interrupted, "Where's Butch? Is he okay?" She had fear written all over her face because he was nowhere to be seen.

"Yes. He was wounded in the thigh, but he will be fine with some rest and tender care. I guess the both of you will need some TLC over the next few months. He is in the second car."

Dan helped her to the car and as soon as Butch saw her he reached out his arms. Dan let them be alone and walked back to Homer. "What is the score?"

Homer looked around and said, "Well, it seems that all of the bad guys are dead or wounded, but that leaves Erickson."

"No he is dead too. Kendra took him down!"

"Okay. You know about Kendra and Butch. Lev took one in the shoulder, but will be fine. Tolliver has a serious wound in the chest and another in his left arm. He will be evacuated by helicopter to the nearest trauma facility. The two drivers are both dead." He didn't need to mention the wound to his arm. The bloody sleeve indicated that.

"We have to go find Willa right now. We know she was being pursued. Lisa may have her. We have to go!"

"Dan, look around you. Every vehicle is of no use. We can't walk, since that would take forever. Lev has called his office so we should have help here any minute. At that point, we'll immediately head out. Okay?"

Dan didn't look around but he didn't move either.

Homer looked at him sadly. He didn't say so and certainly didn't wish it, but he didn't hold much hope in finding Willa alive.

XXXXX

Willa slowly opened her eyes. She was looking straight up at a very small patch of blue sky. *Is this what heaven looks like?* She thought. *I feel fine, so it must be heaven. I thought that I was hit by one of her shots, but she must have missed.*

She decided to get up but screamed in pain and fell back down. No, she had not missed and she looked at her legs. One had blood all over her pants and the other was the same color as it had been just a few minutes ago or hour or day, she had no idea.

She managed to roll to her side and work her body into a sitting position. She used her knife to cut away the pant leg beginning just above the wound. She had, what looked like, a flesh wound on the inside of her right thigh, just above the knee. The bullet hadn't seemed to have hit a bone or a major artery, at least she hoped not.

She cut off some of the material from the pant leg and pressed it over the wound. She then grabbed her bow and removed the string. She wrapped the string around the make-shift bandage several times and tied it off as tight as she could.

She stared off into the distance and saw where the woman had been when she had come out toward her. She strained to see her but couldn't.

She looked around and saw a pile of old growth lying on the ground. It was about two meters away so she dragged herself to the pile and, by the time she reached it, tears were flowing freely from her eyes. She pulled and yanked at several branches until one finally came loose and she pulled it to her.

It was sturdy enough to support her, so she held it and worked her body up to a position where she was standing with her stick buddy for support. Once she steadied herself and figured out how to move with her buddy, she began moving toward the woman.

As she got closer, she began to see that the woman would probably no longer be a threat to her or her family. She saw the first arrow sticking out from her shoulder and the second arrow sticking out from her throat. However, she did not see her third arrow so it must have missed. But, it didn't seem to have mattered. The second arrow had done the trick and the woman would not complete her killing mission.

Willa stood over the body for only a few seconds before she made her way to her pack at the base of the tree she had climbed. She fumbled clumsily in the bag until she found the phone she had saved. She fished the battery and SIM card from her pants and inserted them.

She then stumbled over to a stump and sat. She turned on the phone and punched Dan's number into the keypad.

When Dan answered on the third ring, she said, "Hi, dad. Would you mind coming to get me? I could use a little help."

36. Home

Butch, Kendra and Dan sat in the bright sun on the deck of the Wilde Rover Irish Pub in Kirkland. They had finished lunch and were now enjoying a Harp for the boys and a Shandy for Kendra. They glanced out to the small beach and watched as the three young people sat together on the little grassy area just above the beach. They were laughing and pointing at something.

Willa, Peter and Susie were inseparable when they had a chance to spend time together. Susie now lived with Butch and Kendra in Kirkland and attended Lake Washington High School, where she was a junior and a state tennis finalist.

Willa and Peter lived in Scarsdale with their dad. Willa was in her last year of high school and Peter was attending the Rensselear Polytechnic Institute's branch in Hartford studying for his Master Degree. He was only about 100 miles away, so he came home most weekends.

The two families took turns visiting each coast several times a year and it had been Dan, Willa and Peter's turn to make the trip this summer. It was great timing since they absolutely loved summers in the Pacific Northwest. There were long days of sunshine, hardly any rain and temperatures nice and moderate. But, unfortunately, this was the last day of this visit.

Willa, Dan, Butch and Kendra were all healed from the physical wounds they suffered last year. But, the memories of that experience were still very fresh in the minds of the adults, much less so for Willa.

XXXXX

Help had arrived about twenty minutes after the shooting stopped at Dan's location. Dan was patient enough to wait until the second rescue vehicle arrived at the scene, which was only a minute after the first. At that point, he started demanding they go to Willa and Lev told the second rescue team to go with Dan to find Willa.

Dan called Willa using the number she had called from and she directed the driver to where she was. As Dan and the rescue team came up onto the field, Dan ran across to where Willa was waiting, still sitting on the stump.

Dan stopped in front of her and seemed afraid to grab her, lest he hurt her further. She looked up, smiled and reached out with her arms. They folded into each other. They stayed that way until the first rescue man asked if he could take a look at her leg. Dan reluctantly let go, but kept hold of Willa's hand. The medic told Dan that Willa would be fine. He said he would clean and bandage the wound here, but then she would be taken to the closest hospital.

One of the rescuers verified that Lisa was dead and told Dan. They both looked at Willa and she looked away.

The Russians reported the story as a mob conflict and that the Americans had been innocent victims in the whole thing. No one questioned the story.

XXXXX

Homer and Tolliver were left out of the story and they quietly returned to the states. Dimitri was presented to the public as a hero and champion of justice.

Willa told her dad what she had learned from the woman about her plans for Susie and Peter, the stolen files and Dimitri's culpability in the death of her mom. They decided to keep that to themselves, since he had been so instrumental in helping to find and protect Willa.

Dan did tell Homer in private what Willa had heard and Homer had sighed when he heard her threats toward Peter, Susie and Willa. He didn't seem surprised at Dimitri's involvement in Olivia's death since it was often the way things were done back then. He did ask Dan about whether he had ever seen any files.

Dan had thought for several minutes then said, "I remember that shortly after we all moved to Scarsdale, I came home early to surprise Olivia with some time for just the two of us. I walked into the living room just as she was tossing some papers into the fire in the fireplace. It was winter, so it wasn't unusual to have a fire going but when I asked her about the papers, she said they were just some scratch paper she often used to get a fire started. I didn't think anything of it at the time but now, maybe those were the files Lisa mentioned."

Homer gave Dan a half smile. "My guess is that Olivia finally realized that those files were a potential threat to her family. She probably also felt that she was now safe and that she didn't need them anymore. But, we will never know for sure what they were or what Olivia's motive was for burning them if, in fact, those were the files."

Dan shrugged and said, "I am going to believe that they were the files and that she felt she was protecting her family."

Homer smiled. "Good idea."

XXXXX

Butch and Kendra returned to the states as soon as they were able to travel.

Dan and Willa had wanted to meet Peter, but after Marilyn explained to Peter what she had done, he didn't believe her then got angry and refused to see her or anyone.

Dan and Willa returned to the states after a month of waiting.

As Peter continued to stew over what Marilyn had told him, he began to remember his sister and dad and became less angry. He remained confused by what he had thought he knew and what he was now being told. But, after a couple of months, he agreed to meet them.

Dan and Willa flew back as soon as Marilyn told them that Peter wanted to meet. Their first meeting was on the campus of the university on a park bench in a campus green space. As Willa and Dan approached, Peter seemed to instantly recognize them. Peter had been told the whole story of the search and rescue of Willa and that they still loved him and really wanted to have him be a part of the family again.

Willa and Dan had been shown a number of pictures of Peter by Marilyn as he grew over the past 11 years. But, those hadn't done him justice. Peter had grown to be, as they say, tall, dark and handsome. He was six feet tall, had an athletic physique and dark, almost black, hair. His eyes were blue and his skin was lightly tanned.

Peter stood as they approached and Dan and Willa smiled. Dan offered his hand but Willa wormed past him and hugged Peter without introduction. She sobbed and kept repeating his name. He finally returned the hug. They finally pulled apart and it was Dan's turn to hug Peter. They sat on the bench with Peter in the middle. Willa held his hand as though he might suddenly try to get away.

Peter's English was okay, but Willa told him that he could speak in Russian, if that was more comfortable and she would translate. He smiled and began asking and answering questions with them and they all laughed and cried at times. The first meeting lasted about two hours and, after several more meetings, Peter told them he wanted to come home.

The Russians expedited the paperwork to reunite the family and they all returned to Scarsdale about a month after Peter agreed to go home with them.

XXXXX

About a month after leaving, Willa learned from Susie that her mother had died and that she was now living with a family friend. Willa could tell that she was very unhappy. The truth about what her parents were and what they had done was weighing heavily on her. The family that took her in treated her okay, but there was no affection. They did it more as a duty than to give her a new family.

Willa immediately went to her dad to talk about bringing Susie to America. They were willing and felt that the paperwork would probably go quickly and smoothly so, after discussing this over several days, they were ready to start the paperwork for Dan to become her guardian.

As Dan and Willa started working on the forms, Dan suddenly stopped. He glanced at her, smiled while she looked questioningly back at him. That is when he told her what Butch had told him back in Seattle. Once Dan told her that Butch and Kendra had been trying to have children, she knew exactly what he was suggesting and also smiled.

Dan called Butch and explained what he and Willa were thinking. Butch talked to Kendra and she readily agreed with the idea. He called Dan back and they set the adoption process in motion.

Willa contacted Susie and asked her what she thought of the idea. She hesitated a moment then asked Willa what she thought. Willa told Susie how they had all met, how much they had helped them in their investigation and about how they had helped to save her from Lisa. She told Susie that they really wanted children, but had not been able to have any. She told Susie she was quite sure that Susie would be loved by them as though she were their true daughter.

Susie listened and as soon as Willa finished, she said she wanted to do it.

The Russians were again glad to help.

Susie arrived in New York a few months later and was met by Butch, Kendra, Dan, Peter and Willa. Susie walked out of the international arrivals exit with her Russian escort. As soon as she saw Willa, she ran over and grabbed her in a tight hug. They both started crying. There were tears for the loss of all of those years of friendship, tears of joy at finally being together, tears for what they both had learned from Susie's mother and tears of happy expectations for a bright future. The rest of the small group stood aside silently.

The Russian escort stepped over to Butch and Kendra, whom he recognized from the pictures they had sent. They shook hands and he quietly told them that the paperwork should go quickly and he would be on his way within a few days.

The girls finally released each other, but still stood and looked at each other's face as if to make sure the other girl was still there. They finally turned to the rest of the group. Susie hugged Dan and Peter then moved to Butch and Kendra.

Butch and Kendra had smiles on their faces. Susie finally stepped up to Butch, said hello and gave him a hug. He said hello and that he was so happy she was here.

Susie moved to Kendra who did not wait. Kendra stepped up to Susie and took her in a great big hug. She told her she was so happy to have her with them and would try very hard to be the best mom possible to her.

Susie, Butch and Kendra stayed in Scarsdale for the next two weeks but no one did any tourist stuff. They stayed at the house. Everyone helped with the cooking, cleaning and shopping. Susie's English was rusty, but it came easier and easier over time. After all, she spent the first 5 years speaking only English, so it was well established in her brain.

They played card games or board games or watched TV or movies or just sat around sharing stories. Susie was somewhat reluctant to talk about her past at first and just mostly listened. No one pushed her to talk. It was up to her when she wanted to share.

What four of the people didn't know was that Susie was actually sharing stories from her past at night in the comfort of the room she shared with Willa. The two of them would put the thick comforter on the floor, sit cross legged on opposite ends and talk well into the night.

This was actually excellent therapy for Susie because after several days of doing this with Willa, she began to talk about the same things in front of the others. Whenever Susie felt herself faltering in her story, she would glance at Willa and Willa would give her a smile and a nod. This seemed to help Susie to continue.

XXXXX

The day after the beach scene, Butch, Kendra and Susie went to SeaTac airport to see Dan, Peter and Willa off. They all hugged and Butch told them that they would plan a visit to Scarsdale around Thanksgiving or Christmas.

Willa followed Dan and Peter to the security check point and just before she was to go through the scanner, she turned and waved at Susie, who was already waving back.

On the flight back to New York, Dan told Willa that Amy was going to be in New York in two weeks. She had gotten a promotion and was now head of their Philadelphia office so she would spend the weekend at their home.

Willa liked Amy. Amy and her dad had kept in touch over the past year and they had been seeing each other off and on. Willa had no idea where this was going, but her dad was happy, so she was happy.

Willa had not had any communications from Marcel or Darius but she was fine with both situations. After all, she was going to graduate soon then, head off to college. She was excited about this new chapter of her life and very, very happy.

64258544R00110

Made in the USA
Lexington, KY
02 June 2017